Michelle Lovric

the

Wishing
Bones

KT-162-853

Hodder
Children's
Books

ORION CHILDREN'S BOOKS

First published in Great Britain in 2019 by Hodder and Stoughton

3 5 7 9 10 8 6 4

ISBN 978 1 444 00997 2

Typeset in Granjon LT by Hewer Text UK Ltd, Edinburgh
Printed and bound in Great Britain by Clays Ltd, Elcograf S.p.A.

The paper and board used in this book
are made from wood from responsible sources.

Orion Children's Books
An imprint of
Hachette Children's Group
Carmelite House
50 Victoria Embankment
London EC4Y 0DZ

An Hachette UK Company
www.hachette.co.uk

www.hachettechildrens.co.uk

To Jack

Sorrowful Lily's Letter to the Reader

You want to know what I've been up to, I suppose?

I'm not sure if I should tell you. You see, I've been thinking about you, Reader. Yes, about you. You with a sweet and proper childhood warm under your belt like a good dinner; you enviable creature with nothing more than some apple-scrumping and hair-pulling mischief on your conscience; you with your secret sacred ties to people who love you and have never once tried to kill you.

You and I, Reader, are not made of the same memories. Deep in our meat, we are different creatures.

Here is for why. Do you remember the last time you pulled apart the breast of a roasted chicken and made a wish on its bone? Did you even give a thought to the chicken who died to feed you? Reader, that chicken reminds me of myself. People have wanted my bones, and not just for wishing on.

Yet I cannot claim to be just a victim, or even innocent.

Reader, can I trust you? Perhaps I can. But only because you're living safely centuries after me. So it cannot matter if you tell tales on me or on any of us who have lived through these unspeakable days.

If you're squeamish, close this book now.

Still here?

Well, Reader, be it on your own head.

I'll start with the worst of it, then.

PROLOGUE

The Dying Bed

The Hotel of What You Want, Venice
10 October 1739

Ivo pressed the pillow down on the man's face.

It is but to quieten Mr Dearworthy's cries, I tried to tell myself. *The other guests adore him. It would worry them so to hear how he suffers.*

'Like this, Lily,' Ivo said. 'You'll be doing it on your own soon. Hold his arms down. Now sit on his legs.'

Doing it on my own?

It took all of our strength to subdue Mr Dearworthy. Ivo was just thirteen, only a year older than me. We were both as thin as stalks of wheat compared to poor Mr Dearworthy, who was tall and thoroughly put together. The bed sagged and creaked under his struggles. He flailed and kicked as if he were trying to swim away. But it was slowly, with underwater grace. And he wasn't going anywhere.

'What we do here makes no difference, Lily,' said Ivo quietly. 'He cannot escape his death. It's swilling in his blood already.'

3

Death? Surely Mr Dearworthy is just ill, I thought. *And sad.*

The poor gentleman had been brought low out of malice, so he had. I'd watched the Signorina, the woman who ruled our lives, measure the drops of green liquid into his coffee. The number had gradually increased, day by day, from five to thirty emerald drops. Mr Dearworthy's blue eyes, once candid as a clean window, grew misty under his mop of violently red and curly hair. Too often lately, I'd seen that smiling face contorted with waking nightmares.

That night at supper, the Englishman had finally collapsed. He toppled, all elbows and knees, from his chair to the floor. I'd helped him lurch up to this bedroom.

He used to have such a gentlemanly walk, is what Mr Dearworthy had.

'Uncommonly decent of you, my dear,' he'd murmured, leaning on my shoulder. 'Mercy me! What a kind girl you are, Lily, with those sweet crumpled eyes . . .' Then his mind had wandered back into some heart-wracking dream of his own.

'Uncommonly decent,' he slurred again at the top step. 'And from an orphan who's had mean rations of love in her life, I'd wager, looking at that face. Uncommonly decent.'

But Ivo had been waiting behind the door.

And there was precious little decency after that.

Ivo now threw me a glance that contained equal measures of coldness and annoyance. 'Forget your childish fondness for this Dearworthy. Do you *want* to get your heart broken? He has not a hope in this world. *Thirty* drops. I saw her pour them; you saw it too. No going back after that. Anyway, do you want him to go on seeing those pictures in his mind?'

4

So the pillow is truly a mercy. I tried to see it that way. *Quick death is better than prolonging the agony of his mind. We but ease his passage. Goodbye, Mr Dearworthy,* I thought. *You do not deserve this.*

'Get that look off your face,' growled Ivo. 'Crying helps no one. I suppose you'd have us pray to some saint to save him, convent girl? No doubt you'll know exactly the right one.'

As far as Mr Dearworthy was concerned, Ivo now told me, the one saint worth praying to would be Saint Jude, patron of lost causes.

'Only saint I know,' Ivo said. 'Only saint I believe in.'

From under the pillow, Mr Dearworthy whispered indistinctly, 'It was not supposed to go this far.'

Ivo threw all his weight on the pillow. The movement of Mr Dearworthy's long legs grew feebler; the whimpers turned into sobbing groans and then silence.

Suddenly his legs fell limply apart, still bent, so Mr Dearworthy looked like a long, sad frog. The drops had done their work. Life had been inside him. Now it was not. The thing was simple and terrible as that.

My stomach swooped like a gull around a steep cliff. There were tears crowding at my eyelids, but they did not dare show themselves again, not in front of Ivo.

Lifting the pillow, Ivo pointed to two large jugs by the bed. I could see and smell that they were filled with soupy canal water. He ordered, 'Pour the water over him. *All* over.'

'Why?' I asked. There was no answer.

I tried not to look at Mr Dearworthy's face as I poured until his clothes were soaked through. His red hair darkened. The lively curls were extinguished. A waft of salt arose from his pillow like a ghost of the sea.

Ivo banged three times on the floor with a stick. From below came three answering taps. My stomach swooped again.

'Done,' said Ivo. 'The doctor will be here in ten minutes. Wet those bricks.'

'Why?' I tried again, my heart squirrelling inside my chest.

While I watered the four bricks beside the bed, Ivo stood with his arms folded, gazing down on Mr Dearworthy. His voice was quiet yet rich with bitterness. 'When you look at that face, you see the Englishness. The tightness, the meanness, the greyness of soul and heart.'

'There is . . . was nothing grey about Mr Dearworthy! Or tight! Or mean!'

'You had a weakness for him. That's all,' said Ivo flatly. 'For the English, death is little different from life. No one will miss this one. You did well with your questions to him, Lily. A neat piece of cunning for a convent girl.'

Cunning? All my questions had led to purely sad answers.

One of them was this: for all that he was a most amiable soul, Mr Dearworthy had told me he'd no family. So there was no one to make enquiries or tell if something befell him.

'Shake this,' Ivo told me, handing me a small bottle fragrant with soap and rosewater. 'Keep shaking it.'

I did not bother with another 'why?'.

By the time we heard the doctor's reedy voice on the stairs, the contents of the bottle were foamy and pink.

Just before the doctor opened the door, while the handle was

6

still turning, Ivo seized the bottle, opened Mr Dearworthy's mouth and poured its contents inside, splashing some around his lips and chin too.

'Stop staring like a mad thing,' Ivo barked at me. 'Keep your eyes down.'

A mad thing? I looked sharply at Ivo. *What did he know?*

Doctor Ichthor stepped into the room and leaned over the bed. He didn't ever seem much healthier than a corpse himself, that man. The curls on his long wig seemed held together with dust and cobwebs. His thinness put no pressure on his waistcoat, yet there were buttons missing and buttonholes frayed from fatter times. His shabby looks had not stopped the Signorina from hiring him as our house doctor. Here is for why. Our English guests loved to write in their diaries about how their many ailments were tended by a genuine Venetian nobleman.

Doctor Ichthor was the most reduced specimen of a minor branch of a Golden Book family. Yet he still wore the senators' costume of a black robe with the black girdle four fingers wide, garnished with a silver buckle and a silk stole. Doctor Ichthor's robe was lined with squirrel fur that I always longed to touch, except I never did because the man seemed to swelter a kind of sour mist of disappointment like a second, transparent skin around his body. I did not want my fingers in amongst that.

You had to call men of Doctor Ichthor's class 'Your Excellency', even if what they did was not excellent at all. I had heard rumours at Rialto that he dissected corpses for medical students at the Anatomy School in San Giacomo dell'Orio. What would our simpering English ladies feel about his hands hovering about them, if they knew that those pale fingers had lately been rummaging in the tripes of dead men?

His Excellency removed his threadbare senatorial *berretta* and laid it wearily on Mr Dearworthy's dead knees. That was not sufficiently respectful, is what it was not. I snatched up the black worsted beret and hung it on the bedpost.

'We just pulled him out of the canal,' lied Ivo. 'And after we took the bricks out his pockets' – he pointed to the heap – 'it seemed the kindest thing to lay the poor gentleman on his own bed, in comfort, for his last rest, so to speak. That's when we discovered that the gentleman's diary, which I took the liberty of consulting, is full of the most desolate thoughts.'

He took up the leather-bound book from beside the bed and translated from English with his usual bloodless perfection, '*I am lost on a sea of grief. The waves of pain toss me back and forth, flooding the cracks in my heart with liquid misery. The beauty of Venice makes a mockery of my loneliness. Last night, I saw a skull, perhaps a foretelling of my own, on my pillow. 'Twas only a dream, but I knew it was calling me to my grave.*'

Meanwhile, the doctor was examining the pink foam on Mr Dearworthy's chin and feeling the side of his neck. He shook his head.

'Pen, ink and paper, please. I must record the nature of the death.'

The instruments of a great lie were already laid out for him at the desk by the window. Doctor Ichthor sighed, the shadows lengthening under his eyes. He sat down and dipped the quill into the ink.

'Another suicide,' he said. 'Why do so many Englishmen come to Venice to die? And what is it about this particular hotel that draws them? And why is *this* always the dying bed?' He pointed to where poor Mr Dearworthy lay.

Ivo shook his head, arranging his features in a mixture of regret and mystification. I'd seen him practise that face in front of the damp-speckled mirror in the *salotto*. Now I knew for why.

Me, I'd had no need of practice. I am rare good at expressions of sadness.

I've learned to be.

Sorrowful Lily is who I am, in name and nature. And I was now grieving in all the veins of my heart for poor Mr Dearworthy.

Doctor Ichthor gazed at me. 'What a face you have, girl. They should pay you to accompany coffins at funerals.'

Ivo said, 'Of course the hotel will deal with the formalities. We shall inform Mr Dearworthy's lawyers and arrange a decent burial. It's the least we can do for our *favourite* guest. Such a charming gentleman, so typically English. Such a loss.'

The doctor finished his note. He stood up from the table and picked up his threadbare *berretta*, saying dryly, 'You are too kind. You always are.'

But when he had gone, Ivo told me, 'Go fetch the butcher, Lily. And the jeweller.'

PART ONE

The Island of Murano

CHAPTER ONE

Saint Teresa's Convent of the Barefoot Carmelites
Eight years earlier

Had I been born lucky, and not sorrowful, Mr Dearworthy might have survived making my acquaintance.

But, Reader, I was not born lucky. I was born the opposite of that. I was born mischancy.

Here is for why. My mother has always been gone, so there's been no one to pet me finely. As soon as I was old enough to understand, the nuns at the Convent of Saint Teresa made sure I knew I'd been abandoned there as a newborn. There's your first reason for why they call me 'Sorrowful Lily'.

Then there's that face of mine. If I ever glimpsed my reflection in a window, my green eyes looked as sad as a frozen well, deep and brimming with darkness. Those eyes, with their great fronding of lashes, were framed by a tendrilly tumble of black seaweed-lank hair always escaping from its pins. The same sorrowfulness was imprinted on all my features, from forehead to chin.

It was shadowy-dark inside the high walls of our convent; dark in the lagoon water that jostled around this island of Murano.

13

There was darkness inside me too, as there was inside all the orphans at Saint Teresa.

Imagine a hundred of us young ones confined in a convent as cold as a witch's heart in winter and yet, come summer, hot as the inside of a roast goose. We orphans slept in a long glooming room with little slits of windows too mean to let in a finger of starlight.

Hard words and hard hands on young skin, bat-brown cloth on your body, a rough chemise underneath, a tight scant belly below that: that's how you grow up an orphan.

At least, among the Barefoot Carmelite nuns of Saint Teresa on the island of Murano, that's how you do it.

If you're allowed to grow up at all, that is.

Nuns are married to God. They're not allowed to love anyone else. And it seemed that the nuns at Saint Teresa's positively hated all infants who were not the Christ Child Himself. Otherwise they could not do what they did to babies.

This will send a shard of ice into your soul, Reader, yet you must be told it.

Unwanted babies were brought to *la ruota*, the tall revolving shelf embedded in the gates of every Venetian convent. All deliveries were made via this wheel so that the faces of the nuns would be seen by no man or woman. Sometimes *la ruota* received meat or laundry; sometimes babies. Our convent never turned one away. Behind the walls, babies could be grown with food scraps and beatings into useful workers – provided they were healthy.

14

I was seven years old when I found out for myself what happened to the sickly ones.

It was the first time I'd been sent to draw water at the well. I had to break the ice with the plummet of the bucket, for it was midwinter and the snow was ruched like white wool on the blackened stalks of the cloister's rose bushes. When the water stilled, I heard a small noise on the other side of the well.

And there was a baby in a basket, with a sign above: *Do not Feed or Touch.*

I was learning to read. I traced the words with my fingers. A drizzle of tears lay upon the baby's face. I could see she was a girl from the pink ribbon on her wrist. The heat rising from her told me she had a fever. I understood how grave it was by the blue cast to her skin. I knelt and kissed her hot cheek. I had never kissed anyone before. I liked it. I kissed her again and my heart clutched inside me. I put down my bucket, picked her up and hugged her.

'Put it down!' screamed a nun. She lunged for the child, wrenching her out of my arms. I snatched up the bucket and ran away, hoping the nun would not make trouble for me.

All day, I could not stop thinking about the baby. If no one fed or warmed her in their arms, she would die. I did not want her to die the way I had lived so far, with no one to pet her finely. I did not want it so badly that I could not stand it. When everyone else was sleeping, I crept out of the dormitory and down to the cloister. I scooped up the baby, now cold as a stone, and took her back to my bed. She was too sick to cry or whimper. I forgave her sour smell. I unwrapped her, cleaned her as best I could, and swaddled her in a pillow case. I kissed her until she was warm.

Then she grew furiously hot. I had to bathe her again with water from the stoup. I fell asleep with her making soft snuffling noises in my arms. I held her all night. When the morning bells rang, she was cold and still.

All the other children filed off to their lessons or tasks. I lay on my pallet.

'Are you sick?' A nun poked my ribs.

Then she saw the baby. She hissed. Two other nuns came running in their stilted heron-like way. Refusing to give up the baby, I wriggled and kicked out of their grasping hands.

The *badessa*, who ruled the convent, was summoned to see us like that: an insolent orphan girl abed instead of working, with her arms around a baby, like an oyster holding its pearl. The *badessa's* face loomed above mine, inches away. That face had every element of beauty – nose, eyes, cheekbones all faultlessly sculpted as if from pure marble: lustrous, veinless and white. But a brute coldness tarnished every feature. It was the first time that I'd come to the *badessa's* attention, and it would not be the last.

'This one must be the spawn of some she-devil,' she told the nuns softly. The *badessa's* voice, I would soon learn, was always the most terrible when it was quietest. Each word sounded as tender as a plucked cello string. Yet each word was cruel enough to leave a scar.

Sor Sanctita, the *badessa's* ever-hovering henchwoman, crossed herself. She was a poor sop of a thing, is what she was, Sor Sanctita. She whispered to the *badessa*, '*È la figlia della Pazza.*'

The daughter of the Madwoman? I had often, of course, wondered about my parents. Every orphan does. But the identities

16

of mothers whose babies left at the wheel were almost never known. How could the *badessa* know I had a mad mother? Did that mean my mother was *alive*? So I was not an orphan after all?

The *badessa* laughed. '*La Pazza* left behind a mad little daughter. Of course she did.'

Left behind? So my mother was dead after all. The *badessa's* laughter cut through the seven soft veils of my sorrow and found a dirty hard fury inside me. I said, 'Surely it is a she-devil who kills innocent babies!'

The *badessa* smiled, unperturbed. 'God has taken this baby. No one killed it,' she said.

'Not "it"! "*She*"! She might have survived, with care and . . . love. You *chose* to deny them to *her*. Do you think you're *God*? Deciding which babies live or die?'

As if it were a sword, the *badessa* drew the willow switch she always carried at her waist. She didn't use it straight away. She wanted me to look at it.

'What's her name, *la Pazza's* mad rat of a daughter?' she asked Sor Sanctita.

'Eulalia. They call her "Lily", though.'

'So, Eulalia,' the *badessa* said, 'today you shall learn several useful and unforgettable things. The first is this: the more clever-clever the orphan, the more weals she will find on the backs of her legs.'

She wrenched me out of bed. I clung to the baby.

'Bend over,' she ordered.

The *badessa's* willow cane sang through the air like a wasp. And the pain, as if from the stings of a thousand wasps, spread

17

across my calves and thighs. Sor Sanctita seized the baby and bore her away.

That was not enough for the *badessa*.

She had me harnessed to a wooden cross taller than myself. The wood's splintery edges pierced my chemise to my bare skin. I was made to drag the cross round the cloister a hundred times, until I dropped into a faint. I woke in a locked cell, lying on my belly, with the cross still fastened to me. By then the cross had left an everlasting imprint of itself on me. Until this day, you may still see it, sore and red and angry as Satan on Sunday.

The *badessa* sent for me. 'It's a shame *you* were not left by the well at birth,' she snarled. 'You are one who should not have been allowed to grow big enough to make trouble.'

'No thanks to you that I did grow.'

No, Reader, it was not brave of me. After what I had endured with the cross, how else could she hurt me now? I was not a baby to be tucked conveniently into a tiny mound of earth. I was the daughter of a Madwoman, and I felt entitled to rave.

'You,' the *badessa* said, 'are a fighting girl. There is a large number of interesting things that can happen to mad young girls who fight. Girls with heart-shaped faces, delicate features and long dark hair make the most affecting corpses, too. I promise you – and there is blood in this promise – that your bones could be more useful to me than your living body. Do not forget that.'

I would not forget. The *badessa's* words were now embossed on my memory, Reader, like the mark of the cross on my back.

*   *   *

18

From the day I tried to save the baby, the course of my growing-up was set. It would be solitary and tender-bitter with sorrowfulness. Seeing how the *badessa* had made me the special object of her cruelty, few children dared to show me friendship.

So at night, I said to myself, 'Good night, Sorrowful Lily. Sleep well. Golden dreams, Sorrowful Lily.'

In the morning, I told myself, 'Courage, Sorrowful Lily. You are not dead yet, is what you're not.'

No one else would say it to me.

By the time I was twelve, I was a creature of averted eyes, voiceless apart from obedient murmurs. The cloister shadows loved to swallow me.

I pretended not to notice that the *badessa* punished me more than any other girl in her walled kingdom. She never stopped thinking up ways to make me sorry I'd been born. Between the ages of seven and twelve, I nearly froze to death twice in punishment vigils, standing all night by the well. The nuns had to pour boiling water over the soles of my feet to revive me.

The *badessa* liked to play on the madness in my blood. 'Look at her,' she'd tell Sor Sanctita. 'A creature of nervous tremors, a feeble thing.'

I learned to use this to my purpose. I showed my nakedly sorrowful face to all. I manufactured submissive tears. I never looked at another dying baby. I was never late to Mass. I tried to dissolve myself into the bat-brown flock of orphans. And so I lulled the *badessa* into believing that she'd succeeded in rendering me a dull piece of flesh with no desire to fight her any more.

19

By feigning nervousness, I made myself the *badessa's* girl of choice for her errands to Rialto Market. I would plead pathetically to stay in the safety of the convent, and so she always sent me out. 'Go! You snivelling coward,' she'd say. 'Cry all the way, and all the way back. Wash the streets with your tears.'

'Please,' I begged. 'The crowds, the noise—'

'Why should *you* of all the convent brats be spared the tasks you don't like?'

Soon I knew how to make my way around the inner linings of the city, most regularly to the jeweller's and the butcher's, especially, where I carried sealed boxes and small gold coins.

Only I knew that something was still alive at the heart of me that would be ready to fight when fighting would serve. There were snows falling in my heart and hard icicles in my fists when I thought of the *badessa* and her cruelty. I was suspicious as a water rat. I had other rat skills too. I could scuttle about the convent by night, undetected. I helped myself to bread and goose gravy in the kitchens. I cleaned my teeth with parsley from the herb garden. I even smuggled rose petals under my harsh pillow, to sweeten my sleep.

By the time I was twelve, I'd learned a great deal more about the *badessa*. I had made it my job of work to know. I'd turned myself into a ghost-rat of a girl who could eavesdrop, unseen, on the gossip of the nuns.

In this way, I'd learned that the *badessa* was not Venetian. She'd come here more than a quarter of a century before from Sicily, an island to the south of Italy, a place of orange trees and fiery African sun; a cursed island too, of famine, plague and earthquake. Sicily was a place where the people really knew how to hate, the nuns whispered, where revenge was sweeter and bloodier than anywhere else.

Well, Sorrowful Lily could be Sicilian too. I swore to take revenge on the *badessa*. I took my vow as the clock struck midnight on the last day of the year of 1738. The bells tolled bleakly through the bare corridors. To me, they seemed to chant, 'No more, no more, no more . . .'

No more of this, I thought. It was time to leave my mischancy childhood behind. From now on, I'd make my own luck. The *badessa* would not have it all her own way. As the last bell tolled, I, solitary, vengeful Sorrowful Lily, pledged myself to the end of dead babies and beaten children at the Convent of Saint Teresa.

And I vowed that the year of Our Lord 1739 would be the one in which I'd get that thing done.

CHAPTER TWO

Shall I tell you about Venice in 1739?

I speak of the Venice beyond the walls of the convent, the city I knew from snatches of glimpses when I did my errands, the place I knew from Venetian blood beating inside me.

Venice was a grand, ramshackle, peeling-paint masterpiece of a place, a playful, disrespectful city, who borrowed her streets from the sea, which sometimes, at high tide, took them back.

She was a city full of wet stinks and exotic perfumes, of bewildered foreigners, of tail-pluming cats and alcoves where stern Madonnas watched with disapproving eyes over all the pretty wickedness of our *Carnevale*, as well they might, for that wild party raged from October till April. And there was *nothing* you couldn't get up to under the cover of a mask.

She was a city addicted to colour. On my errands, I saw that colour in the cut silks and dappled damasks of her women and in the art that throbbed on the walls of her churches. I saw it in her gaily painted boats, her flowered balconies, in spun-sugar towers in the confectioners' windows, and I saw it in the painted masks that even the noble children wore.

There was a touch of magic about Venice. Our streets and apothecaries were named for wolves, astrologers and wizards. There were always rumours of mermaids, mythical talking beasts and ghosts who lived in meltings of past and future. Miracles were a *commonplace* here. Many were painted on our church walls.

Most magical of all – or so it seemed to me, Sorrowful Lily – was that in Venice the secret sacred ties between mother and son, father and daughter, cousin and cousin, were stronger and more precious than elsewhere. Venetians lived in the intimacy of narrow streets across which they sang and shouted their love and frustrations with one another. Venetians walked with arms linked and hearts open for one another. When I wore my sorrowful face out into those joyful streets, there was often a smile for me, an apple pushed into my hand, a *'povera orfana'* muttered tenderly behind me. The Sicilian *badessa* had no idea that sometimes when she sent me out to Rialto, I helped myself to generous rations of Venetian affection, and that it made me stronger, like food.

For all her *Carnevale* mischief and her otherworldly mysteries, Venice was also a city of God – with one priest for every fifty souls and a sky bristling with bell towers. Apart from the secret sacred ties between them, the Venetians were very serious about only one other thing – the relics of saints, by which I mean their *wishing bones* – for that is how Venetians thought of their holy fingers, knee-bones, skulls, noses, ribs, toes and teeth.

The holiest saints were the ones who were made to suffer long tortures before their deaths – boiled in a bath like Saint Cecilia, or roasted on a gridiron like Saint Lawrence, or having their flesh torn with iron tongs and their hair set on fire, like Eulalia, my own patron saint. These martyrs were thought to be closest to Jesus Christ, because he too died slowly and cruelly, nailed to a cross. Venetians prayed to these saints because they believed their perfect souls were still alive in heaven and, even up there, could do you a rare amount of good.

But your prayers worked even better if you had a piece of the dead saint to pray to. You could catch holiness yourself, like a cold, from a fragment of a saint's body. In the old times, every time a saint died, Christians would try to touch his or her skin and even bones, just to get a smudge of holiness on their fingertips. The devout would collect the blood, tears or sweat of saints in sponges or cloths. A saint's last breath could be saved in a bottle; his shadow might be trapped a flask. Oil that oozed from saints' dead bodies was said to smell of roses in Paradise. But by far the best kind of relic for wishing on was the bone of a saint.

Naturally, saints' bodies were divided into as many pieces as possible so that more people could enjoy the benefits. And each relic, no matter how tiny, was as holy as the entire body. And so these little bits of saints – these wishing bones – were prized, and sold, and traded; wars were fought over them; legends and wonders were spun around them.

But now, let us come back down to earth, with a flump and a bruise.

For where there is wonder, there is a way to make money out of it.

*   *   *

24

At our Convent of Saint Teresa on Murano, the *badessa* made money from the Venetians' love of saints in every possible way.

She put it about the town that she'd secured the services of a saint hunter in the Holy Land. I knew, from the ledgers I spied on, that she paid men to sit in taverns and talk of him. This so-called hunter had only to lay himself down to sleep and visions of saints' resting places would cross his dreams. Another interesting thing about this hunter was his ability to find the same saint's finger, toe or nail many times over, especially if it could raise a high price. He sent everything he found back to the *badessa*.

The truth of it is that there was no hunter at all. Instead there were slave orphans in the dim classrooms of the convent. Our task was to make convincing fakes of every kind of holy relic.

I'd scratch marks on the dormitory door with a chalky stone every time the *badessa* sold the holy hammer used to drive in the nails at Our Lord's crucifixion, or a rusty nail 'stained' with 'His' blood. Or an 'authentic' Crown of Thorns, which had in fact tortured not Jesus but the fingers of the orphans, who had to twist spiny branches into wreaths and then rub them with dung and ash to make them look as ancient as if they'd been rammed to the head of Christ seventeen hundred years before.

The *badessa* also sold 'soil from the blood-soaked ground around Christ's grave'. And 'oil that spent the night in front of the place where Christ was crucified'. You could buy olive stones 'from the Mount of Olives', straw 'from the holy manger', flasks of 'holy water' and 'tiny fragments of the True Cross' on which Christ died. As you can imagine, Reader, that dirt, that oil, those stones, that water and those twigs had never been closer to Jerusalem than have I, Sorrowful Lily.

The *badessa* had holes drilled in stone tombs at our convent, rigging tubes so we could collect fragrant oil 'exuded from the bones of saints'. This 'manna from heaven' had the sweet aroma of Paradise because of the rose and lavender petals we orphans rolled and pushed into the holes before filling the tombs up with oil. The tombs, I scarcely need tell you, were in fact empty of any saint, and often held a dead rat or two.

We orphans owned the slender fingers necessary to refashion fresh white bones into antique-looking relics. We battered them with tiny hammers. We worked the dark sumac powder into goose fat and then rubbed the dark sludge into the pitted bones. The supply of new white bones seldom faltered. We all knew better than to ask where they came from.

Our most skilfully dissembled relics were put inside elaborate cases called 'reliquaries'. To make these items, the *badessa* called in her jewellers, Bastian Olivo and Isepo Luzzo, whose shops were by the Rialto Market. Some reliquaries were in the shapes of whole golden arms or legs. Others were miniature silver mansions studded with precious stones.

As well as money, the *badessa* earned praise. Sermons were preached about her marvellous ability to charm relics out of the stony ground of the Holy Land. 'You should think of a saintly relic,' our own priest instructed us at Mass, 'as a light that is never spent, that continuously illuminates all around it. And you should think of the Convent of Saint Teresa at Murano as a jewelled light in the lagoon.'

In the whole of Venice, it seemed, only a hundred nuns and orphans knew that our convent was as far from a jewelled light as a butcher's shop is from a white wedding.

Speaking of butchery, the *badessa* had a passion for roast goose stuffed with prunes, garlic, sage and butter. She liked it simmered in the convent ovens for hours, till the meat was almost falling off the bones. Too impatient for a knife or fork, she'd rip the dark tender flesh off the drumsticks and wishbones with her bare teeth.

On Saturdays, a special goose was prepared by her favourite butcher. I struggled home with it, trailing blood all the way from Rialto. It was stuffed with a rabbit stuffed with a pigeon stuffed with a quail. Right in the centre quivered a single truffled oyster.

The *badessa* ate the whole thing herself.

The drawers of her desk were full of gnawed bones.

Meanwhile, we orphans ate soup made from the giblets, livers and parsons' noses. Our little portions of goose would not even flavour a thin gravy. Instead, they were minced into a brown-tasting soup into which we dipped mould-rimmed hard bread.

Because she especially hated me, the *badessa* liked me to serve her fat suppers. I was strong, with an infinitely flexible spine – strong enough to carry a pewter platter of goose all on my own.

'Eulalia,' she would say, 'doesn't that goose smell *delicious*? Doesn't it drive you *mad* with desire for a taste of it?'

I looked as half-witted as possible, saying, 'Yes, Reverend Mother. Delicious, the goose smells. Sweeter than honey or money. I hear the saliva of angels dripping from heaven. Do you not hear that sweet tinkling?'

'Mad questions like that will get a slap for an answer,' she replied, ripping a wing from the goose and burying her teeth in its flesh.

As the ghost-rat of the convent, my wits – and all of my senses too – had sharpened with my years. Now, many nights, while the other orphans nightmared on their pallets, you'd find me examining ledgers in a shaft of moonlight in the *badessa*'s office, to which I had fashioned a skeleton key from a goose bone.

My first mission was to find my own self – the record of my secret depositing at the convent wheel where mothers left unwanted babies. I craved knowledge of any secret sacred tie to a father or mother, even if that mother was mad. I eventually found myself and my birth-date, 18 February 1727.

Un'altra anonima bambina, another unknown baby, that's who I was. I read that I'd been christened 'Eulalia' by the *badessa*'s priest.

Parentage dubious, it said. *Mother, Madwoman, deceased. Father unknown. No dowry.*

And that's all there was to me. The story of my family was as closed as the ledger I now slammed shut. My father had left me nothing: no money, not even a name. My mother had left me just one thing: a mad taint in the blood, that weakness the *badessa* loved to mock.

But wait! I thought. *There are lies in this ledger entry about me.*

For if the *badessa* and Sor Sanctita knew that my mother was mad – *then they must have known who she was.*

For some weeks after that, I stayed away from the *badessa*'s office. I did not like to handle the book that offered me as much mystery as truth. It simply added frustration to my sorrowfulness.

Eventually I crept back. Here is for why. I missed rifling through the *badessa*'s account books. They were a kind of story, telling how she robbed people with her lying relics and how she spent the money. There were thousands of ducats tucked away between those pages.

The more I discovered in the ledgers, the more I felt like a person who was important. I was so stuffed full of bad facts about the *badessa* that I was like a whole courtroom, including the judge and jury.

It gave me a diamond-bright, devilish, rat-twitching feeling to know so much about my enemy and her crimes. So when I heard rumours at Rialto that Venice's favourite lady saint – a real one – was in danger of kidnap, then my thoughts naturally turned to the *badessa* too. If there was saint-thievery afoot, I was sure she'd want in.

CHAPTER THREE

Although we didn't much care for foreigners in general, the Venetians had welcomed the corpse of Saint Lucy with open arms. Our blind warrior Doge Enrico Dandolo sent her back from the crusades in 1204. A church was dedicated to her; a magnificent tomb was built to cradle her. Through its glass sides, any Venetian – even an orphan straying from her errands – could behold the mummified remains of the tiny woman, wearing a silver mask to hide what the centuries had done to her face.

Saint Lucy was patron saint of our best-beloved Venetian sense – sight. Her own eyes had been put out by a Roman officer. Another story had it that she plucked them out herself to discourage a suitor. (Like all lady saints, the only bridegroom Lucy wanted was God.) All paintings of Saint Lucy show her holding her two eyes on a plate. Yet in that mysterious way of saints, another pair glows in her lovely face.

A prayer to Saint Lucy could stop you from going blind. It could restore perfect sight if the world had gone dark on you through age or illness. A box beside her tomb overflowed with spectacles left there by Venetians whose sight had been saved. She was so important that there was a prophecy that if Saint Lucy left Venice then our city would lose her colour.

Take away our colour and we'd all be ghosts.

Worse, the prophecy said, without our colour, there would be a great severing of the secret sacred ties between Venetians. Mothers would turn against sons, daughters against fathers, cousins against cousins. There would be hate in people's hearts and blood in the streets.

Lately nervous gossip flew about the city that someone planned to steal Saint Lucy. The rumours arose from an attack on Saint Lucy's tomb. A side door to her church in Cannaregio had been kicked in, and her glass tomb split by an axe. One of Saint Lucy's tiny feet had been ripped from her body as the thieves tried to pull her through the glass.

But a passer-by, hearing the commotion in the church, had interrupted the thieves and called in the *Signori di Notte*. By the time the guards arrived, there was no trace of the tomb-robbers: just poor Saint Lucy, her silver mask askew and her mummified left leg finishing in a stump at the ankle.

Pigeon-coloured skies loomed over Venice from the day Saint Lucy's foot was stolen. Without the sun, the water lost its jades, turquoises and golds, exchanging them for unpolished pewter and tarnished silvers. Then came another terrible sign – two mothers were beaten by their sons and one father nearly strangled his daughter. A once-loving pair of cousins fatally wounded each other in a duel. Most of Saint Lucy was safe, but it seemed that

31

secret sacred ties of the Venetians were already beginning to stretch and break.

Fishwives began to keep small statues of the saint in their baskets. The congregations at Saint Lucy's church swelled with every Mass. There was a tang of anxiety in the air whenever Saint Lucy was mentioned. People pushed drawings of her stolen foot into the spaces between the stones of her church, always with the same message scribbled underneath: *Give it back*!

As Saint Lucy came from Siracusa in Sicily, now every Sicilian was a suspect. Merchants with Siracusan accents were sworn at and rough-handled into gondolas.

But here was what I thought: what was the *badessa* but a Sicilian? And what about her trade in saints?

I ransacked her office by night, hunting for Saint Lucy's foot. I even pulled away the skirting boards, inspecting mouse holes with a candle. I offered to clean the dankest parts of the convent by day, hoping to find a leather packet or box with the saint's little foot behind the stoup in the necessary room, in the mortuary, in the spaces behind the troughs in which the nuns' habits were washed.

I could not stop thinking about Saint Lucy's little foot.

I was still thinking about it when the convent caught fire.

CHAPTER FOUR

On the night of 10 March, the *badessa* was careless enough – or so stupefied by her vast supper – that she left a ledger open on her desk. Even after all my years of midnight spying, this particular ledger was a new one to me, though an old book in itself. Long, thin, bound in black leather, it had been handled so much that its corners had surrendered their colour and were white as my own fingers in the moonlight.

The ledger was arranged in alphabetical order. Neat columns showed orphan names, year of birth and the day of each baby's delivery to the convent. Among them, in fresher ink, were the names of some orphans whom I had known personally over the years.

Beside each name was a list. My gaze fell on the most recent entry. It was for Cecilia, a sweet girl who had worked beside me at the relic manufactory tables. Next to Cecilia's name was written:

1. *little finger, left hand, Saint Ursula: 3 ducats*
2. *right leg, Saint Tryphon for Saint Clemente: 20 ducats*
3. *assorted hair, Saint Teresa, Saint Catalina: 35 ducats*

33

4. *spine, Saint Marta: 67 ducats*
5. *wages from Hotel of What You Want: 10 ducats*
6. *cost of feeding and clothing till 13 years: 34 ducats*
Profit on operation: 102 ducats

Under '102 ducats', two thick lines were drawn, which seemed to indicate that the 'operation' was over.

I suddenly remembered the last time I had laid eyes on Cecilia. It was months ago now.

Girls from Saint Teresa's were regularly sent to work as chambermaids at the Hotel of What You Want, a mysterious establishment in the heart of Venice. Cecilia had been one of those girls. A few weeks before Saint Lucy was attacked, she'd come to the convent to fetch some damask napkins laundered by the nuns and the tub of goose grease which, for some reason, the *badessa* sent every month to the hotel. Cecilia had seemed in strange spirits, even feverish, when she'd dragged me behind a tree in the cloister. The pupils of her blue eyes were large and black as grapes. She'd said, 'Lily, I know things that could bring down this whole convent and put the *badessa* in prison.'

'You mean the false relics?' I asked her. 'Or is it to do with Saint Lucy? I wouldn't be surprised—'

'No, worse and far worse than that,' she gabbled. 'Look!'

She lifted her sleeve. On her white skin, her name was clumsily carved in bleeding letters. 'In case they find my body and don't know who I am.'

'Why should they find your body? Who are "they"? You're not well, are you, Cecilia? What are they doing to you at that hotel?'

34

Footsteps pattered close by and Cecilia showed me a terrified face.

'If anything happens to me, Lily—'

'What might happen to you?' I asked.

'Even you could not imagine it,' she whispered, and fled.

I'd not laid eyes on Cecilia after that day. I continued to rake through the ledger, recognising the names of other girls I had known, all divided up into bones and ducats. What had become of them?

My fist closed around the little tinder box on the *badessa's* desk until it made painful grooves in my fingers.

I opened up my fist. The tinder box lay warm on my palm.

When I set fire to that ledger, I little thought how the mildness of the March night would feed the flames, igniting a drawer of oily goose bones, the dusty curtains and the *badessa's* willow switches. Soon the whole office was afire.

I could not hide my crime. The flames licked my apron and I ran from the room with a lapful of fire. The flames had by then wrapped themselves round my body and had begun to feast on my chemise. The ends of my hair danced and sizzled with fire, as if I were becoming one with my poor burned patron saint, Eulalia.

My heart was so tightly wrapped in fear that it could not run to its proper time but stuttered and raged inside my chest. My breathing came when it felt like it, which wasn't often. Only outside the burning office did I think to roll myself on the stone floor and quench my own flames.

That was where they found me, still writhing.

The first to come was a girl named Barbarina. She beat the burning embers of my dress with her bare hands while mouthing prayers to Saint Agatha, the patron saint of putting out fires. When the smoke hurt her eyes, Barbarina swore. By then the nuns were there, stamping out the flames. Soon the ruins of the *badessa's* office lay smouldering under jugs of water carried by ranks of running orphans.

As for the *badessa* herself, she simply stood over me, looking. But that look was enough to set tears spurting down my blackened cheeks.

At the Chapter of Offences, I was judged guilty of fire-setting. My legs were switched raw by the *badessa* in front of all the other orphans. But I did not cry out until the *badessa* started on Barbarina, who was beaten for her unsaintly language.

'The rest of your punishment,' the *badessa* announced, 'will take place in a certain room below the tideline, where you can scream your heart in half, Eulalia, and no one shall help you. You'll have company, however.'

She pointed to Barbarina, who shrieked, 'No! Not there! Please!'

What did the girl know about that room below the tideline?

With Barbarina resisting like a tigress, the two of us were dragged down to the watergate and thrust inside the gloomy storeroom beside it. When my eyes accustomed themselves to the mean light, I saw that the only furniture consisted of two chairs nailed to the walls at head height.

'For why?' I whispered to Barbarina.

'For when the high tide comes.'

From the slot of the window, I watched clouds like black hands with long wandering fingers making shadows on the water in the shapes of wolves and serpents. Then the first wave hissed in under the watergate. Every minute, more cold tongues of tide edged in. Soon we were soaked to our thighs. Lifted by the rising tide, we climbed up on to the chairs. Even on the chairs, our legs dangled in the water.

'When will it stop coming?' I asked Barbarina.

She shook her head. 'The tide does as the tide wants in Venice.'

Like most Venetians, I could not swim. I began a prayer to Saint John Nepomucene, patron of silence and of floods. He had been thrown off a bridge in Prague and left to drown in the Moldau River.

'Shall we die here?' I asked Barbarina.

'Did you think the fire hurt you, Lily? Or the beating? That was nothing, Lily. *Nothing*. The lesson here is the cruellest one of all. The *badessa* doesn't care if we die or not. If we drown, she has two fewer problems. If we live, we'll always know that no one cared if we died.'

Another wave flung itself against me. I watched Barbarina's face distort with fear. She watched my fear. We clung to one another as the water crawled up our skin.

The water came as high as my eyes. I swallowed plenty, choking on its salt. But by tilting our heads up and stretching our necks, we managed to keep alive until the tide began to turn three hours later. Out with the tide went too my cries, and my dignity and any remaining sense that this world might be a good place. Worse, for a Venetian, that tide took with it my pleasurable ease with the water. As long as I lived, I'd be afraid of it now. I'd take no pleasure in a jade-green canal, nor a fluting giggle of drain water, nor a soft whisper of rain – a mischancy state for a girl who lived on an island of canals in the middle of the Venetian lagoon.

At dawn, a grim-faced boy arrived in a boat and handed me aboard without once meeting my eyes or answering a single one of my questions. I might as well have spoken to the seagulls who laughed loudly at me all the way across the lagoon that I trembled to feel roiling beneath me. The silent boy rowed me from Murano to San Felice in the heart of the old city of Venice, to the Hotel of What You Want.

Like poor Cecilia, who disappeared with her name carved in her wrist.

PART TWO

The Young Ladies' Academy
County Kildare, Ireland

CHAPTER FIVE

In that incubator of monsters that they called an academy, Esmeralda Sweeney led the war on me.

The tribe that cleaved to her – Oh, Mary O'Mealie, Oh, Brigid Malone, Oh, Theresa McTeer! – were just as bad. Great walking maggots of girls they were so. Always wanting someone to bash, and me being but the height of their brawny elbows, they thought me a fine candidate for a bashing.

On the very first evening I arrived at the Young Ladies' Academy, your woman Esmeralda had me by the scruff with my head down a chamber pot that was several inches from empty. Her teeth afloat in malice, she told me, 'You shall not see another day of happiness, creature that you are.'

When I spluttered protests, she asked the O'Mealie, the Malone and the McTeer, 'Do you not see the creature going vicious on me?'

'It isn't picking daisies that she's doing,' agreed the Mary O'Mealie.

'So what am I to do but defend myself against the filthy article?'

Esmeralda Sweeney pulled my head up only to ask, 'Are you

liking that now, Miss Dearworthy?' before plunging it back in the pot.

I was not at my fighting best just then, being at the Young Ladies' Academy on account of a recent great robbery of my happiness. My adored father, my darling mother, had been wrenched from me in a carriage accident but days earlier. Meanwhile, my kindly English guardian was away in Venice on some mysterious business. Uncle Red, my guardian, was not quite a cousin and not quite an uncle. Yet he was my only living relative. On his instructions, the maid-housekeeper had delivered me to the academy with a kiss on the cheek and a large trunk, and there was the sudden end of my life as a beloved daughter, in a loving family, in a lovely home a few paces from the Liffey in Dublin Town.

Uncle Red wrote, *My dearest hope is that it shall comfort you to be among nice girls your own age until I can come back. Then we can settle your future together. Be brave, sweet girl. Mercy me! I wish I could be with you at this terrible time. But lives depend on my absence just now.*

My Uncle Red did not wish himself with me as hard as I wished it myself, while the cold contents of the chamber pot dripped down my hair. Esmeralda Sweeney lifted her head to caw her pleasure like a dirty crow after dipping its beak in the guts of something dead. And no one, for the love of little baby Jesus, came to stop her. Not one school-mistress, not one maid, not one stable-boy. It was as if the whole academy was pure afraid of her.

My very name made me easy prey for my enemy: 'Deirdre

Dearworthy' has such a sentimental ring to it. Esmeralda Sweeney re-christened me 'Dear *dear-dear-oh-dear-me*-Deirdre Dearworthy'. I resolved to deny her the satisfaction of seeing how that vexed me. So I told everyone I adored my new name. It drove the bullies quite to distraction when I said, 'Please, my friends. Treat yourselves. *Do* call me Dear-oh-dear-me *Darling* Dearworthy. Or just "Darling", to save your jaws cramping with the fatigue.'

'Darling' was the name that stuck.

And that's not the only way I got at them. My enemy brought out the lion in me. Not being endowed with lion's teeth, I sharpened my tongue instead. I had to be clever with it, because, as I'm after telling you, those girls were twice my size and counting so.

I plumed myself a reputation as a dangerous curser. At midnight, from under my blanket, I'd growl bloodthirsty threats in the dormitory. I swore I'd buried sticks with my tormentors' names carved on them in the earth in secret places in the academy garden. If anyone hurt me, I vowed I'd go and stamp on those sticks until they were fit only for kindling. And then those girls their great selves would dry up, splinter and die!

How they wept and trembled, the O'Mealie, the Malone and the McTeer! Except Esmeralda Sweeney herself, who had not one drop of imagination, and only brawny fists. She said, 'You can lose the mouth, Dearworthy. Or you'll lose some more of that red hair.'

If I've a talent, it is for tongues. I'll soak up a new language the way an Irish bog takes in rain. My parents had indulged my pleasure, bringing in governesses to teach me French, German, Italian and

43

even Russian. Now, at the Young Ladies' Academy, Uncle Red made me a gift of private Italian lessons from a young woman who was the daughter of a gondolier. Finding me absorbent, she taught me her Venetian dialect too. It made me feel closer to Uncle Red, to speak the tongue of the place where he now stayed. I found books about Venice in the academy's pitiful sham of a library – breathless volumes about gilded palaces, galleons, gallantry and art to drive you mad with a glorious excess of colour. Even Venice's abominable traitors went by delicious names like 'Bajamonte Tiepolo'. Meanwhile, I smiled every day at a painting of the city in our dining room. The Grand Canal shimmered like the Liffey would – if the Liffey were got up in ball-dress of green silk and lace.

Of course the tribe of Sweeney took its revenge on my smile. They would not tolerate my looking happy. Next, Esmeralda Sweeney contrived to snatch away my spectacles, so I couldn't see anything and began to falter at my lessons until new ones could be made.

There was a certain cupboard up in the attic of the academy. The tribe of Sweeney would drag me up there and lock me inside with the spiders, the cobwebs and the rats that were so potent and fierce in themselves that they snickered at the rhyming rat curses every Irish child knows. Sometimes they even left me in that cupboard overnight. They'd roll a blanket under my bedcover. They'd cut off one of my red curls, so they could leave it to peep out. The schoolmistresses were mostly old and short-sighted, so they were none the wiser.

Not one girl dared offer me friendship for fear of bringing down the wrath of Sweeney.

Uncle Red wrote to me, *Can I send you more funds, my dear? Is there anything you need? I shall be with you as soon as I can.*

I wrote, *By the way, I've changed my name from Deirdre to Darling for the sake of expedience. I beg you to ask me no more about the matter. Apart from new spectacles, a project I have in hand, there is nothing I lack for at all. The sight of you would be a pleasure, however.*

There was nothing I needed that he could give me just then. I could not forget that lives depended on him staying away a while longer.

I had a great need to cry, for my lost mother and father, for my loneliness and for all the insults and offences I had to bear under the monstrous regime of Esmeralda Sweeney. So perhaps it was right that Uncle Red left me there a while, to get those tears all done.

The only thing that kept me from utter despair was the thought that, as soon as Uncle Red came to find me, I'd be leaving on his strong and pleasant arm with the scent of his cologne agreeable on my nose, and the kindness of his voice soft on my ears.

And that would be the end of tears and the beginning of better.

PART THREE

The Hotel of What You Want
San Felice, Venice

 **CHAPTER SIX**

11 March 1739

All the way into Venice, my mind dwelled on just one thing. Whatever awaited Sorrowful Lily at the Hotel of What You Want, at least she'd be far away from the *badessa's* persecutions. Even the surly face of the boat boy could not ruin my pleasure in that.

So, Reader, I ask you to imagine the churn of my belly and prickling of my hands when, at the hotel's reception desk, I found a woman who looked so similar to the *badessa* that she might have *been* her. This woman, perhaps a year or two younger, had the same hardened kind of beauty, like a dark sky the moment a storm strikes. I stood gaping at her, unable to compose a sentence.

'Eulalia, known as Lily, I believe? Why that stupid moon-face? My sister Arabella says that you're cleverer than it's good for a girl to be,' said the woman. Even her harsh accent was the same as the *badessa's*.

Was the existence of this sister what Cecilia had tried to tell me before she disappeared?

'You will call me "Signorina",' the woman said.

49

When I looked into the Signorina's brown eyes, I felt the convent walls closing in about me again. Even here, a long crow's flight over the water from Murano, I'd still be the prisoner and slave of a woman without pity or decency. The only difference was that this place was saturated with the damp smell of tea instead of roasted goose.

The door was open. I breathed the air of freedom and took a step towards it.

'Aldo!' shouted the Signorina. 'Show her what happens to girls who try to escape!'

I fled. But my first turn led me into a blind alley that ended in a canal. At a safe distance from the water, I leaned panting against the bricks watching the ripples of the waves that were reflected like starbursts on the underside of the arch. We Venetians have a word for that watery, wavering light: *sbarlusso*. Of course, with Saint Lucy's foot gone, the light was sunless and today the *sbarlusso* winked sadly, like a widowed uncle.

'*Sbarlusso,*' I said aloud, still panting. That's what my life would be like – free, scintillating, lively – without sisters from Sicily to insult, bend and beat me. I would find decent work. I would make some secret sacred ties of my own.

I felt the rumble of footsteps before I even heard them. Then my arms were pinioned behind my back and a sack thrown over my head. I smelled garlic, meat and anger through the coarse weave.

A man's voice told me, 'Thought you'd get away? Don't make me laugh. I know all about you. You are the daughter of a madwoman. You are not destined to live free. Your wits are not up to it, girlie.'

This coarse high voice must belong to Aldo, I realised, the man the Signorina had summoned.

'And if you try that again,' he whispered, 'I won't bother bringing you back. I'll drown you like a kitten in a bucket. Who's going to miss you?'

CHAPTER SEVEN

'I see you've returned whence you were scarcely missed,' the Signorina told me, glancing up.

Aldo had dragged me back to the hotel, where he ripped the sack off my head and shoved me against the reception desk. The Signorina stood behind it, holding a large document.

An elegant but ugly man now stood next to her. He picked up the document and began to fold it. I saw the words *certificato di morte . . . nessun erede*. Death certificate . . . no heirs.

She turned to the man. 'Would you not expect this penniless orphan to be grateful for honest employment? Yet the first thing she did was insult my hospitality by running away!'

There was a warmth in her voice that made my fingertips feel oily. 'This gentleman,' she told me, 'is the English Resident in Venice. Our dear guests are under his protection.'

I noted his thick fingers, his long head, the cold pebbles of his eyes. He did not have the air of a protector. A flash of green appeared behind him. A tiny vivid bird circumnavigated his head. He made vain attempts to bat it away. The Signorina lowered her eyes tactfully until he had recovered his composure enough to remember my presence.

'A runaway?' He stared at me. 'Venice is full of ungrateful boys and girls. If she wasn't so pretty, I'd throw her back on the streets, Signorina Magoghe.'

I kept my eyes downcast, humbly eating the floor of the hotel. My mouth strained into a straight line of submission. I murmured, 'Please forgive me.'

'No,' said the Signorina. 'But I see that you've found some manners, so I take it you are ready to serve.'

The Resident laughed, like a burst of killing shot from an arquebus. The bird flew around his head again. This time he swore horribly and ran out of the door, chasing the creature with arms outstretched.

'Until Thursday, as usual,' the Signorina called after him. Then she thrust her face down to mine. 'Here you will learn both charm and the English language. I don't care how sorrowful and mad you are, so long as you hide it under a believable veneer of charm. Now why are you standing there when there are floorboards to scrub? Let's have that nice young flexible back bent over *now*.'

The rag I smeared over the floor snagged on a fragment of broken glass.

I used it to carve the words '*Sorrowful Lily*' into my arm.

It took just a few hours in the hotel business for me to learn that the *badessa* and the Signorina were related not just by their features but also by greed. Where the *badessa* was greedy for goose, Signorina Magoghe was greedy for revenge. And the people she wanted to take revenge on were the English – particularly the wealthy, dull, lonely English. Somehow, she saw to it that this was the only kind of guest who came to the Hotel of What You Want.

The hotel charged a power of money per night – as much as the famous hotels like the Sturion or the Leon Bianco, whose tariffs I'd seen chalked discreetly on boards. And yet the Hotel of What You Want was tucked away in a ravine of back alleys fronting the undistinguished San Felice canal, with its street door in the humble Calle della Racchetta.

What set the hotel apart from the other dilapidated buildings in Venice were its windows and their swollen curved awnings, pleated like an old lady's drooping eyelid and painted the same pleasing tender shade of pink. At least that's what they looked like from the outside. Inside – well, Reader, that's a tale to be told.

At other Venetian hotels, a fashionably dressed *portiere* was employed to greet guests with bows and compliments and to assure them that nothing was too much trouble. Our *portiere* was Aldo Momesso – the man who had caught me and threatened to drown me like a kitten.

Aldo Momesso was no elegant popinjay. And everything was too much trouble for him. He was all-over dirty and rude, with huge ears that followed a meandering whorl of grey flesh into a very dark space behind his small black eyes. All the filthy, nasty gossip in Venice ended up in there. He knew who'd betrayed whom, who had left stinking rubbish in front of whose street door, whose dog had the mange. Although he spoke their

54

language but poorly, Aldo Momesso treated our English guests with utter contempt, as if he knew all their secrets too.

The English did not understand. When he insulted them, they tittered that Aldo was 'a one'. They said, 'Oh, I shall write a little something in my diary about our Venetian *portiere*. Such a *character*.'

Relieving Aldo Momesso at his desk every morning, I ran my finger down the names in the guest ledger: Miss Mullvein, Mr Bungus, Mr Winchelsea, The Honourable Lownton Fishcold, Sir Sebastian Sourcollar, Mrs Sprigge and Miss Birthwort. And my favourite, Mr Dearworthy, of course.

As well as names and ages, the hotel ledger listed their home addresses. Then there were two extra columns, labelled *Status* and *Next of kin, if any*. Looking down the *Status* column, I saw a long line of *bachelor*, *spinster*, *widow* and *widower*. And they were always *childless*. It seemed to me an odd coincidence that so few of the guests had ever been married and most of them were of an age where their chances of romance were somewhat smaller than those of my own self becoming Queen of Bohemia.

The *Next of kin, if any* column was also rather uniform. Often there was a simple dismissive dash. Occasionally, it read *Distant cousin, elderly*.

Most usually, it said, *Apply to estate solicitors*. And many of them bore a singular symbol beside those words.

That symbol consisted of a black teardrop inked inside a hollow black heart.

*　　*　　*

So why did they flock to the hotel, these lonely, delicate Englishmen and women?

Here is for why. The secret of the hotel's success was hidden inside the windows' pink awnings, each of which held a theatre stage in miniature. The guests were treated to a series of enchanting scenes brought to life with wind-up devices, candles, painted backdrops and cloud machinery. Thanks to these clockwork scenes, which the Signorina called 'our dioramas', the guests could order that their bedroom view of a shimmering Venetian canal be replaced by an exotic market in Constantinople, a panorama of the Alps or a Parisian boulevard.

'The English have no imagination,' the Signorina said. She was teaching me to assemble each of the dioramas, which was to be one of my daily tasks. The work was intricate, perhaps even a little like making a saint relic. Little fingers were required.

'The English,' she continued, 'hate foreign travel, foreign places, foreign music, foreign drinks and foreign food. All they want is reliable plumbing, a cup of East India Company tea, bread and butter, a slice of barely dead beef, and a cowardly little peek at the big wide world.'

Setting a model camel in place, she said, '*La locanda di ciò che si vuole*' – she used the Italian words for the hotel's name – 'gives the English what they think they want. Meanwhile *they* don't have to move a muscle or sniff an unsavoury odour. They can feel superior without getting hot or bothered or having to deal with starving beggars.'

And indeed each room was a little England. The Signorina sold her guests the story that the jugs by their beds held English spring water from the hills of Malvern, even though our *bigolante* – a tall-hatted lady with a yoke dangling two buckets – pulled it up from the well in Santa Fosca and delivered it to the tall terracotta jars in the kitchen each morning. The Signorina did, however, supply genuine prints of English hunting scenes on the wall and English-style chintzes draping the windows.

Another strange thing about the Hotel of What You Want were the sculpted black lionesses that lurked in every corridor. I always ran past them.

When the light caught their sleek sides they gave off a shine as white as lead paint. Their triangular ears were cocked for my step. Their noses quivered with my scent. I could not escape the sensation that those lionesses wanted to flay me with their teeth and put me inside themselves. I measured my errands on the guest floors in lionesses – how many I had to pass to get to each room and accomplish any tasks, how many I survived.

Sometimes I felt hot lioness breath on the back of my neck as I passed.

Then I was more frightened of the madness in my blood than of those sleek black beasts.

PART FOUR

Young Ladies' Academy
County Kildare, Ireland

CHAPTER EIGHT

For tears, all you need is life and a quiet safe place to shed them.

So you'd not be counting the pillows I soaked in the privacy of the night at my Young Ladies' Academy. I missed my mama and papa sorely. My heart had not closed around the wound of my orphanhood. Months later, I was still cradling my pain as if it was newborn.

Meanwhile my tortures at the hand of Esmeralda continued long and deep. Uncle Red kept not arriving to take me away. He dallied unconscionably long in Venice, until I was fed up to the tops of my eyebrows. Two months, three, four.

What was he doing out there at all?

Venice – I longed to see that place as much as I longed to be delivered from Esmeralda Sweeney and her desire to beat the head off me. Perhaps in Venice, I could be of use to Uncle Red in his mysterious business – the one that lives depended on. I was already fluent in Italian and Venetian. My teacher, the gondolier's daughter, told me that her father wrote to her from Venice to say that a terrible cold winter had started far earlier than was natural. I hoped that Uncle Red was not too distracted to dress warmly.

61

But don't think me an angel. I am not that nice. I also nursed a selfish little hope that the cold might drive him back to Ireland to sweep me up and out of this cursed place.

Adding to my troubles was a sore change in Uncle Red's letters. Once they'd arrived as regular as church bells tolling and were full of sensible kindness. But lately the man was not himself. The few letters that came were strange, rambling. Sometimes I did not know if Uncle Red was describing a nightmare or if he had plunged into some dangerous real-life trouble.

My dear, he wrote, *this beautiful city nurses a horrifying secret. Secretly, I must send you these missives. Secretly, I must go about my business. I fear they are watching me.*

He did not say who 'they' were.

PART FIVE

The Hotel of What You Want
San Felice, Venice

CHAPTER NINE

Seven months later
1 October 1739

Balancing the tray on my knee, I checked the sign outside Chamber Seven.

Tuesday, goes to sleep in Paris, it said.

Underneath: *Wednesday, wakes in Constantinople.*

It was a Wednesday, seven months since I'd left the convent.

Saint Lucy's foot was still missing, and grey skies had continued to brood over Venice the whole time I'd lived and served at the Hotel of What You Want.

I was still alive, to my surprise. I'd already lasted twelve weeks longer than Cecilia. The weals from my beating had healed to scars; my dreams less often tumbled into nightmares about rising water. I was dressed as Cecilia had been, in an *imbusto*, a tight blouse; a *còtola*, my skirt of green and red stripes; and the long rust-red *vestina* or jacket that went over it all. In that coldest of autumns, I wore stockings tied at the knee with blue ribbons. It was the first time in my life I had worn anything that was not bat-brown or grey, and I could not quite get over the sight of myself in the many mirrors of the Hotel of

What You Want. I looked like an exotic bird darting from room to room.

My white face, however, remained quite as sorrowful as ever.

I knew better than to let the mirrors in the corridor distract me from my duties. Speed was of the essence, if I was to avoid a slap from the Signorina or a pinch from Aldo Momesso. I set the breakfast tray on the floor outside Chamber Seven and proceeded as usual to the large cupboard at the end of the corridor. From a shelf, I lifted a large and heavy painted box labelled *Constantinople*. Glass tinkled uneasily inside it, and pieces of cardboard slithered like lizards. With difficulty, on tiptoes, I pulled down an empty box marked '*Paris*' and balanced it on top.

Back at Mr Dearworthy's room, I opened the door. The curtains were still drawn around the bed. Light, agreeable snoring eased out through the green damask.

Quite a cosy sound, I thought. Mr Dearworthy was kind, always helping me with my English without laughing at my mistakes. I liked the rich red hair that tumbled around his wigless head and the soft eyes that rested on me with grave attention whenever I spoke.

I set the boxes on a bench under the window and the tray on a table by the bed. I reached into the pleated eyelid of an awning to remove the glass plate that showed Notre Dame and the Seine dreaming under a dark blue sky and pale moon. I lifted down clockwork dolls of modishly dressed ladies and tiny strutting dogs with ruffs and waistcoats, two painted carriages and their white horses, followed by a block of inviting shops, careful not to dislodge a single tiny apple from the pyramid of rosy fruit on the stall outside the épicerie. I left till last my favourite piece: a miniature barrel organ with its painting of the palace of Fontainebleau on one side. I wrapped each piece in a cloud of sheep wool and placed it in its special compartment in the *Paris* box. Finally I removed all the spent candles that had warmed the delicate mechanisms behind each model and kept the entire Parisian cast strutting and strolling half the night inside the curved awning of Chamber Seven.

I glanced out of the window. The light was growing stronger. I needed to work faster to accomplish my task before Mr Dearworthy's tea grew tepid. The stage inside the awning was empty now.

I opened the lid of the *Constantinople* box and slid out the backdrop of the domes, minarets and palaces, all seeming to float above the waters of a great bay cleverly created by a mirror smeared with watercolour paint and oil. Next, I turned to the upper part of the diorama. Here was what Signorina described as 'cloud machinery' – frames of painted glass hinged on pulleys. After lighting the small lanterns underneath, I tilted the glass this way and that, until the sky appeared haunted by the light and humid clouds of an oriental dawn.

In quick succession I lifted out, wound up and set down cunningly carved figures of men, each in a red fez, a camel, three slender street cats with long black legs. The snake charmer and his cobra went to the right of the scene, a stall of bright spice powders to the left. I arranged the buildings and stalls of the souk. I set sailboats upon the water. I smiled at a lovely veiled lady peering mischievously through the curtain of a litter carried

67

by four slaves. I placed candles behind each mechanical device. For this diorama, they were perfumed with cinnamon, saffron and cumin. I wound the little tin box that played music of the snake charmer's flute. I lit the aromatic candles. Immediately the struts behind the little models began to whir softly. The room filled with the scents and sounds of old Constantinople.

While I handled these pretty toys – which I'd now done so often that it was automatic – my brain ranged over new and better plans for revenge on the *badessa*. This was my habit, and my pleasure. The dioramas gave me ideas; and ideas led to delightful daydreams of my enemy lunged at by the snake-charmer's cobra or trampled by a vicious camel.

While I worked, I also thought sometimes, as all Venetians did in those grey days, of the plot to steal Saint Lucy and all our colour. And that worry led me to thoughts of Cecilia. In all these months at the hotel, I'd not heard anyone utter her name. How could you erase a living girl so completely?

One last task: I replaced Mr Dearworthy's comfortably shabby slippers with a pair of jewelled Turkish ones and laid a red silk robe and a fez on the chair beside the bed.

It was time to open the bed-curtains and rouse the victim.

I know I should have written 'the guest'.

But it was not quite like that.

CHAPTER TEN

There was one more special service provided by the Hotel of What You Want. The Signorina supplied her guests with 'English Night Mixture' to help them sleep.

That mixture was no more English than I was. Taddeo the cook concocted it from mysterious bottles I was sent to fetch from the Apothecary of the Crowned Wolf behind San Marco.

Worse, Night Mixture forced nightmares on our English guests. By night, the hotel corridors rang with groans and whimpers. By day, the drug made the English dim, dreamy and disconsolate. Yet anyone who tasted it always asked for a larger dose the next evening.

It was my task to empty the bottles of whatever English medications the guests had brought with them, and to replace the contents with even more of Taddeo's brew.

The Signorina told me that the Night Mixture helped the guests 'appreciate' the dioramas. 'If they're a little addled, the scenes seem even more delightfully magical to them.'

Because *she* said it, and because she was the sister of the *badessa*, this had the quality of a terrible lie. And to give the lie a sharper sting, there were grim jokes played on the guests. I hated hearing footsteps on the stairs in the middle of the night. Because of my secret rat-skills, I knew they belonged to Ivo Peruch, the hotel's boy-of-all-trades, who'd be creeping down to set a ghastly wax head on some unfortunate guest's pillow. He was the same boy who had rowed me from the convent to the hotel, without a word of comfort or advice when both were so sorely needed.

The wax head's lips glistened as if just licked. It had stiff horsehair eyelashes. The skin was peeled off the face in pale pink flaps. The muscles and the bone were revealed, as were the grinning yellow teeth. A drug-blurred midnight awakening beside this head drove our English guests to think tragic thoughts and write wretched entries in their diaries. I guessed that, like me, the poor people worried that they'd been tainted by madness.

In the morning, the guests woke with the night still inside them. They sniffed blearily at the aromatic French coffee or Turkish spices in their dioramas. But their tired faces melted into smiles when they saw the miniature towers of the mosque of the Hagia Sophia or the souk in Aleppo, or the pyramids of Egypt, all the places it would be so hot and bothersome and vexatious to visit in person. And beside their beds, they'd find a neat package of rose-scented Turkish delight and a pair of embroidered slippers with turned-up toes. They forgot their nightmares and began to feel pampered again. And so, somehow, they fell back in love with the Hotel of What You Want. The enchantment of the dioramas worked every time, is what it did.

To entertain her guests, and to add to the tumult of their senses that bitter autumn of 1739, the Signorina had brought in

70

a tall well-made boy called Giacomo Casanova. She got him up in an expensive wig, a powder-blue frock coat in figured velvet with deep round cuffs and scalloped pockets, a ruffled shirt tucked inside a long damask waistcoat, satin breeches, ribbon-tied stockings and heeled satin shoes with turnover tongues.

Not that I personally was given to staring at the boy, of course.

In other words, the Signorina's gift to the guests she hated was a scaled-down model of a great Venetian gentleman of fashion. The truth, like everything else at the hotel, was less lovely. Aldo Momesso made sure I learned that Giacomo was nothing more than the son of an actress and the grandson of a shoemaker.

But no one could say he was not clever. Giacomo had studied law since the age of twelve. Rising fourteen, tall as a man, he was now training to be a priest. Law and liturgies were in his head, but the stage was in his blood. Giacomo Girolamo Casanova – he liked to roll his full name off his tongue – never, never stopped giving forth. He would recite long poems with all the theatrical gestures. He could play word games in Latin with any English schoolmaster, and win. He could play the violin as if it were part of his own body. Giacomo would do anything that would make people happy, especially ladies. A *particular* love of making ladies happy, is what Giacomo Casanova had. '*Sweetest* heart,' he called them, even if they were the most shrivelled old maids, like Miss Mullvein and Miss Birthwort.

Giacomo wasn't handsome, exactly. He had something more interesting than that about him. I attributed his charm to his endless curiosity about other people. 'My goodness,' he'd say, no matter what bit of boringness the English ladies confided in him. 'Fascinating. Tell me more, *sweetest* heart.'

71

I too felt happy when I was around Giacomo, because he made it seem that I was absolutely the most delightful person he had met that day. Yet he was a confusion to me. You learn not to expect affection, growing up as I did. Simple things distracted me out of all proportion. Especially a smile. A smile was a diamond. Orphans and diamonds: we do not go together. At the hotel, in the street, if anyone seemed to smile at me, I would look behind me, sure it was intended for someone else, someone loved, someone with a secret sacred tie to the smiler. When that smile was really for me myself – and it came from Giacomo Casanova – what a feast it was.

'Fascinating Lily,' Giacomo called me. 'Not "Sorrowful Lily"! Lovely Lily, my dear friend of the infinite eyes.'

Giacomo did not know that I could not have a dear friend. My need for a dear friend was too big, too hungry, too untidy. I would swallow a dear friend whole.

I let Giacomo's smiles warm my face. But I did not let them into my heart. I stayed alone, and Sorrowful.

And I stayed fearful that I was mad, like my dead mother.

CHAPTER ELEVEN

No doubt the Reader would like to hear that it was charming Giacomo who taught me English. But, as the Reader knows, I was born mischancy. So it was Ivo Peruch, the hotel's charmless boy-of-all-trades, who was tasked with my teaching.

Ivo's English was coolly correct. From a few bitter comments he made, I gathered that perfect English grammar had been beaten into him by his former employer, the British Resident – the ugly man haunted by the little green bird. Ivo always disappeared when he visited. And he never rowed Signorina Magoghe to her Thursday tea parties at the Resident's palace.

Ivo was nothing like a normal boy of thirteen, gangling all over the place like a puppet whose strings have been half snapped. He walked as quietly as a ghost and kept his voice low. Yet he was what any reasonable soul would call a rasper, that boy; a character who makes your skin flinch like an ant in your chemise, like a flea in your bed.

But it was easy to see why the Signorina had hired Ivo to work in her hotel. He hated the English as much as she did. The first words Ivo ever addressed to me personally were: 'The English come to Venice to die. No one misses them. In the meantime, however,' he sighed, 'you must learn to talk to them.'

My English lessons were conducted with heartless precision. Ivo made me repeat phrases after him until they were flawless. He never laughed at my mistakes. He never forgave me when I failed at a word he thought he'd ground into my head.

'It would help if you smiled when I *do* get something right,' I told him.

'It would help if you'd do that more often,' he answered coldly.

It was such a waste, is what it was. We could have been comrades, Ivo and me. We suffered the same daily cruelties from the Signorina and Aldo Momesso. And we had other things in common. We were both orphans who'd misbehaved and been sent away. But I did not hear this from Ivo.

I overheard Taddeo the cook telling his friend the butcher that Ivo had been taken in as an orphan and had worked three whole years for the British Resident, who'd then dismissed him for some outrageous act of disobedience.

I was just leaning in closer for more detail when I felt humid breath on the back of my neck. I turned around to see one of the guests, Mr Bungus, also listening. Yet how could that be, when Mr Bungus could barely stammer a few words of Italian, let alone Venetian dialect? He muttered something about needing to order a weak broth for luncheon and hurried away.

At our next lesson, I asked Ivo, 'What did you do, to get yourself sent off by the British Resident?'

Ivo looked pointedly at the list of pronouns I had copied out.

74

'I met the Resident, you know, on my first day. Why does a green bird follow him about?'

'How should I know?' Ivo flashed. He was clearly resolved to be as slippery as a black eel, so I did not pursue the subject of the Resident. I was simply grateful that the Signorina absented herself from the hotel once a week for a few hours with that unpleasant man. The atmosphere lightened then, because Aldo Momesso also vanished during that time.

Occasionally I would follow Ivo if my errands coincided with the times he left the hotel. I only ever saw him go as far as Santa Fosca, and then he always disappeared. Try as I might, I could not see where. One moment Ivo would be there, treading his invisible tightrope with his far-too-careful walk.

And then he'd be gone.

By the time I had lived eight months at the Hotel of What You Want, my English had grown rare good. Meanwhile, three guests had taken their own lives. Mischance-ily, none of them was my least favourite guest, the whining Mrs Sprigge.

The more English I understood, the more suspicious I became.

In my lessons with Ivo, I was learning how to question the guests, in a falsely casual way, while tidying their rooms or when bringing them a glass of Night Mixture. I had to hold the exact answers in my head until I could run down to record them in a particular ledger kept under the reception desk.

'And what brings you to our lovely city of Venice, sir?'

'Forgive me, but do you not have an air of sadness about you, madam?'

'I could not help noticing that you seem very much alone?'

'Ah, a lost love is always tragic.'

'No family *at all*?'

'No close friends?'

'So *nobody* knows that you are in Venice?'

The English guests would shake their heads mutely, unable to speak. Then, down in reception, I would put the necessary marks against their names in the ledger.

Another of my tasks was to watch who cried when Giacomo Casanova sang his songs of lost love. Then I had to put the teardrop mark inside a heart against their names in the green book. Giacomo's voice was not the most beautiful in the world, yet there were more passionate feelings crammed into every one of his songs than there were drops of blood in a happy mosquito full of her victims' vital fluid at dawn.

Every so often, when he was singing, Giacomo would look at me, and I would feel as if little pink crabs were scuttling all over the back of my neck.

Who'd have thought that sensation could be so very pleasant?

Reader, does it surprise you that the guests liked me? They praised my 'cut-glass English accent'. They did not realise I merely mimicked their own voices, adding a tremor of empathy. I received many tips, which I saved in an abandoned mouse hole in the skirting board of my tiny attic bedroom. I did this because I already knew – deep inside me – that someday I'd need to leave the hotel in a hurry. Then I'd need a little money behind me.

The hotel guests themselves collaborated in my English lessons. Their sentimental hearts loved the *idea* of an orphan girl with crumpled eyes – once Mr Dearworthy had pronounced them so, everyone had used those words on me.

Every morning, I brought him tea in bed. Mr Dearworthy began mock-complaining as soon as I opened the bed curtains. I enjoyed his complaints. So did the gentleman himself, because he uttered them with a twinkle in his blue eyes, is what he did. It was as if he prepared them especially, in order to detain me in pleasant conversation.

'There are no straight lines here in Venice!' he'd exclaim. 'And the houses are as densely packed as the bowels inside my belly. How does one find one's way around?'

'I suppose we just know, sir,' I said. 'We Venetians are born with a map inside us.'

Mr Dearworthy continued, grinning like a fox. 'And as for the gondoliers and their songs! They sound like spleen extractions. Mercy me!'

'Mercy me!' I agreed, laughing out loud.

'Ah, you can laugh, my dear Lily,' he said. 'I so hoped you had it in you, despite those eyes of yours. A girl who doesn't laugh is like a cat who doesn't chase butterflies!'

That morning, Ivo caught me smiling as I came out of Mr Dearworthy's room.

'Don't you go getting a soft spot for any of those guests,' he said.

77

Ivo missed nothing.

That evening, when I brought him his Night Mixture, Mr Dearworthy looked me straight in the eyes and said, 'Lily, if you ever wish to talk to me, quietly and in confidence, I shall listen and be discreet. Truth is a great relief, my dear. Why not try it?'

CHAPTER TWELVE

From that time onwards, many was the time I was ordered to Mr Dearworthy's room to question him yet again. I was sorry to see how, over the months, he showed the dismal signs of heavy dosing with the Signorina's English Night Mixture. Mr Dearworthy was transforming from a twinkling, teasing Englishman to a long twitching hare of a man.

One day I noticed a new symptom. He started violently at the clatter when I laid his tea tray on the table beside his window, which that day hosted a busy diorama of Marrakech. His hands would not stop shaking. He answered my questions in an absent-minded way, his voice smeared with sadness.

'I hope . . . I hope you feel better, sir,' I said. 'Perhaps don't drink the Night Mixture any more.'

Then I glanced around quickly in case Aldo, Ivo or the Signorina lurked in the corridor. What if it was suggestions like that which had got Cecilia disappeared?

* * *

'Cecilia who? I don't know who you're talking about,' Ivo always insisted, every time I asked about her.

'It is quite amazing what you don't know,' I said bitterly. 'The length and breadth of it. And what you don't remember.'

I could not help but think that Cecilia's fate was a pattern for my own. Anxious about Mr Dearworthy, I was more rat-twitchy than ever. I began to hunt for clues, deploying all the old rat-skills I'd used for spying on the *badessa*. Given my extensive duties, nothing in the hotel was out of bounds to me except one storeroom, next door to Chamber Seven. It bore a sign that read opaquely *Awaiting collection*. It was locked, always, with the key kept in a pigeonhole supervised by Aldo Momesso. I observed that if the *portiere* was not there then neither was the key.

One evening, when Aldo was slumped snoring on the desk, I borrowed the key from its pigeonhole long enough to make a swift impression in soap. Then I whittled a copy out of a chicken bone. Late the next night, when all the guests lay sleeping, I lit my candle and crept to the storeroom.

Inside were piles of green ledgers. There was also a serving outfit just like the one I wore myself, hanging on a butcher's hook like a hollow corpse. I knew instantly that it was Cecilia's, because it still held the size and shape of her body inside it, and because of the bloodstains on the sleeve that had covered the place where she'd carved her name.

As I approached the far wall, one of my feet dropped into nothingness. I collapsed to the floor, clinging to the edge of a hole as wide as a wine barrel. My candle dropped a long way and landed with a thump, a roll and then a splash. My scream was silent – the breath was choked out of me with shock. I needed both hands to haul myself back to safety. Lying on the floorboards, I heard the waves lisping two storeys below. I knelt to peer over the edge. When I touched the rim, my hand came away sticky and stinking. The smell hit first my nose and then my mind with bitter memory.

Goose fat.

I rose, hurried out and closed the door. I stumbled into Miss Mullvein in her elaborate nightdress and a lace cap, holding a candle. In her other hand was something that looked like an apothecary's glass beaker.

'I heard a noise,' she said. 'Are you quite yourself, dearie? You look shaken. What do they keep in that room, Lily? It's always locked.'

How did she know that?

'Very . . . strong soaps for . . . scrubbing skirting boards after flood tides,' I improvised. 'Dreadful-smelling, it is. Best keep away.'

Her eye fell on the adjacent door, the one behind which Mr Dearworthy slept. 'Poor gentleman,' she said. 'Not himself, lately.'

A few hours later I was one of the last two people to see Mr Dearworthy alive.

PART SIX

Young Ladies' Academy
County Kildare, Ireland

CHAPTER THIRTEEN

I barely recognised the handwriting in Uncle Red's next letter, so wild was it. But I was comforted that it revealed that at least he was not alone in Venice: *I cannot tell my companions what I've discovered. That would not be safe for them.*

I wrote to enquire about those companions: *And don't I hope to make their acquaintance very soon?*

There came another disordered letter that spoke only of sadness and bad dreams. After some weeks, the letters stopped altogether, though the funds continued unabated. I did not know what to do with all the money. A seamstress was sent for, to prepare me a sumptuous wardrobe fit for a duchess. Why else would I need all these clothes unless Uncle Red meant to bring me to Venice? I worked on my Venetian until my mouth was dry.

I read and re-read Uncle Red's last letter, which had made little sense, especially a reference to '*the head on my pillow, which makes me think . . .*'

Whose head? His own?

Then it came to me. *Romance* might have befallen Uncle Red in Venice! Was he distracted and deranged by love? Perhaps I was being outfitted for a wedding? Ladies always loved Uncle Red, but his mysterious assignments invariably tugged him away from any hope of settling down. These months in Venice were the longest he'd spent anywhere. For once, perhaps, his heart'd had time to catch its breath so. I wished him happy, sincerely I did, but I also wished him *quick*: quick to confide his news; quick to summon me to meet his sweetheart. She must be a charmer. We would get along famously, because I am not without a charm of my own.

Meanwhile, didn't Esmeralda Sweeney still look at me the way boys look at cake? And didn't she pounce upon me daily, committing clever offences against my person that never showed up in a bruise you could show to someone in order to get help? My hats were mutilated. My new velvet travel cloak was found snipped to a black snow of threads. The seamstress wept: it was her masterpiece. Still sniffling, she began another. Even when it was finished, I was still at the Young Ladies' Academy, still on the edge of my rump, still waiting for news.

Finally, there was a letter. Not from Uncle Red.

From the offices of a solicitor in Dublin.

PART SEVEN

Venice

CHAPTER FOURTEEN

10 October 1739

I take up my account again from the hour of Mr Dearworthy's death – imagine me running through the corridors of black lionesses.

At the dying bed, I had not screamed, 'Murder! Help!' I had not stayed Ivo's hand on the pillow. I had not stopped Doctor Ichthor recording suicide where there had been a killing. Now, as I panted down the hall, I was screaming silently, mad with grief for Mr Dearworthy. I imagined I saw the lionesses' muzzles glistening with black blood.

It was a relief to put myself outside that murderous place, the hotel, to pound the streets all the way to Rialto to summon the jeweller and the butcher. For what, I could not guess. All I knew was pain, confusion and sorrow.

A fitting darkness had creaked down on Venice while Ivo and I had done what we did. The darkness had been sealed with a great closing of rusty gates to keep out foreigners, thieves and homeless mad orphans with no secret sacred ties to bind them to the good. I felt it personally, every locked door. Tonight, I knew I deserved it. Images of Mr Dearworthy rose up in my mind. Now they were memories of a dead man. Mr Dearworthy would never speak to me again in that kind gentlemanly way he had, never tease me, never ask me to tell him the truth. My hands still trembled for their part in his silencing.

The butcher and then the jeweller, Isepo Luzzo, looked up, sombre, unsurprised at my late-night taps on their windows. To them, I was part of this now – I was just another creature complicit in the filthy business of the Hotel of What You Want. They too counted on me keeping its ways, its silence, its obedience.

In their eyes I read it – and I see it in my Reader's eyes too – the hotel had swallowed Sorrowful Lily and turned her into a murderess.

Ivo avoided me all the next day. The Signorina and Aldo Momesso, in contrast, took every opportunity to stare at me appraisingly.

I was astonished at how the guests grieved for Mr Dearworthy. One after another, they drew me and Ivo aside, begging for details of his last hours. The men were stern, writing things in pocketbooks and comparing notes. Miss Mullvein and Miss Birthwort, dressed in deepest black, applied lace handkerchiefs frequently to their red-rimmed eyes.

Mr Winchelsea slammed his fist on the reception desk, saying, 'This is not right. There is something not in order. No right-thinking gentleman would . . .'

'I am sorry from my heart, sir,' was all I could reply. It was the truth and it was not enough. And it was not enough of the truth either.

When Signorina told them crisply, 'A private funeral has already taken place. The gentleman left express instructions,' the ladies erupted in sobs and the gentlemen shook their heads.

Ivo grumbled, 'Why are they so upset? He's nothing to do with them.'

At nine that evening, Ivo and I were having one of our English lessons at the reception desk, as if nothing had happened, as if no one had died. As usual, but with added urgency now, I tried to distract Ivo from grammar, to extract some information from him.

'Example of pluperfect conditional, Ivo? If Mr Dearworthy had not died, it would have been a far better thing.'

The air vibrated with my fear and indignation.

'Can you at least tell me for *why* the Signorina hates the English guests enough to do this evil?' I asked Ivo. 'Do you know?'

Clearly relieved at a question not directly about Mr Dearworthy, Ivo loosened his tight tongue for once. It turned out that he too had a liking for midnight visits to his mistress's desk. He had also risked daytime inspections of her room during her Thursday tea parties at the Resident's palace. He had pieced together a story from his investigations.

'Some years ago, an Englishman broke her heart and shamed her. She keeps a miniature portrait of him in her bed-chamber still, mounted inside a glass ball, sitting in a bowl of black vinegar. Not a nice face. Thin and weak-chinned. He told her he loved her, promised to marry her – I've seen the letters – but after two months, he sashayed back to London to marry an heiress. The

91

man wrote to tell the Signorina of his marriage, as if she were simply a maid in her own hotel. "*My bride and I shall happily accept your felicitations.*"'

I shivered. 'Did she weep?'

'Momentarily, apparently. But she quickly rebuilt herself out of anger.'

'And now she hates all the English?'

'All of them. The Signorina wants to make money, because it will protect her from scorn. She was scorned because she wasn't as rich as an heiress. By an Englishman. Now any Englishman, any Englishwoman will stand in for the man who hurt her. So – my turn,' Ivo said. 'Your *badessa* – is she like her sister?'

'She's greedy enough for five fat ladies! And mean! She would cane your hide for sneezing in the winter.'

I explained the roasted geese and trade in false relics to his troubled face. 'So yes, the *badessa*'s like her sister. She uses children and young people to do her dirty work. '

'Children are more easily bullied than adults,' said Ivo.

'You don't even need to hit them,' I agreed. 'Once you've got them frightened enough, you can hit them just whenever you feel like it.'

A spasm of pain clenched Ivo's features. I guessed he'd been beaten himself, whenever someone felt like it. I took advantage of his moment of weakness, demanding, 'What happened to Mr Dearworthy's body? Why did the butcher and the jeweller need to come here in the middle of the night? And what happened to Cecilia?'

'Have you not worked out what goes on here? I gave you

credit for being more intelligent, Lily. You watch – no one is more watchful than you.'

'Pardon my ignorance! I've not read many books about how to poison innocent travellers with misery drops . . . or . . . suffocate them. And nor did we receive lessons on these subjects at the convent.'

'You've been an apprentice English-killer for weeks, Lily.'

'How dare you? I am *no girl* to be killing Englishmen or any other living creatures, even rats.'

Nonetheless, even as I said these words, the knowledge crowded my chest that I had marked Mr Dearworthy for the grave. Nor would Ivo allow me to evade my guilt.

'The answers you extracted from Mr Dearworthy made him the perfect candidate for his death. Are you so soft-witted you didn't understand what you were doing? *You* who spent your childhood – such as it was – making false saint bones?'

'I did not know the consequences of those questions . . .'

'Yet you asked them so well.' Ivo's words cut through me.

When I could speak again, I asked, 'Does Giacomo know about the Night Mixture?'

'Giacomo has no idea,' he told me, 'and we mustn't tell him. His heart is too soggy, and his mouth is too wide.'

I said hotly, 'What's wrong with a kind heart, Ivo? And Giacomo's mouth gives pleasure to so many people.'

'I know you're partial to him,' said Ivo coldly.

'I am not,' I said quickly. 'So no one else knows?'

'Aldo Momesso, of course. And the butcher. And the jewellers. And the English Resident' – he spat out the name – 'registers the

93

deaths of the citizens under his so-called protection. And there's one other person who knows,' Ivo said. 'The clerk of the Anatomy School at San Giacomo dell'Orio.'

He looked startled at having let this knowledge slip.

'Where Doctor Ichthor teaches? The doctor told him – the clerk?'

'Her, actually. The anatomy clerk is Alina Magoghe.'

Magoghe. That name again. The *badessa* was Arabella Magoghe and the Signorina was Anna Magoghe.

'Another *sister*?' I exclaimed. 'Two were enough of a blight on this place!'

'And Alina might well be the coldest-blooded of the three. She's ... strange. Even the *badessa* and the Signorina avoid actually spending time with her. She looks cruel.' He used his fingers to pull down his mouth into a grimace. 'Like this.'

'Like one of those sharks at the fish market?'

'Exactly,' said Ivo. 'Yet she's beautiful, somehow. Her eyes are like those black opals from Ethiopia that you see on reliquaries of the most famous saints. Except when she looks at a corpse. Then her eyes are flat, indifferent. It's not a very ... human response. Perhaps that's why she doesn't mind running a place for dismembering the dead. And it's obviously very profitable.'

'What does she do with all that money?' I asked.

Ivo said, 'She has a weakness for jewellery. Earrings like chandeliers! But mostly she just piles up her gold for the love of it. I've found there's a spot on the bridge where you can peer into her office and watch her arranging the coins into perfect pyramids. Then she pushes them into a great heap and starts arranging the money another way, slowly and lovingly.'

I wondered, *What's suddenly made tight-lipped Ivo so chatty, so indiscreet?*

But as he was in a spilling mood, I decided to push my luck. 'And Doctor Ichthor?' I asked. 'How much does he know?'

'As much as he cares to, which isn't much.'

A step in the hall by the watergate made us start. Aldo Momesso poked his head around the door, making the entire room ugly. 'Do you think the Signorina pays you two to sit there looking guilty as a jailhouse?' he asked. 'Get to your duties, my poppets. It's gone ten. School time's over.'

'What happens if someone comes to ask after the dead hotel guests?' I demanded at our next lesson. 'Not one word of English until you tell me.'

'There are occasional mistakes. An unexpected nephew or cousin appears. The Signorina potions their coffee before telling them, "Oh, your dear uncle . . . so tragic. Such a nice gentleman. He was so charmingly *uninhibited* about his fascination with belly dancers of the souks in the Constantinople diorama. He asked us to import a real dancing girl – after all, he said, 'This is The Hotel of What You Want. That's what *I* want.'"'

'A dirty slander, I assume?'

'Of course. But it ties in with the fevered diary notes about a head upon their pillow. Then the Signorina tells the nephew or cousin that we wanted to avoid any embarrassment. She says, "If *you* wish to tell the authorities about your uncle's *exotic* tastes, well, of course . . ."'

'Does that always work?' I asked.

'They assure her, "We shall not be making any further enquiries."'

'And if they are still difficult?'

'They begin to feel quite unwell,' said Ivo.

I snatched more conversations off Ivo when he could not avoid me, such as when we were set to two-person tasks like turning mattresses or taking down curtains for the laundry. To my favourite subjects of Mr Dearworthy, Cecilia, the three Magoghe sisters, I added a new one: what Ivo got up to at Santa Fosca. The more I pried at his tightness on this subject, however, the more he closed up. At the mere mention of Santa Fosca, his face grew as impenetrable and dark as a slab of yew wood. He turned away from me.

To his back, I theorised, 'Perhaps they were poor and alone when they arrived here, those sisters,' I said. 'Money is the only thing that they can trust, hang on to, pile up and use to make people treat them well.'

'You are poor and unloved,' said Ivo bluntly, 'yet I've not noticed any tendency in you to pile up gold coins. Or bones.'

It was not that I hadn't thought of the latter. My dream revenges on the *badessa* were sometimes dirty with blood and screams. When I shocked myself, I reminded myself that it was the *badessa*'s fault that my mind ran those crazed corridors. Even at a distance, she fed on my spirit, my sanity.

And now I was beginning to fear that I'd fallen into a trap. Why did the Signorina push me and Ivo into spending time together – if not to make sure we could go over and over the crime we had committed against Mr Dearworthy? The more we talked of it, the more we were her creatures, saturating in her evil. This was how it worked, wasn't it? You were tricked into complicity and then guilt kept you at the evil work. And whose side was Ivo on, in the end? I was new to this, but he'd been at it years. Had his deeds tipped him over into the Magoghe camp already?

But if I don't become like Ivo, I realised, *then I might become like Cecilia.*

Something new appeared on Ivo's face just then – compassion? Or was I just trying to see it there? His voice gave nothing away when he said, 'As you cannot leave the subject alone, come with me to the Anatomy School. Tonight. I'd quite like to see for myself where Alina Magoghe hides her gold.'

'Do you want to steal it?' I breathed. 'What would you do with that kind of money?

Ivo's face assumed its usual mask of evasion.

'We all have expenses,' he said.

CHAPTER FIFTEEN

That night, the snow started. Snow in October? It had never happened before in my lifetime. Market gossip naturally put the fluttering skies down to the loss of Saint Lucy's foot. Yet from where I shivered, walking behind rather than beside Ivo, the snow seemed like a special malediction just for me, falling on my head to chill my bones and blue fingertips. My *vestina* was utterly inadequate to the task of warming me. It didn't skim the cream of the cold. Ivo's company, as ever, bestowed as much warmth as a tin nail.

The snow had chased Venetians indoors to their firesides and early beds. Ivo and I seemed to have all Venice to ourselves as we crossed the Rialto Bridge, making our way to San Giacomo dell'Orio and the honey-combed poor streets behind the Anatomy School. We paused at the nearest bridge, presided over by a Madonna – a creamy-white statue – in her miniature iron chapel. At the top of the bridge, Ivo nudged me to lean over the parapet and look into a lit window. 'It's her office,' he said.

The first thing I saw in the lamplight was the body of a large man glowing redly in a tray of sand. His head was missing.

'Is that Mr Dearworthy?' I asked. 'Is *that* what they did to him?'

Wetness rushed to my eyes. Tears sharpened my vision. Suddenly I could see that the figure in the tray had his skin peeled off, revealing plum-coloured muscles, red and violet veins, and even ivory-coloured bones. The muscles were tightly plaited, the throat a mass of knotted flesh. His skin was arranged in loose folds around him.

'No, Lily,' said Ivo. 'Can't you see it's made of wax? Alina Magoghe keeps him for Dr Ichthor to use when teaching student doctors, if there are . . . no fresh corpses to be got. The head – that's the one the hotel borrows to—'

'Decorate the guests' nightmares.'

Again, the flood of ugly truth, when it suited Ivo. *What's in this for him? Has he used my curiosity to lure me here? Have I been fatally stupid to come?*

'If that's not him, where's Mr Dearworthy then?'

'Lily, that was three weeks ago,' was all the answer I got.

Turning back to the window, I whispered, 'She's the most dreadfully beautiful of all the sisters!'

As Ivo had promised, Alina Magoghe was counting her money, her face and the gold coins lit by the lamp. She was like a jewelled dragon burrowing through stolen treasure. Her tongue flickered out of her mouth with delight. She wore a dress of opulent red velvet with ermine trimming at the sleeves. She did not turn a hair at the sight of the wax man's poor pillaged body. I breathed, 'She must be the coldest person in the world.'

As we watched, Alina Magoghe's expression of greed grew dreamy. She leaned back in her chair, her fingers stretched out among the coins.

99

'Well then?' Ivo asked. 'What do you think is going on here?'

I stared at him. 'You brought *me* here to see if I could give *you* information?'

Then my eyes turned back to the headless wax man in his tray of sand. For a heart-lurching moment I thought I'd seen his left hand move. But that, of course, was impossible.

The bells of San Giacomo dell'Orio were tolling midnight. As they faded, I heard a creak like an old door easing itself open in the wind. I was sure the noise came from inside the Anatomy School, from the room where Alina Magoghe crouched over her coins, with her back to the flayed man.

It did. The wax man slowly rose from his tray. The skin peeled from his torso flailed behind him like boneless wings. The sound of flapping must have disturbed the clerk's golden reverie. She turned.

Her face convulsed with terror and rage. She cried out something that sounded like, 'Aleeeeesha, damn you and your tricks!'

'Who's Aleeeeesha? Is that the man's name?' I asked.

The headless figure stood between the clerk and ourselves, momentarily blocking her from our view. But I heard her scream with fury as a pile of coins toppled. Ignoring the clerk, the man turned towards the window – and me and Ivo on the bridge. He saluted *us* with one hand and strode out of the room. A few moments later we saw him emerge from the door to the canal. There were only yards between us and all his horror. He rose on his toes. His loose skin flapped and stiffened into voluminous wings. He took off into the night, a pale shadow stippled by the snowflakes that had begun to fall more heavily now.

Behind us, a voice – a woman's voice – cried out, 'Oh, *why* did you let that happen, you foolish creatures?'

There was no one else on the bridge. Just the marble Madonna and the Christ Child in their little stone chapel. Ivo and I looked at one another and back at the Madonna, whose face was as still as the stone it was carved from.

'Did *she* speak?' I asked, a shudder forking down my spine. 'Our Lady over there?'

'We must have imagined it,' he said.

'What, both of us? Together at the same moment? Are we so close, Ivo, that we share visions? And did we imagine the wax man getting up and flying off, or the terror on Alina Magoghe's face?'

As I spoke, the Madonna's marble features suddenly became mobile, lines of agitation flowing from her forehead to her chin. Her eyes glittered with life. 'It was midnight! The Flayed Man was just waiting to be witnessed! Do you not know that you must never look directly at a Flayed Ghost at midnight? The light of your eyes feeds their souls and gives them strength. Even that empty-hearted woman in there knew *that* much and kept her back to him as the clock struck! Imagine what he's up to at this minute. Flayed Men crave the fresh moist skin of others! Headless ones are not above helping themselves to another head, tearing it off the neck of a living mortal.'

My fingers flew to my neck as she continued, 'What are you two doing on a bridge at midnight staring at evil? What are you even doing out of your beds at this hour? What would your parents say? Mortals, I just can't be doing with them!' she complained. She kissed the top of the Holy Infant's head.

'There must be Baddened Magic about,' she murmured. 'It is the only way to account for this whole bad business.'

At a footstep on the other side of the bridge, she stiffened to a motionless posture. A priest appeared. Ivo and I instinctively folded our trembling hands as if praying to the now mute Madonna. The priest nodded approvingly.

Even when he was gone, the Madonna refused to talk to us again. The headless Flayed Man was nowhere to be seen. Alina Magoghe sat in shock at her desk, her fluttering earrings becalmed around her beautiful face, the glittering money unseen in front of her.

'That Madonna *spoke*!' I could not keep the fear out of my voice. 'The Flayed Man *flew*! That is magic. Are the Magoghes *magic*? In a bad way? Don't pretend you don't know.'

Ivo's voice shook. 'This is new. I don't know. I'm not pretending.'

The snow still whispered and uttered heavy sighs. I began to shuffle away, one eye on the sky lest the Flayed Man swoop down to take my head. Ivo followed me, a pace behind, as if he could not bear to look at me or talk to me.

It was annoying as a wasp to have him dogging my footsteps. Yet I would have been even more frightened alone. I blinked away tears and warmed up my anger. I turned to Ivo, finally. '*Baddened* Magic? What is that? The anatomy clerk was horrified and angry about the Flayed Man. Something is not going right, even for the Magoghe sisters. What was that name she called out?

102

Aleeeeesha. Who? What has this to do with poor Mr Dearworthy and why he had to die?'

Ivo shook his head, stubbornly. At Santa Fosca, I watched to see if his glance betrayed anything. He flicked his usual look towards the Apothecary of the Golden Hercules, and his expression suddenly softened, but his footsteps did not falter.

We arrived back at the hotel as the bells of San Felice were tolling one.

I was exhausted and frightened and in no way ready for what awaited us.

For the last thing I expected was that Mr Dearworthy would have someone who loved him, or that she would turn up in the middle of the night at the Hotel of What You Want.

CHAPTER SIXTEEN

'Shop!'

A clipped little voice, and an insistent pressing of the reception bell, summoned me and Ivo away from the horrible tasks we were struggling to catch up with after our visit to the Anatomy School. It was two in the morning. I was up to my elbows in cold water in the laundry room, washing meat stains from the cook's aprons; Ivo, in the kitchen, was scrubbing the bone china cups deeply stained by stewed English tea. Aldo Momesso's night off had just started and we were supposed to man the *portiere*'s desk till dawn, as well as attending to our own work.

At the fifth squeal of the bell, Ivo and I rushed to reception from our different rooms, arriving with such speed that we collided in a painful clash of knees and noses. The bell was still vibrating horribly. Any moment Mrs Sprigge would be descending in her limp nightcap to complain about the noise and the Signorina would appear in all her frightfulness to punish us.

Approaching the desk, all I could see was a hat – a most appalling black hat infested with drooping snow-dusted feathers. Its brim rose to my own eye-level next to the counter, motionless.

After the scarcely believable things I had just witnessed at the Anatomy School, I was almost prepared to think that a ghost hat – even one as frightful as this – could float in the air and ring the reception bell of the Hotel of What You Want.

Then a small white hand reached up to the desk and slammed the bell again. 'Shop!'

Ivo slapped his own hand down on those white fingers. A furious squawk issued from under the hat. In perfect Italian but with an unusual lilting accent, the owner of the hand shrilled, 'For the love of little baby Jesus, how dare you touch me, you dirty boy?'

My mind's eye flew to the tetchy marble Madonna on the bridge by the Anatomy School, and *her* little baby Jesus. This was turning into a night of unearthly encounters. Was it magic – and was it good or bad magic? – that had brought this strange little person here at this spectral hour?

The voice continued, far from ghostly, 'I am Darling Dearworthy, ward of Mr Gregory Dearworthy. You, girl, have a truth-telling face on you. I demand to know what happened to him.'

A tremor rocked my shoulders. I could not utter the correct answer, which would be, '*Murdered, body disappeared. For further information, apply to this boy at my side.*'

I glanced at Ivo. He too was apparently silenced by shock.

Leaning over the counter, I saw a pair of violet-blue eyes, heavily fringed with lashes, behind a pair of black spectacles halfway down a tiny nose sprinkled with russet freckles. The hair was red as a rash, as red as the hair of Mr Dearworthy himself. It hung in damp draggles over a sable tippet and a voluminous swish of velvet cloak beneath, its hem weighted with melted snow.

Not a ghost, then. Mr Dearworthy's *ward*? She must be an orphan like me, to be in need of a guardian. I wondered what had happened to her parents. Clearly, she was related to Mr Dearworthy by blood. That tigerish hair confirmed it.

Yet, like all the guests, Mr Dearworthy had told me that he'd nobody in the whole world. As the Signorina's drug began to work on him, he'd muttered with increasing misery of his loneliness. Why had he withheld information? Who could *forget* that he had a girl as lively as this one in his life?

Ivo shot me an accusing glance. I had failed in my questioning. He had given me rare praise for my 'neat piece of cunning', and I had not deserved it.

'How do we know you're not some brazen fortune hunter?' Ivo finally asked the girl.

Darling Dearworthy slapped her letter of passage on the counter. 'I'm full sure of who I am, boy. Read it if you don't believe me.'

Written under her name were the words *Ward of Gregory Dearworthy, Esq.*

She slapped down a second letter. It was headed, in copperplate, *Masters Solicitors, London*, I saw. *I regret to inform you of the passing of your esteemed . . . You are his sole heiress . . . provisions for . . .*

'What,' she demanded, with an edge of tears to her voice, 'is this tottering tripe about my Uncle Red taking his own life? Do you think that I came down in the last shower of rain? Uncle Red would *never* do such a thing. Especially when he might well have been . . . in love.'

Uncle Red? It suited him. *In love?* No, *in danger* is what he'd been.

Darling Dearworthy was small for her age, which was, I noted from the letter of passage, almost exactly the same as my own. Her chin thrust sternly forwards. She'd apparently travelled all the way across Europe on her own, arriving in the middle of the night. She must have bullied a sleepy gondolier at Mestre from his bed to bring her into Venice through the snow across the dark waters. She'd commandeered a Venetian porter to carry the large trunk I'd just noticed behind her. Would I have had the courage or tenacity to do any of that? In this most foreign of cities, beset by snow falling out of season?

A girl like this deserves to know the truth about her guardian, I thought.

As if reading my mind, Ivo reproached me with another of his looks. 'Chamber Seven is vacant,' he said. 'A lovely view of Cairo set up tonight. Would you like to see the pyramids, miss? The English usually do. Terms are a week paid in advance.'

I wondered if Darling Dearworthy's Italian was good enough to detect the contempt seething in Ivo's voice.

Chamber Seven, where her guardian died?

'Is that really the only room?' I asked, reaching for the ledger.

'Don't patronise me, boy,' said Darling Dearworthy. She pushed the delicate iron spectacles up her nose impatiently. 'I don't care if you show me the sphinx or a pea sandwich. And I'm Irish, not English. Away with your "English"! Now, I want a jug of hot water and a bed with no lumps. Or wrinkles in the sheets. You may take it from me that I'm a fierce one for a smooth under-sheet. I want bread and hot milk with three heaped spoonfuls of sugar. You may carry my trunk. We shall deal with the matter of my Uncle Red in the morning when there's someone of authority to answer me so. I'll have no more dealings with *boys.*'

The spectacles on Darling Dearworthy's nose were lightly steamed by the warmth of the skin. They hid from her the full sight of Ivo's face, which was turning into a portrait of icy dislike. She carried on as if she were doing him a mighty favour by allowing him to shoulder her trunk. 'Wipe your hands before you touch it! What are you called, boy?'

'Ivo,' he glowered.

'I do not love the name "Ivo",' she said, in English. 'It sounds like "Evil".'

His back stiffened.

'You, miss,' she said to me. 'Come with. And don't creep about like a rat.'

I came with, reluctantly, hardly eager for my own dose of expert scorning. As we passed the lionesses in the corridor, Darling Dearworthy paused to kick each one. 'Nasty beasts,' she said. 'And I feel the need of kicking something. I daresay Master Evil will not stand by to be kicked, much as he doubtless deserves it.'

You have no idea, I thought.

Yet inside Chamber Seven, Darling Dearworthy looked at me kindly and thanked me for helping remove the pins from the monstrous hat. She let down her red hair, which tumbled past her waist. Like her guardian's, it was rich in purple highlights. It rolled around her shoulders in constant motion as she gestured and talked.

'I vastly hate bullies,' she said confidentially. 'And that boy is a clear case of it.'

While I lit the fire in the grate, and encouraged it with bellows, she walked to the window and began to sniff at the spices of the miniature souk in the diorama. She took the tiny fez off one of the male figurines and placed it on the head of a camel.

'That Ivo's got a pocketful of nothing but begrudgery.' In English she added, 'Mercy me!'

My hands prickled. Mr Dearworthy had used that phrase, 'Mercy me!'

She shrugged off her shawl, letting it drop on the floor.

'Why are you called Darling?' I asked, hastening to pick it up. She seemed an abrasive little person to bear such a sweet name.

'Well, my real name is Deirdre – which means "sorrowful" – in full, it's Deirdre of the Sorrows. She a beautiful Irish heroine, you know.'

What did I know of Irish heroines? I'd never left Venice. I'd never even thought of it, so I hadn't.

'Your Deirdre – was she a saint?' I asked, knitting my brows. 'I've not heard of her. Like Saint Rita, patron of broken-hearted ladies?'

'Deirdre? No saint, her! In fact, she was a rather stubborn and naughty girl,' said Darling. 'Deirdre was punished for it and made pure sorrowful.'

'Like me!' I told her. 'I am called Sorrowful Lily.'

'We are twins so!' she said enthusiastically. 'Why are *you* sorrowful? You've a pair of eyes on you that a body'd be wanting to drown in and a great look about you of being *haunted*.'

109

'I am perfectly content,' I lied.

'Sure if that face on you is not sorrowful, I'd hate to see you when you're sad.'

'But why are you called Darling if your real name is Deirdre of the Sorrows?'

'I am not without a sorrow of my own. Long story, starting when my parents were killed in a carriage accident.'

So I'd been right. Darling Dearworthy too had no mother to pet her finely.

'Nor do I have mother or father,' I told her. An invisible yet almost touchable warmth filled the air between us. Darling squeezed my hand.

'Uncle Red adopted me as his ward,' she continued, her voice rich with rage or tears – I could not tell. She was entitled to both. 'We already shared a surname, though he is not quite an uncle and not quite a cousin.'

As I did with all newly arrived English ladies, I began to lay out all the Irish girl's toilette items – the onyx candle-holders, tweezers, a basin in the shape of a scallop shell, bottles of perfume. Her trunk was red lacquer beset with an extravagance of brass fittings and locks. From it, I lifted a gold paper knife, a writing set with more onyx panels, decorated scissors.

Darling Dearworthy had money as well as style. And now she was her guardian's heiress too. She looked soberly at her luxurious possessions as if reading my thoughts. 'Gifts from my Uncle Red. I'd have preferred more visits from the man, who was so kind and charming in himself. He was frightfully busy with something important, however. "There is something to be sifted," he would say, his eyes split wide with distraction. And sure wasn't it something here in Venice, lately? He wrote, *Lives depend on it.* So I didn't like to bother him. I told him I was as snug as in Saint Brigid's pocket at the Young Ladies' Academy. Which was the dirtiest of black and bloody lies. It was a lonesome shadow I cast behind me there. I hated the place and was hated back by certain heinous individuals.'

Brave, I thought, *to keep such suffering to herself.*

I envied her uncrushable spirit. But I couldn't help wondering, *How well would it have fared in a war against the* badessa?

'Your Italian is almost flawless,' I remarked, to fill the sad silence. 'And the Venetian too.'

'Mercy me! I love a foreign tongue in my mouth! Ah, I see from your face that this expression needs some refining. Sorrowful Lily, *you* shall perfect my Italian for me. Uncle Red paid for private lessons, so I could speak Italian as fluently as he does . . . did.'

Mr Dearworthy had *never* spoken to me in Italian! Only in English. Here was yet another thing I should have known.

I asked, 'How did you come to arrive here in Venice so . . . suddenly?'

'How could I let Uncle Red be buried without finding out what befell him? The lawyers' letter about his . . . passing . . . came with a roll of bankers' drafts for my immediate needs. As my immediate need was to leave the academy, I called for a carriage and left for Dublin, where I bought this desperate hat and booked my passage that very day. So here I am in Venice – which seems a pretty kind of place, if freezing like an ice-house, and full of madmen and women wearing silly masks. However, I

111

love it that, behind those masks, they are chattering away in all the languages I could ever wish for.'

'It is our *Carnevale*,' I said. 'Six months of the year, one goes about in masks. The town is one big party. I fear it seems an insult to your grief.'

Ivo poked his head around the door. His eyes lingered a moment on the Irish girl's red curls. I hoped he was thinking guiltily of Mr Dearworthy. Without even glancing at me, he said, 'Lily, there's *work* to finish.'

'Are you mad in the head?' asked Darling Dearworthy. 'It's a frightful hour for working, gossoon. I've a *bone* to pick with you – *killingly* pompous as you are—'

Ivo disappeared, closing the door behind him. I wondered how long he had been listening outside. Long enough to hear me neglecting to ask Miss Dearworthy the usual questions about her state of mind and lack of relatives? She was, of course, already down by one guardian. A needling pang in my heart told me that Signorina would absolutely require this inconvenient girl disposed of.

I already liked Darling Dearworthy too much.

Harden your heart or you'll get hurt, I told myself. I did not want to remember her smile, or her laugh, or her violet-blue eyes with the long-fringed lashes and her gesture of pushing the spectacles up her freckled nose, or the way she stretched the syllables of 'vastly' and said 'so' at the end of so many of her sentences, and 'sure' at the beginning of them.

Wretchedly, I began to ask Darling Dearworthy the prescribed questions as I helped her undress.

'So you're all alone in the world now that Mr Dearworthy is . . . gone?' I asked as she slipped a fresh chemise over her head. The delicate fabric could not protect her, or me, from the indecency of my questions. But at least, in that moment, she could not read the guilt on my face. I added, 'Do the lawyers know where you are?'

But Darling was sharp as scissors. And not blunt, pretty grape scissors either, but those tiny flashing scissors that barbers use to snip the hairs out of men's nostrils. As soon as her head emerged, she fixed on me. 'Did you put these same questions to my Uncle Red so? They are vastly odd questions, if you ask me.'

My neck suffused with an uncomfortable heat. There was fire around my hairline. *I'm blushing*, I realised. Instead of answering Darling Dearworthy, I moved towards the door, muttering, 'I must attend to the reception desk.'

'The desk?' she asked. 'Is it known to scamper off if left to its own devices?'

So I filled a hip-bath for her and softened the water with rosemary to soothe her travel-weary bones and I took her a glass of warm milk in her bed, first smoothing the under-sheet so that there was not the merest wrinkle to trouble her sleep. Without her iron spectacles, Darling Dearworthy looked even younger, like a violet-eyed doll propped up in bed awaiting her owner's arrival.

She patted the counterpane. 'Tell me more about yourself, Sorrowful Lily,' she commanded. 'For a start, what have you to sorrow about? Is this not a pleasant hotel with smooth under-sheets and sparkling crystalware? These knick-knackatory devices in the windows beat all my old dolls' houses to dust! Are you not

113

a lucky specimen, not to be shut up in a frightful Young Ladies' Academy somewhere in the back of an Irish beyond – but instead a girl free to earn an honest living in this city where the whole world longs to come?'

Every word punched my conscience, especially the 'lucky' and the 'honest'. I had no pert answers ready for her. Since I came to the hotel no one had shown an interest in me, except Mr Dearworthy and Giacomo Casanova. And Giacomo was allowed to notice me only if the Signorina wasn't looking.

Darling was saying, 'Sure this hotel is tucked away from the splendours of the Grand Canal, yet it is quieter for that. And all day and night, the waves play their music for your pleasure.'

'I am . . . afraid . . . of the water,' I admitted.

'A Venetian afraid of water? Sure there's a story in that!'

She was powerfully persistent, this undersized Irish girl. To distract her, I was obliged to quickly concoct a beautifully sane mother who'd petted me finely but had died young of a fever. I sketched out a sea captain of a father. I grew myself two older sisters, married off to merchants and living in opulence in Cyprus and Dalmatia. My imagination shambled to a halt after ten minutes.

'For the love of little baby Jesus,' said Darling Dearworthy, 'what a talentless kind of liar you are, Lily. You've bored the legs on me stiff with your sugar-coated details, and me starving for a savoury crumb of truth.'

Even from my downcast eyes, I could see her smiling. She was not angry with me at all. Her smile infected my own lips.

'You're even prettier when you laugh,' she told me. 'I'm sleepy

114

now,' she said, draining the milk glass with gusto. 'But you must come and tell me your real story when we're rested. Be assured, girl, that I shall get to know you, whether you like it or not! I think you *shall* like it, however. And then, Sorrowful Lily, you shall tell me the truth about Gregory Dearworthy's death, be it ever so sorrowful. Uncle Red was a truth-seeker, you know. He always said so. And I am the same so.'

I earned a slap on the ear for being the one who imparted the sore news to the Signorina. She said, 'Watch her. Stick to her like honey. Pretend you are her best friend. Find out everything about this Darling Dearworthy, do you hear? And charge her double the usual rate. She's rich now.'

So I was licensed to spend as much time as I wished in Darling's room. Just as her guardian had, she loved to watch me set up the dioramas – Marrakech, then Paris and next Constantinople. Yet even as she chattered about the wind-up dolls, she interspersed questions about her Uncle Red, about the hotel, about the other guests – none of whom, strangely, seemed surprised at her existence. When she asked me about my own life, something commenced to loosen inside me. My caution and fear – which had served me so well – were dissolving into a heartfelt desire to tell Darling everything she wanted to know.

If I'd told Mr Dearworthy the truth, might he still be alive?

On the third morning, when I delivered Constantinople and her breakfast tray, Darling opened her eyes and repeated her guardian's very words to me: 'Truth is a great relief, Lily. Why not try it?'

I walked back to the door and locked it. She nodded and patted the bed. She poured me a cup of hot chocolate from her tray, guiding my trembling hand to my lips. The sweetness ran down my throat and opened it.

So my own story spilled and gushed into Darling Dearworthy's ears: everything – the murdered babies in the convent, the false relics, the goose-stained teeth of the *badessa*, the wooden cross I'd borne on my shoulders for a week. I told her everything except what happened to guests – and girls like Cecilia – who disappeared at the Hotel of What You Want, guests like Gregory Dearworthy. That I could not bring myself to tell her, because of my own part in it. I couldn't bear the pain, the shame, Darling Dearworthy's hatred. And I did not tell her of the Flayed Man or the speaking Madonna – for I could not afford for Darling to think me mad.

For each dreadful thing I told her, she expressed the *proper* outrage. 'Dreadful doings!' she said. 'Inconceivably cruel! You sad little love! I don't understand, Lily, why you did not fight back all this time. I'd have been taking shooting lessons if I were you.'

'Me, I'm just a rat, creeping about,' I muttered. But I felt the rightness tilting back into things. That's the power that Darling Dearworthy had: a power of correctness, and a power of entitlement to what was right.

She must have been loved rare well, I thought, *and petted finely.*

She had a fearless anger at what was wrong. She burned with

116

all the fire that had been scorned and beaten out of me, or, more lately, subdued under a grey weight of guilt.

How furious the Signorina would have been to know who was the questioner and who the answerer every time she sent me up to Chamber Seven.

'Keep acting,' the Signorina nagged, 'as if you actually *like* the chit, mouthy little madam that it is. And double her Night Mixture. Two drops in her hot milk!'

'We're getting on very agreeably – as far as she knows,' I promised, trying to look sneaky. 'Today she's asked me to take her to buy her own *Carnevale* mask.'

'Get her a *moretta* then!' growled the Signorina. 'For any time she's not answering the necessary questions.'

The *moretta* was a black velvet muzzle kept in place by a button that the wearer had to hold in her teeth. I say 'her' because only women wore the *moretta*. Anyone who wore the *moretta* was also, perforce, silent.

Little did the Signorina know how I loved to hear Darling Dearworthy speak. Over those days I had come to like her with a shocking intensity. I never saw it coming – a sudden fondness for a real girl. I'd done without fondness for so long that I'd got to believing I could manage without. But Darling had only to show me a tiny few bits of affection and here was me thinking I'd like to follow her around like a stray kitten, mewing for smiles, as if smiles would keep me alive better and longer than a bowl of milk.

Of course, Darling Dearworthy would not be my friend if she

117

knew what I'd done. She wouldn't be my friend if she knew about the taint of madness in my blood. She wouldn't be my friend if she knew that she too was surely in danger. Yet I could not warn her – not unless I admitted my complicity in the carnivorous habits of the Hotel of What You Want.

Then she would stop petting me finely. Instead, she would start hating me, as I deserved to be hated.

CHAPTER SEVENTEEN

So far, I'd contrived to empty Darling's milk tainted with Night Mixture into the canal every evening, replacing it with a harmless glass. But I'd seen the Signorina staring with suspicion at Darling's still-bright violet-blue eyes. 'The Irish chit has a constitution of iron,' she muttered. 'They must dose them hard and regularly at that Irish Young Ladies' Academy of hers?'

'So she told me,' I lied.

The days of Darling Dearworthy were filled with legal documents to do with her guardian's large estate. She snatched a little sightseeing with Giacomo between meetings with a lawyer and Ivo's former employer, the English Resident, whom she pronounced 'a bullet-headed swizzler'. She too had seen the green bird that hovered around his head. She'd laughed at his fury: 'All that grandeur and he can't command God's tiniest creature to cease and desist. I'm sore tempted to ask the man what he did to offend that bird, apart from looking crooked at it.'

She happily came with me to buy her *moretta* mask, remarking good-humouredly, 'Well, nothing else would silence me! And now I look like a proper Venetian too.' But her red hair spilled out behind the mask, bright as burnished copper, speaking eloquently of her Irishness: no Venetian grew such colour on their head. And she sometimes perched her spectacles comically over the top of the mask, something no vain Venetian girl would ever do, no matter how short-sighted.

By night, Darling's interrogations of me continued. Every morning she woke the wiser by a memory of mine, including the time I'd been left to drown. 'Esmeralda Sweeney should have a taste of that!' she said. 'She, unlike you, deserves it.'

A week after Darling's arrival, the Signorina summoned me to the kitchen where she herself warmed a pannikin of milk. 'Why is it taking so long to extract the information from the Irish girl? This not *The Arabian Nights* and you're not Scheherazade, spinning stories. Are there more inconvenient relatives in the Dearworthy woodwork, or not?'

Mimicking a scowl of annoyance, I said, 'As you know, the little madam has a wild mouth on her. And the will to talk about notions of her own choosing. I don't believe that anyone has ever with success asked her to change the subject.'

The eyes of the Signorina narrowed. 'There's admiration in your tone. Are you getting a fondness for the chit? That's not your place.'

'I deceive her that I'm fond, that's all.' I hardened my voice. 'To me, she's no different to Mrs Sprigge.'

The Signorina unlaced the flask that hung from her belt. She measured eight drops into a glass vial. Of course, she thought Darling had been unaffected by the smaller doses – the ones I'd secretly disposed of.

'This'll get what we need out of her.' She poured the hot milk into a cup. 'Tonight I'll serve her myself.'

Eight drops. I could not let Darling drink them. She'd not built up any resistance. They would make her rave and vomit. She was so slight they could even kill her.

'I'll come with you,' I said. 'To reassure her.'

Together we paced the lioness-infested corridor to Darling's room. The Signorina caressed the beasts' black heads as we passed. I could have sworn one of them uttered a great rolling purr. *Baddened Magic* was my first fevered thought. But I told myself that fear had made me imagine it.

Darling Dearworthy was sitting cross-legged on her bed, frowning at some legal documents. When she saw the Signorina, she frowned some more.

'I don't want you. Lily may stay.'

The Signorina smiled. 'Of course, my dear young lady. But first *Lily* and I have brought you a tonic.' She held up her vial. You are looking sad, my dear. I must warn you that, in this town, death loves sadness.'

'Sadness and I are old friends these days,' said Darling cheerfully. 'We rub along nicely so.'

The Signorina flinched but then continued smoothly, 'Even so, there is a fever about and we wouldn't want you to get it, would we? Here – I'll mix it with your hot milk and you'll not taste a thing.'

'That's a purely nasty shade of green.' Darling squinted at the vial. 'I'll take my chances with the fever.'

Yes, I thought, *yes, don't drink it. There is death lurking in that cup.*

121

'It contains only the finest ingredients from the best Venetian apothecary . . .' coaxed the Signorina. 'The green is . . . a costly seaweed with medicinal *and* beautifying properties.'

'Take it away. Send up hot chocolate, and some for Lily,' said Darling, returning to the papers.

The Signorina took a step closer; her shadow hung over Darling's face.

She said tightly, 'If only your dear guardian had taken this tonic, he would not have fallen into such a low state. The fever, you see, lowers your spirits . . . makes you a danger . . . to yourself.'

She poured the Night Mixture into the milk and held it out to Darling.

I couldn't watch. I kept my eyes on the floor. The worst thing was that the Signorina's lies sounded so credible. If I were Darling, I would have reached for that cup, just to honour Mr Dearworthy's memory.

Darling's hand was now stretching out for the pale green milk. Because I had evaded the truth, for my own shame, Darling Dearworthy was now in exactly the same danger as her Uncle Red, the danger he had not survived.

I thrust myself between Darling and the Signorina. I plucked the cup from the Signorina's grasp. Trying not to gag on the dizzying fumes, I drained it.

The Signorina slapped my face but it was already half-numb.

'To your room,' she ordered. 'Immediately.'

Of course. She doesn't want Darling to see the effect of those drops!

Darling's face was pinched with amazement. 'Why did you do that, Lily? Why?'

122

My voice had disappeared down my throat along with the Night Mixture. I was already swooning before I reached my bed. I fell unconscious on the bare boards of my room. What would they do with my unconscious body? I could not fight them now. Would my clothes join Cecilia's in the storeroom with the greased chute? My last thought was that, if I died, I had still not warned Darling about what exactly she needed to fear at the Hotel of What You Want.

So I might as well have murdered her myself.

I was almost shocked to wake up on the floor in profound darkness. They had not disposed of me – yet. Perhaps I would not live long. But I could use the time to warn Darling so that she might save herself at least. My head swam too violently to make walking possible, so I crawled like a rat down to Darling's room.

This is too easy, I thought. *No one watching outside my door. No one lurking in the corridor. Where are they?*

I climbed into Darling's bed. Darling was quick to spot the bald truth in my drowsy gabbling. Her mouth dropped open.

'Poisoning? Boys laying wax skulls on pillows? These people are like the villains in some horror-drenched fairy tale. This Signorina is a female Bluebeard. Her sisters are – but Lily! Is this what happened to my—?'

I said, 'Can you forgive me? Ever?'

Would I forgive a person who had colluded in the murder of someone I loved? Of my last living relative?

'For the love of little baby Jesus, Lily! I don't blame *you*!' Darling said, wide-eyed. 'Obviously, *you*'ve no part in it at all. I knew there was something terrible happening. The Signorina, Master Evil and that Momesso monster watch me like craggy vultures. They've been through my things. I was not allowed to visit you when you were taken ill. Would it have killed them to let me do that? Wait! Do you hear that?'

The door seemed to sigh, as if its very wood were breathing heavily.

'There's someone outside,' I whispered. 'Listening.'

They let me get this far, I realised, *so they could learn what I know and what I would tell. Now I've damned Darling to the same fate as myself.*

'Darling!' I shouted. 'You're in danger!'

I blew out the candle. *In the dark,* I thought, *we are all equal.*

Darling's voice rang out of the blackness. 'In danger from Master Evil? The surly eavesdropper? Really, Lily, why do you tremble so? He's nothing but a sourpuss.'

'You'd better hope it's only him,' I whispered.

Together we listened to the door handle turn.

The moonlight sketched a blur of black and lace rushing at us. It gripped my throat. Another person slammed into me, thrusting a sack over my head. Two arms held me tight, dragging me out of Darling's bed. The breath was trapped in my lungs, and fingernails bit into my flesh like iron pincers. The sour smell confirmed the identity of one of my assailants: Aldo Momesso, as did Darling's cry, 'Tell that goose-looking horror to take his hands off Lily!'

124

The Signorina hissed at Darling, 'Do you know that this girl is a lunatic? Or could it be that, amid all her crazed confidences, she's omitted to tell you that she's the daughter of a known madwoman?'

'You're putting lies on Lily, Signorina.'

'Am I?'

The truth has a different taste to a lie, is what it has. I could almost *taste* Darling remembering how I had lied to her about my family. I had never supplied the real story. I'd left a vacancy. The Signorina had just filled it. Meanwhile, I was struggling like a mad thing inside the sack, making noises less human than animal.

The Signorina continued, 'The taint of lunacy is in the girl's blood. She preys on the serenity of our guests with ghastly fantasies of murder and potions!'

A bottle was forced under the sack and between my lips. Liquid was tipped down my throat. How many drops now joined the potion that still weakened me? The darkness grew more intense.

Darling cried, 'Leave Lily be!'

'Miss Dearworthy, you have been duped,' hissed the Signorina, 'by a liar. Did she not try to befriend you with false sweetness? Did she not insinuate herself into your confidence? Did she not ask you a thousand questions, acting as if she cared about you like a sister? Such are the wiles of the mad! Cunning, subtle, credible.'

'Good thing I'm smart enough to know the truth when I hear it,' said Darling. 'Lily was just halfway through telling me something extremely interesting and I *insist* on knowing the rest. *I insist.*'

'Smart as a whip, you are, Miss Dearworthy,' said the Signorina. 'A girl with plenty of this and that.'

Aldo Momesso sneered, 'Smart as a whip. A whip – now there's an idea.'

'Sure you would not dare, beast that you are. I'll pay for Lily,' shouted Darling. 'It turns out that I've teems of money. You haven't the least notion of how much! I shall buy Lily out of your service. She shall be my companion.'

I wanted to say, *You cannot pay for what I know, and that is for why they will kill me now.* But the drug was coursing through my veins like a pride of black lionesses and my tongue was numbed.

'Does your man Ivo have something to do with this?' shrieked Darling.

As I was dragged from the room, the *portiere* told Darling, 'Don't worry. We'll fix your lunaticky young friend. We'll fix her real nice. You won't hardly recognise her when we're finished with her.'

CHAPTER EIGHTEEN

When I woke up, I was bound with a web of ropes to a plank. Only my tear-sore eyes were free to roam. They explored stone walls and a slit of window. Then my nose recognised the stink of boiling goose bones. I was back in the place I had hoped never to see again – Saint Teresa's convent of the Barefoot Carmelite nuns on the island of Murano.

While unconscious, I must have been taken from Venice on a boat and carried through the Murano streets to this place. How many people had handled me? And how roughly? Many and very roughly, it seemed, for I ached all over.

Was Ivo among them? Perhaps he'd rowed me here. Then I thought of Darling. Had she believed the Signorina? It was too easy to picture Darling's stern little face screwed up in horror at her choice of friend – a madwoman in bud.

Then I realised that for her own sake, Darling *had better* believe that I was a mad liar. If she showed signs of thinking otherwise, then she'd not survive long. I hated the thought of Darling shedding our friendship like a dirty glove. Yet I had to hope that she'd done exactly that, giving loud voice to her pure disgust with me.

I drifted back into a mercifully deep sleep. When I woke again, the *badessa* was grinning down at me. 'We shall make a fine nun of you, Eulalia,' she told me, in that string-plucking voice of hers. 'And where better to hide your madness than in the quiet of the cloister? We shall *soothe* your delusions with prayer. And service. And scrubbing.'

'I shall never be a nun!' I screamed.

'No one wants you, Lily,' the *badessa* told me happily. 'No one cares about you. No one has ever cared about you. Girls like you have no choice but God.'

I struggled against my ropes. 'I know what goes on at the Hotel of What You Want,' I said.

'And that's just why you'll soon be begging to become a nun,' was the *badessa*'s answer. I shrank back against my board, awaiting her slap. Instead she produced a large piece of paper from her sleeve. 'So, either you tell me everything Darling Dearworthy knows – or *she* shall become *this*.'

Leaning over the crucifix above my plank, she spiked the paper on the nail that staked Christ's feet to the cross. Then she left, turning the key in the lock.

The letters on the paper were large enough that I could read them from where I lay. *From Darling Dearworthy,* said the note.

Left hand – Saint Tryphon.

Right foot – Saint Blaise.

Toes of left foot – Saint Agatha.

As I read, I imagined each of those parts being harvested from Darling's living body. Feverishly, I thought, *She can survive that. And that. Without her right foot, she can walk with a crutch. Without her left hand, she can still write. They might bring the butcher to her, and she might be less than she was, but she shall live.*

Then I read the last line. *Heart – Saint Philomena.*

When Darling's heart left her body, my soul would fly away too. I felt it leaving already – little sparks of life, of hope, flickering their last.

Days passed. The *badessa* kept her distance. I was allowed to rise from my bed and pace my cell. Food and water arrived on trays. I walked backwards and forward like a madwoman, just to keep my blood circulating. Otherwise I might have frozen to death.

That autumn of 1739 was continuing the coldest Venice ever knew: a devil of an autumn, in which ice floes had already begun to roam the Grand Canal and the whole lagoon showed a desire for freezing over. That made a special *Carnevale* for the rich, idle Venetians, fat as butter, who could skate in their lush furs. I heard their screams of joy through the convent windows. There were no skates for orphans, of course, and no socks either.

The temperature was too bitter to allow more that fitful sleep. So I had a luxury of dark hours for worrying about Darling. Without me to protect her, how long would she last at the Hotel? Giacomo was adorable, but he did not know the truth. As for Ivo – whose side was he on, anyway?

My helplessness was so extreme that my thoughts, the only free thing about me, rampaged far and wide. I thought of all the other girls confined against their will in Venetian convents, forced to become nuns, growing old without ever being allowed to be young. And when they died, who knew what happened to their bones?

When I next awoke, my pillow was wet with tears and the *badessa* was once again gazing down on me with satisfaction. It must have felt so good to her, so nutritious, to see me brought this low.

'We just need *this* cut off,' she said, lifting up a long strand of my black hair. 'And soon you'll be the humblest nun ever born.'

It was Barbarina – she who'd shared the water torture with me – who was sent to do the deed. As she walked into my cell, her face was hard and closed.

Yet when she'd shut the door and checked at the small grate that no one was watching, Barbarina's mouth erupted in a grin. She held up her hands – her fingers were raw and pocked like red coral. So they had set her to lace-making, another of the *badessa*'s profitable enterprises.

A pair of lace scissors hung at Barbarina's belt.

'Please don't cut my hair,' I begged. 'Let me keep it. She's taken everything else away from me.'

'I wouldn't dream of it,' she said. 'Far too pretty it is, dark as ink and soft as a smile. I'll show you how to oil it and coil it away to nothing under this wimple.' She produced a small bottle and a white hood. 'But I need to give you a spiky little fringe up front, so it looks as though that's all you've got.'

Her kindness blurred my eyes with tears. Yet her chatter disturbed me.

'I'm getting out of here,' she told me. 'Once I've mastered the lace trade and repaid my keep for all these years with extra cleaning, then I can go to Burano and marry a fisherman.'

I wanted to warn her, *You know too much, Barbarina. She'll never let you go.*

But I couldn't bear to destroy her happiness and her hope.

And, selfishly, I was too grateful for my hair, which made it feel as if I still owned a little bit of myself.

I was now called Eulalia – in full – after my patron saint and moved to a high part of the cloister reserved for novices.

I wasn't Sorrowful Lily any more. That was the name of a girl who had briefly existed in the living world of Venice, a girl who had dressed in a bright red *vestina*, who had for a short while known the freedom of the streets, who had made an extraordinary friend called Darling Dearworthy.

Now, to keep my friend alive, I would accept a kind of living death.

It is only fair, I thought. *I helped to take her Uncle Red's life. I owe her.*

My new life as a nun-in-waiting made being an orphan at Saint Teresa seem like a time of careless pleasure. My cell was seven paces long by six paces wide. It was located just above the dung hole. The only window was shuttered with a padlock. There was a wooden door with a movable grate for handing in food. By way of furniture I now had a pallet of straw and a battered praying stool, above which hung a crucifix.

When I lay on my pallet, my eyes always flew to the list of Darling's body parts that were now pinned to the wall. The *badessa* had never cared if I lived or died. Now I would never escape her, except if I died. And then I could be sure that my body would not rest in peace or stay intact.

No, I must live and live like this. I screamed, a sound excavated from my sorrows, from the sorrows of all my sister-brides behind high walls all over Venice. My scream scooped up their despair and carried it around the cloister of Saint Teresa. I felt my little world stand still.

From the force of my scream, the *badessa*'s paper teetered on its pin and then fell lazily to the floor.

But no one came to attend to me, or even to quieten me.

Then I understood. My screams were meat and drink to the *badessa*. She wanted me to scream. She loved my screams because they painted her power on the walls. And she wanted all the nuns and all the orphans to hear what would happen to them if they dared offend her as I had.

I closed my mouth and kept it that way.

If I prayed, it was this: 'Go back to Ireland, Darling, and forget about me. That's the only way you'll be safe.'

CHAPTER NINETEEN

Barbarina had taken over as the *badessa's* errand girl. She relayed the gossip of Venice, where the sky still hung low and grey as it had ever since the foot of Saint Lucy was taken. The autumn fruits, Barbarina reported, had rotted on Murano's trees without ever getting ripe. Snow fluttered down and was overtaken by hard rain as it landed. People reminisced, Barbarina told me, of bone-meltingly hot Octobers, and even Novembers when Venetians walked the streets without catching their deaths of cold.

Barbarina was the only person in the convent who gave me a second glance. The *badessa* had made sure that everyone knew that Eulalia, the new nun-in-waiting, was dangerously mad. Even the children pulled their skirts away from me as if I was vermin, as if the taint of insanity was contagious.

I trusted Barbarina because she consented to talk to me, because she'd saved my hair, because we had shared the water torture. But I should have paid attention to the deadness in Barbarina's voice when she volunteered information that the nun who taught lace-making had found a way to send secret notes to her brother in Venice. I should have noticed how Barbarina did not meet my eyes when she told me that the letters were hidden in packages of lace that reached the outside world via the wheel set in the convent wall. I should have worried when Barbarina agreed with hesitation that she'd smuggle ink and paper into my cell and slip a note for me into one of her rolls of lace. I should have wondered about all these things, but the lure of a pen and paper was too dazzling. With a pen and paper, I need not be alone. I could write a secret letter to Darling and urge her to flee Venice. I could tell her that I had embraced my vocation as a nun, and that she must forget all about the terrible things I'd said.

Scanning the address written on the outside of my letter, Barbarina was unsurprised. I should have noticed that.

She said, 'You'll never guess what happened there – at the Hotel of What You Want!'

'What?'

'A burglar came in the night and robbed a young Irish girl. I recognise her name on your letter! Such a strange name, Dar-ling Dear-worth-ee! I heard at the Rialto Market that the girl happened upon the robber about his work and he beat her without mercy.'

'Is she . . .?' My heart hammered at my breast.

'She survived, and gave him something to think about, the boy says.'

All this while, I'd believed my own problems the most consuming subject in the world. I thought I was saving Darling by submitting to the *badessa*'s will. Meanwhile Darling had been attacked. But she was still in Venice. She'd not gone back to Ireland.

Yet to save her life, I had to make her do so. I snatched back the letter and scribbled a few last words: *Please excuse the mad*

134

things I said to you, I concluded. *I was not myself then. A life of perfect piety is all I seek now.*

'Don't fret, Lily,' said Barbarina as I refolded the letter. 'The errand boy shall collect it this evening with the lace. Dar-ling Dear-worth-ee shall be reading it by this time tomorrow. Easiest thing in the world.'

Next morning I was escorted to the *badessa's* office. My letter to Darling lay open on the desk.

The *badessa* said, 'How wonderful that Darling Dearworthy shall read these pure facts for herself in your own handwriting, Eulalia. Thank you for that. Yet your sneaking act requires punishment.'

That night I spent down in the room by the water, waiting for the tide to come in, and then fighting once more to stay afloat and alive in its grip.

After that I began to live as a nun and I learned the hopelessness of a nun.

It had taken the *badessa* just four weeks to destroy me.

I dragged myself around the parts of the convent that were allowed to me. I breathed in the steel-cold air, and kept it inside my body, as if it offered a protection against loneliness. For I wished to be numb, inside and out. I felt nothing when Barbarina came to show me her sorry face. I walked past a baby mewling in a basket in the cloister and did not pick it up.

Yet there was no quiet corner of my mind, no place of safety for my feelings, no place of pleasant blankness. My mad thoughts kept me constantly and cruelly roused.

Madness – I felt the grains of it rubbing against the soft matter in my head, inflaming it. I was too aware of the skin under my fingernails, too conscious of each blink. The sensations exhausted me, as did the beating of my blood. I no longer believed in myself as a person. I was just one of those faceless nuns, stamped out like books, hundreds at a time, all the same. I shuffled like a nun. I lowered my eyes like one. There was no point in looking up. I still sometimes thought of Darling, and of Ivo and of Giacomo, but in a dim, foolish way, as if they were creatures from an old fairy tale. The only sound that made sense to me was that of the gulls laughing at me outside my cell.

I was not allowed to join the nuns in the refectory. Food was brought to me in a new cell that was tucked in the northernmost – and so the coldest – outside wall of the convent. It was only gradually that I realised that my rations were dwindling. The *badessa* told me, 'Dead girls don't need to eat.'

So that was it. Now that I'd written those lies to Darling, the *badessa's* work was done. Business – that is, murdering and dismembering – could go on as usual at the convent and at the Hotel of What You Want. The *badessa* was free to starve me to death. She could blame my madness for my wasted corpse. Perhaps she'd done the same to my mother. It was a gentler destruction than I had feared, even though the *badessa* would enjoy its slowness. I fell into a dreaming state, each day feeling less and dying more.

*   *   *

I was in that state, days later, when a pair of hands arrived at my window sill. I considered the sight of them yet one more proof of my madness.

Dully, I noted Ivo's red face above those hands and a bolt-cutter snapping the lock on the shutter.

Ivo smiled at me. That smile in itself seemed the substance of a dream. Ivo Peruch did not smile at *me* – he only ever looked so gentle and concerned when he glanced at the Apothecary of the Golden Hercules in Santa Fosca.

'Hello, Lily,' he said. 'Barbarina told me where to find you. I assume you're ready to leave? We've come to take you away.'

'We?'

'Darling waits below. Did you think she'd believe that ridiculous letter?'

He flung two ends of a rope ladder into my cell. 'Tie them to the door handle,' he told me. 'Can you stand on your bed to reach this window sill?'

He drew in his breath at the sight of my gaunt wrists. Then he helped me climb on to his back and carried me down the rope ladder.

 **CHAPTER TWENTY**

Darling put her arms around me. Her face was hidden in the muzzle of her *moretta* mask. With the button between her teeth, she could not speak. She pointed to the canal and the boat that Ivo had borrowed from the Hotel of What You Want.

Safely aboard, Darling spat out the button, revealing the blackness around her eye where she'd been hit. 'It's fierce pleased I am to see you,' she whispered. She snuggled up to me, drawing a blanket around both of us. I let the warmth of Darling's body soak into mine.

'There's nothing of you!' she exclaimed. 'In a few weeks you are become purely bone and skin. You can't weigh more than a herring. What have they done to you? What *haven't* they done to you?'

Better than what would have happened to you, I thought, *if I had not submitted to becoming a nun.* But I didn't want to talk about that. 'You were attacked, Darling?' I asked. 'Your room was ransacked?'

'Mercy me!' said Darling, ''Twas nothing worse than this your woman Magoghe could contrive for my discomfort. I was not

138

without giving a punch or two of my own. I'm fine as fivepence.'

'Did you see who it was who came at you?'

'Not herself, I believe. All swaddled in black he or she was. Not a glimpse of a face on show. But it *smelled* like Aldo Momesso. Dank and vastly nasty. And I notice he's wearing a nasty bruise under his hoary chin now.'

'Quiet!' ordered Ivo. 'Do you want the whole lagoon to know that Lily is not in Saint Teresa's?'

'Of course, *you* are so naturally secretive,' Darling told him, 'that you could teach snakes to sneak. In the Garden of Eden, *you'd* be *best friends* with the serpent.'

We all sank into silence, stunned by the cold. From the boat, Venice looked a crust of a city, nursing her lost summer heat deep in her terracotta bones as she floated uneasily on a well of dark blue iciness.

Ivo rowed us back into the tiny canals. He returned the boat to its mooring, while we waited for him in an abandoned courtyard a few streets away. Darling lifted my bat-brown habit over my head. She helped me struggle into a pair of boots and one of her own dresses, which she'd brought rolled up under her arm. She handed me bread and cheese that she'd tied into her sleeves. Between mouthfuls, I asked, 'Where are we going?'

'Master Evil won't say. He claims it'll serve for one night. And that we mustn't be seen arriving there by boat. Don't eat so fast. Little bites,' she urged.

I said, 'Be careful of him, Darling. He *seems* to be helping . . . yet as soon as you unpick any of his lies, he weaves new stories out of the same words—'

139

'I've the measure of young Master Evil,' she told me. 'So crooked he couldn't hit the water if he fell in a canal.'

I wondered how the two of them had managed to stay civil enough to contrive the plan to save me.

'Ivo!' Darling's strained tone warned that he was approaching from behind me. 'Where in the name of little Baby Jesus *are* we?'

'Of course *you'll* get lost around a single corner from the hotel,' sneered Ivo.

'There you go again, Master Evil, rejoicing as to how you Venetians have it over non-Venetians, with all your secret sacred ties and the city's map printed inside your heads. To a person of normal wits and sensibilities, one humpback stone bridge over a green canal *naturally* looks the same as the next.'

'I pray that you are never alone in Venice, Darling, but always have me to help you,' I told her.

'Come,' said Ivo, tugging my arm. His face was pinched as we hurried along the narrow streets.

'Would it kill you to tell us where we're going?' Darling asked him.

'It's best if I don't name the place,' said Ivo, 'in case someone forces you to tell them.'

'Very well, so, Lily,' Darling said to me, 'the night you were taken, you were about to tell me about Uncle Red's death—?' She pulled my letter out of her sleeve. 'And you wrote *this* pack of lies to put me off the track. You chose to let the *badessa* have her way with you, in order to save *my* life, did you not?'

'That,' snapped Ivo, 'is another matter not to discuss in public.'

I threw a scornful glance at him. How long did he think he

could hide the truth from Darling? She wasn't slow to voice her suspicions now: 'You're acting the maggot, Ivo, which is Irish for you're up to no good.'

She tore the letter into a dozen jagged pieces and dropped them on the ground, her eyes fixed on Ivo.

A couple in the street stopped to stare at us. 'What's going on here?' cackled the woman.

'*She* looks foreign!' The man pointed at Darling. 'Those clothes! That red hair!'

The man took Darling's shoulder in a rough grip.

'Run!' I shouted. A few streets away from the couple, we paused. Darling was in a bother with the panniered hoop trying to rise above her knees.

'Y-y-you are walking all wrong, you two,' I panted. 'You have to learn to look as if you don't exist!' I lectured them. 'As if no one loves you. As if no one's ever loved you. Then people won't even see you.'

I showed them how to inhabit the air like nuns: eyelids downcast, body clutched into itself, inaudible steps, mouth sealed. Darling's eyes were hot with concern. But Ivo had an aptitude for invisibility already. I guessed he had learned it during his time in the English Resident's service.

We left the well-known parts of Venice far behind. Buildings grew humbler, sparser. We crossed an orchard. Apples crunched juicily under the ice beneath our feet, releasing a sweet rotten perfume. Then a rough terrain tangled up our feet and made us stumble.

'There are no houses here,' I observed. 'Where are you taking me?'

'No houses, no spies,' said Ivo.

'Another question deftly sidestepped,' muttered Darling. 'He loves an evasion, does our Ivo so.'

The big gulls swooped overhead, noting our presence with cries like silk being torn.

'Gulls always laugh at me, is what they do,' I told Darling. 'And do you know what? Our Venetian word for them is *magòghe*, almost identical to the name of those sisters from Sicily.'

'Lily,' she said. 'Mercy me! You see everything darkly now. Your feelings have been trampled so. Sure the sisters borrowed the Venetian-sounding name by way of a cover to help them slide more easily into Venice society.'

Ivo looked quickly over his shoulder and jumped down on to a shingle beach lapped by the grey waves. Then he drew aside some bushes, calling, 'Come!'

We followed reluctantly, ducking our heads and crouching down to a crawl. There was a faint light inside from a shaft in the rock. The sourness of rotting seaweed twitched my nose.

Ivo tinder-lit the lantern he'd brought and held it aloft. We were in a small cave. The sand was damp and giving under my feet. The water outside was uncomfortably close. To me, the roar and crunch of the waves was as frightening as the howl of a wolf.

'Ivo, you gossoon!' said Darling, reading my face. 'This is beyond dreadful. For the love of little baby Jesus, Lily cannot sleep here.'

'It's the best I can think of,' said Ivo. 'This is where I wanted to bring—' He stopped, deciding not to share that information with us. To me, he said, 'Here's my cloak. You can keep the lantern and tinderbox.'

Darling suddenly threw her arms around my shoulders and pulled me to her bird-boned frame. I felt her bird-light heartbeat close to mine.

'It is fierce sorry I am to put you here, in this sorrowful place, Lily,' she said. 'I wanted to buy you a room in a hotel. But Venice is so small, Ivo tells me you'd be spied on and denounced. Aldo Momesso has his ear to every slippery corridor of gossip.'

I nodded.

Darling's brows knitted. '*This* place is not what I dreamed for you at all. And you should not be alone, Lily. It's a crime so to leave you here in this frightful cold and dark, with your health not what it should be and your spirits down a hole.'

So she too fears for my sanity, for all she tries to tell me I'm not mad.

'But Darling absolutely needs to show herself to the Signorina at the Hotel of What You Want, and so must I,' said Ivo impatiently. 'And Darling must still act sad and bewildered about your disappearance.'

'Go!' I ordered them. 'I'll do perfectly well here,' I lied. 'It's more comfortable than my cell at the convent, is what it is.'

In that, at least, I told the truth.

'Put your mask on!' Ivo told Darling. 'That's it. Put that button in your mouth.'

'So you don't want to hear my thoughts on Lily's accommodation, all the way back to the hotel? Fancy.'

As the sound of their arguing faded, I propped the lantern in the sand and unwrapped the rest of the bread rolls Darling had brought me. I devoured them as slowly as I could. I stretched out in the sand and wrapped myself in Ivo's cloak and slept the sleep of shock, exhaustion, relief and freedom.

But mine was not a dreamless sleep.

CHAPTER TWENTY-ONE

I dreamed that I was sleeping in a cave. As you do in dreams, I saw myself as if watching from above. Dream-Lily wore gloves of sand; her hair was wrapped in crumbling veils of its whiteness. Her dress was coated with sand so that she seemed halfway to a marble statue. Dream-Lily lay still as a statue, except for ripples of shivering.

In spite of everything, Dream-Lily felt safe, not sorrowful.

Darling's smile hovered in my memory. I had been embraced tenderly before being left alone. I turned over in the sand and wrapped my arms around myself as if they were Darling's.

Then Ivo's face floated into my mind, along with sore misgivings. At that moment came a hellish clamour from outside the cave. In your dreams, you know things. So I knew that the noise was God fighting with the *badessa* in the lagoon.

I crawled to the opening of the cave. Dream-Lily's eyes ranged out to sea, for dreams lend you a telescope as well as full knowledge of things beyond your own brain.

They fought with thunderbolts and lightning on God's side,

and shrill curses on the *badessa's* side. The lagoon lit up and fell into a blackness punctuated by horrible streams of insults.

I saw myself, pathetic as I was, a half-starved girl, peering at a battle, sitting with her stick-legs in front of her – a figure so insignificant that you'd notice her solely because of the amount of misery densely packed into her scarred and famished body. I sat there, one little young person, the only witness to a battle between good and evil.

But it was also personal. God and the *badessa* were fighting over *me*.

And it was possible that God might lose.

The fury of the battle rose and the tide soared with it until the sea unrolled a long black tongue into my cave. I heard the *badessa* say, 'Ah, there you are, Eulalia,' and I screamed, waiting for her face and her body to join that terrible voice.

The badessa *has beaten God*! I thought. *And now every good thing will go from this earth. Venice. Darling. Everything.*

All my sorrows seemed to be living things. Pain was feasting on me. Then the stink of goose grease filled my nose, and I fainted with the horror of it, and what it meant.

I was woken from my nightmare by the first icy wave washing over my legs.

I shuffled back, deeper into the cave.

Of course, I thought dully, *the water*. In Venice water is always inevitable. *It comes like the saliva in your mouth is what it does, over and over.* The water kept coming. I wrapped my arms around a rock and clung to it as if it were someone who loved me. If the water took me, then I would likely freeze to death even before I drowned.

The water wrenched me from my rock and tumbled me on the coarse sand as if it wanted to polish my skin. The white fingers of the retreating waves pulled me with them far out to where the water was infinitely black and deep below me. My spine flexed like a worm. I felt loosened from my bones. I no longer knew what was dream and what was life, what was death. I thought, *The badessa has sent these waves for me. Because she won.*

The waves made fists, kneaded me between their wrists and thumbs. My eyes were harried by the million teeth of the salt-stinging water invading my nose and ears, lastly my mouth.

I paddled my arms frantically, but the truth was, I had no idea which way was up to the air and which way led to the depths where the weight of water would crush my lungs. I might be desperately saving myself or frantically killing myself. I might be swimming towards an undulation of poisonous jellyfish, or away from them. How would I know?

The waves delivered me into a canal and flung me from side to side. I scrabbled at the shell-encrusted walls. Without pity, those walls scraped away the tops of my fingers, and shrugged me aside.

I wept, *Why does Venice turn her stony shoulders against me, her orphan daughter?*

My black hair billowed around me. A prayer bubbled out of my mouth, letting more water in. A prayer? I don't know where it came from inside me – from me, Sorrowful Lily, who knew just how often saints' relics were false. From me, Sorrowful Lily, who

147

had known no blessing or mercy from a life lived in a house of God's brides. Yet, as the water claimed me, I folded my wet hands together and prayed. But not to God, or the Madonna, but to Saint Lucy, the favourite saint of Venice.

'Save me, Saint Lucy!' I begged. 'If there is Baddened Magic, like the Madonna said, then surely there is *good* magic too? Isn't that what faith is – good magic? I swear, if you spare me, in your name, I shall put an end to the *badessa* betraying saints with false relics. I shall make her sorry she ever faked a saint's kneecap. Or beat an orphan. Or left a baby to die. And I shall find your stolen foot, I swear, and restore it to you.'

Inside my head, I heard a soft female voice chanting, '*The vow has been made and the saint has accepted it.*'

Suddenly, I lost the desire to fight, or even to scuttle away like a rat. I wanted to be taken into the water's cold arms. I did not try to swim against the tide that wanted to take me. As my mind faded slowly to blank, a wave dragged me under the rim of the sea and water began to cram itself into my mouth and nose.

I separated from myself then. I re-entered my dream. I stopped hurting. For the first time ever, I was without pain, or anger or loneliness.

I watched as my own body roamed the reefs as a jellyfish moves, my skirts ballooning, shrinking, undulating.

In my dream, I saw fish kiss my lips and breathe bubbles of sweet air into my mouth. Then the currents would seize me again.

I believed in my dream-heart that I would be the sea's creature for long years afterwards, a bruised, fish-kissed thing, a peeled thing, and finally a bone thing, propelled by my hair through byways of below worlds, my parts white and smooth as a shell, the cragging of my ribs made mother-of-pearl and my skull a lantern for fish.

Then my dream stopped telling me my fate. Darkness fell, even on my mind. The kind of darkness that no lamp could ever light up.

I have nothing more to tell you, Reader.

PART EIGHT

Venice

CHAPTER TWENTY-TWO

I was woken by the newsboys crying the early morning *avvisi* through the streets. The words sounded oddly like, '*Headless Flayed Man seen flying over city? Mermaids stolen from the church of Santa Maria dei Miracoli!*'

I was not without a question mark and an exclamation of my own. *Headless Flayed Man? How would a flayed man fly without his head or eyes to guide him? Who would steal a mermaid? And why would you be wanting mermaids in a church?*

More like a fairy tale than the news: I must have misheard. My thoughts returned to Lily, crouched all alone in Ivo's horrid cave. I hoped she'd caught a little sleep and not her death of a chill on that cold sand. I should have brought her two of my dresses to wear, one over the other. A single dress had been a selfish notion. I thought of the pangs in her poor belly, fed only on bread rolls after a month of sparse rations and plentiful cruelty.

Outside the newsboys kept shouting. Their words insisted on penetrating. '*Church stripped of mermaids!*'

Sleep was done with. This had to be investigated. And then I would make Ivo take me to Lily with a basket of hot pies, that second dress and my best warm shawl.

I dragged my cloak over my nightdress and rushed down to the *calle* where I relieved a newsboy of an *avviso* in exchange for a coin and a morsel of cheeky banter that is better left unrecorded. For I am *not* your girl to dwell on the pollution that comes out of a boy's mouth. Is it the red hair on my head that excites those unnecessary remarks from every low species of boy from Ireland to Italy?

I placed the *avviso* on the table in the breakfast room and ordered a cup of hot chocolate from Aldo Momesso. Then I could not bring my lip to the rim, suddenly certain he'd spat in it on his way back from the kitchen.

The *avviso* waxed vastly lyrical about the mermaid-napping.

The church of Santa Maria dei Miracoli was built in the 1480s to house a miracle-working painting of the Madonna. Sad, stern, tender – Our Lady's portrait is surrounded by mermaids carved from flesh-creamy marble. Little stone angel-babies reach out to them with plump hands. The mermaids lean towards the pretty babes. But their open mouths and their wild eyes reveal other desires too – namely for some handsome sculpted Tritons nearby. The sculptors' work is so exquisite that the young mermaids seem to own real beating hearts. And now those restless girls have forsaken our most graceful church, and—

Venetians! I thought of Giacomo Casanova, that big-eyed boy who played the violin and liked to stare at Lily. *Always on about their desires! Mad in their little heads about them!*

But there was something in the description of the young mermaids that reminded me powerfully of Lily – Lily trying to love a dead baby at the convent. Or perhaps it was because Lily was never far from my thoughts. When I'd kissed her goodbye at the cave the night before, poor Lily's face had the same look of yearning the *avviso* described. Poor Lily wanted more than she'd ever had of human warmth. Life had been marble-cold to her. Truth is, Lily and I were both lonely as stones, or we had been before we met one another. The difference was, I had known love before, and I believed it could come again.

I shall teach Lily to believe she can be loved and be safe. What use is Uncle Red's money, if it cannot make a sorrowful girl's life come right? Two sorrowful girls' lives, in fact.

As I folded the *avviso* and rose to my feet, I noticed another paragraph below the ones about the mermaids.

To add to the misery of the exaggerated cold weather, Venice suffered a vicious storm and unexpected high water in the middle of this night just passed. Records broken for an October acqua alta. *A dangerous tide swept secretly into the city while Venice lay sleeping. It is not yet known if anyone is lost.*

'Ivo!' I shouted, running to the reception desk. 'Evil, you are so!'

His face appeared at the door to the kitchen.

'This, again?' he said wearily.

I thrust the *avviso* into his hand, pointing to the word *lost*.

CHAPTER TWENTY-THREE

Detritus from the water's savage invasion clotted the streets. As we ran towards Lily's cave, our ankles tangled in long arms of seaweed crackling with ice. Elbows of driftwood tried to trip us. The cold mustiness of the sea still hung over the land. A mist hovered about our heads, tasting like the breath of drowning men.

At the mouth of the cave, I saw something that broke my heart.

There was no Lily. Instead – a poor little scrap of Lily's plain convent chemise, snagged on a rock. I recognised the coarse fabric. Scratches trailed down a rock, as if from dragging fingernails.

'Look! She tried to fight!'

'She would,' said Ivo. 'Lily would always fight.'

I did not like the finality of his tone, the giving-up in it. Ivo was mumbling, as if praying. 'I never saw the water come in. It was always dry here. It's where I wanted to bring – always dry, it was.'

He just kept saying it, again and again: 'Always dry.'

Did he believe that a prayer could bring Lily back?

'You never liked her,' I said bluntly. 'She knew too much,

157

didn't she? And some of what she knew would get *you* into trouble, wouldn't it? I remember now – the sand was *damp as a fish's bed,* Master Evil. It sank under our feet. Water *was* here even before this storm. And poor Lily so afraid of it—'

'Darling,' he said, 'there was frost lying on the sand, that's all. You cannot be thinking that . . .?'

'I could so. In your mouth the truth grows wings and flies away, so it does.'

Why should I trust him? Lily had – and look what had happened to her. Ivo had taken her from the convent only to drown her.

Wasn't it all just a great black-tongued story he made up, that a hotel would not be safe? He probably knew the water was coming for her. No matter what the newspapers say, Venetians surely feel those things in their blood. I'll wager there's a little tug inside them every time a great tide is due. Another one of those secret sacred ties between them and the city. Lily was too done in to feel it. Ivo took advantage of it.

I stumbled out of the cave, scanning the shore for a bedraggled little body. There was nothing but weed flung out by the waves. The air was grey and looming, with a speckling of blackness in the sky. A flock of birds wheeled and swooped, lifting their wings like heroes. With Lily gone, it was suddenly clear that I too had nowhere safe to go. I turned away from those birds. I did not have the courage even to watch them, flying off as they did, without hesitation, brave enough to soar into the cold heart of an infinite sky.

'We should get you back,' said Ivo. 'We'll be missed.'

'Do you think I'll take advice from *you*? You? You who's

probably been working with the Signorina and *badessa* both to get rid of Lily, with all the evidence washed cleanly away? You *kill* me, Master Evil, with your amusing ideas for my safety. *Killing* funny, they are.'

I turned my back on him and busied myself fashioning a cross from two twigs tied with a blue ribbon I inched out of my petticoat. Safe above the tide mark I dug a hole with my bare hands, relishing the scrape of the moist dirt, the cold hurt of the rough sand. I placed the scrap of Lily's chemise in the hollow. I patted earth over it and planted the cross deep with the force of my pain. I beat it lower with my shoe. Ivo stood in silence. I saw the mouth on him tighten. It did not look like it should look. It just seemed mulish and angry, without an atom of rightful guilt.

I ripped some tough flowers from the grass, the roots snapping like bird bones, so I knew I had killed the lives of those plants. The brittle sound of their little deaths was too much. Down they came, my tears, cold like pebbles on my cheek. I cried enough to rust all the pipes in Venice.

Then Ivo cried too; fierce hard he cried. He slapped the tears off his face. Much as I hated him for putting Lily in the cave, I thought a better use for his fingers would be to hold mine. I could not explain the vast gap between those two feelings, first of furious suspicion against him and then my need for the grasp of his hand. My heart tilted this way and that, in heart-ripping confusion.

When we had finished our weeping, Ivo started pushing words into the air. 'The *Magoghe sisters* killed Lily. By driving us to hide her here . . .'

159

'No!' I said. 'Don't you even say her name. Her name is too good for your mouth. We put Lily's life in *your* hands, Lily and I did. They were the wrong hands!'

'Blame me,' he said. 'Blame me. Everyone always does. I'm used to it.'

He trudged off ahead of me. Over his shoulder he called out bitterly, 'One day I'll get tired of being the villain and I'll tell the world the truth—'

'Truth?' I demanded. 'How does *your* being the victim help Lily? You must look the thing in the eye. You won't even look *me* in the eye. Take responsibility. Honour up!'

Ivo's neck flushed red and he stopped where he stood. When I caught up with him, his face was closed up tight like a bear hunched in winter sleep.

Was I any safer with him than Lily had been?

I had no one else.

So I followed him silently back into town. He didn't need to ask me to put the mask on. I had nothing more to say to Master Evil. I was happy to grind the *moretta*'s ivory button between my teeth. I still clutched a trailing fistful of dying flowers I'd torn from the earth to place over Lily's makeshift grave. I had forgotten to lay them there. It was fitter that way, for there was nothing beautiful about Lily's death, neither the manner nor the means of it.

The Signorina was at the desk when I walked in. Ivo had already slipped in the servants' entrance and stood beside her, taking a scalding scolding for his absence.

'*Buongiorno*, Miss Dearworthy,' said the Signorina, handing me my key with a look that soaked up almost all my bravado and rifled my belly with cold fingers. 'Pleasant sightseeing? Yet you've an air of sadness. It reminds me of your dear guardian in his last days. I'll have Taddeo fix you another cheering Night Mixture, my dear.'

Ivo stared at her, his mouth fixed in a thin, trembling line.

'Your kindness . . . I hardly know how to thank you,' I said. 'But pray don't run to the bother of Night Mixture. I shall shortly be moving to alternative accommodation. You won't have to suffer my sad face any more.'

Her eyelids came down like one of those pink awnings in the hotel's windows.

'Did someone borrow your lips, Signorina?' I asked. 'Have you nothing to say to me?'

'We shall be sorry to lose you, Miss Dearworthy. And we'll keep your room for you, of course, just in case you change your mind,' she said finally. 'Meanwhile, I do hope you enjoy your last night among us.'

161

CHAPTER TWENTY-FOUR

I lay in bed letting grief for Lily swim through my blood to every finger and toe. Only when I was soaked through with sadness did I begin to shudder and quietly howl. I was crying for Lily, but I was crying for myself too. I cried for having possessed a real friend for scant days, and for having lost her so cruelly. I wrapped my arms around a bedpost as if it were the mast of a ship that might carry me, in my great flood of sorrow, out to sea to join her.

I cried so much that I grew a great thirst, exacerbated by the over-salted fish supper served in the hotel dining room. The last thing I did before finally falling asleep was drink deeply from the jug of water by my bed. It tasted brackish, but I put that down to the tears lining the back of my throat.

I woke up in the night with a skull grinning on my wet pillow in the moonlight. I screamed and shrank back in the sheets. Then I lit the taper with shaking hands. I knew about that skull. Lily had told me all its evil use, how it made guests think that they had gone mad. I punched the hollow where its nose should be, and sent it spinning across the room.

Ivo was the one who laid the skull on people's pillows. Lily had told me so.

And he must have laid it on Uncle Red's pillow too! My guardian had written of a head on his pillow in that confused last letter! He had not been in love. He had been in the grip of a poisoner.

So I was right, after all. Ivo was in on it all the time. Now he wanted to drive me mad too. He had got rid of Lily. I supposed that earned him a tip from his Signorina. Was that all Lily was worth to him? A ducat? And me – probably less.

I tried to feel more angry than hurt, more vengeful than lonely, but I could not. Pain seared hotter than rage.

My aloneness stared me in the face, mocking me. With parents, then Uncle Red and now Lily gone, there was no one left to care if I lived. And several who'd prefer me dead.

I lit another candle. A book lay open on the desk, its blank pages inviting the relief of writing. A quill and ink were ready beside it. *While writing,* I thought, *I'll suffer only half the pain as the rest of me will concentrate on the mechanics of recording my feelings.*

I staggered to the desk, dipped the quill and let it hover over the page.

Lucky Lily. Her suffering was over now. Mine was just beginning. What would happen to me? Nothing good. My mouth was dry with envy. I reached to the glass by my bed and gulped the water before I remembered how stale it had tasted. I wiped my wet mouth on the bed curtain and stumbled back to the desk, suddenly dizzy. I began to write fevered words.

What if they creep in on me while I write?

I would not wait there like a sorry stack of peat to let them do to me whatever they had done to Uncle Red. I would find that cockroach of a boy, Ivo, wherever he slept – if his conscience let him sleep – and tell him I knew what he was up to. Him with his skull and his sneaking ways.

Slowly, unsteadily, I rose from the desk. It felt as if my whole body had dried out, shrivelled by the tears I had shed over Lily. *That must account for the giddiness on me*, I thought. *And the fact that my mouth's as dry as toast*. I drank more water straight from the jug. In the moonlight, that water had a great look of greenness about it.

I pulled on my clothes. The buttons were disobedient, refusing to visit inside their customary holes. One stocking was enough, I decided, tying a great rabbit ear of blue ribbon at the knee. Despite the cold, I didn't need my cloak, not when the thing loomed up at me on its hook like a vast bat. Anyway, I felt as if I were burning up. My dressed itched like forty fleas. I crammed a ducat in my pocket and staggered towards the door. A moment later I hit the floor.

Lying there, I finally understood.

They had poisoned me.

The liquid I'd been gulping was dolloped with the potion they used to kill Uncle Red. They'd made me thirsty with salty fish at supper to make sure I'd drink glass after glass of it. Soon I'd be unconscious, and they would make me disappear before I was even dead.

Using every fibre of every muscle, I slithered on my belly to the bed and used the bedpost to drag myself to my feet. If I was going to die, I would not let them have my body. I would go to the place where Lily died, and let the currents take me to wherever they had taken Lily. It would be a clean death.

My shoes were beyond my fumbling fingers. Fluthered on Night Mixture, I set off on one bare foot and the other in a stocking, weaving from doorway to doorway with a fever in my head, and the stones of Venice icy under my feet.

Perhaps, without the potion inside me, I'd never have found the place. Under the sway of its power, I dream-walked there, unfaltering, through the darkness, without even a lamp to light my way. My heart ached. It felt as if even the night wanted me dead, the stars sniping at the tender space between my shoulder blades. What had we done, Lily and I, to offend this universe?

The sky was lightening to a leathery colour by the time I reached the cave. The tide was coming in again. I sat in the wet sand with my legs sticking out in front of me. The water watched me for a while. Then it came to nibble my feet. It swarmed foamy as Irish beer around my knees and then my thighs. It took away my untied stocking. It sucked at my skirts and petticoats.

The Signorina's poison made it hard for my head to stay upright. I drooped backwards into the sand, thinking, *Lily, wait for me, out there in the lagoon, wherever you are. I am coming. Be full sure of it.*

I felt the sea spray licking my face like twelve hungry cats.

Good, I thought, *my last night is ending. Lily, I shall be with you soon so.*

CHAPTER TWENTY-FIVE

There were hands under my arms, dragging me away from the water.

'You idiot of a girl!' Ivo's voice was saying.

'Ah, it's your man Ivo, the miserable fellow with earache from the keyholes he listens at!' I mumbled.

'What do you think you're doing?'

'Drowning so,' I mumbled. 'Like Lily.'

Ivo's face loomed close to my own. 'No!' He flinched away. 'I can smell it on your breath.'

'You mean the potion you use on guests you want to . . . to . . .'

I could not keep my words walking in straight lines. My tongue was numb and my teeth clattered like tin buttons.

'What brought you here following me?' I asked thickly.

'I read what you wrote in the diary in Chamber Seven. Then I just imagined where the craziest girl in Venice would go.'

Purple spots bloomed in front of my eyes. My head sagged till I felt my chin collide with my chest. The next thing I knew Ivo was splashing my face with cold seawater and then hauling me to my feet.

'What's the hurry on you?' I grumbled.

'You need to keep moving,' he said. 'We must get you to a coffee house and put something hot inside you.'

'You think in your great wisdom that I am going anywhere with *you*? Or drinking anything *you*'ve had a chance to interfere with first?' I demanded. 'Why pretend to be shocked about poison on my breath? Didn't *you* drug my water? Didn't *you* lay the skull on my pillow?'

Ivo shook me. 'Of course not! It must have been the Signorina. Or Momesso. I woke in the night, worried. I couldn't forget the look she gave you when you came in. Or the way she said, "Enjoy your last night among us." As if it was to be your last night on earth. I went to your room but the door was open. The skull was in pieces on the floor and you were gone. I read those wretched words you wrote.' Then he cursed. 'I forgot to tear out the pages. She'll have them as evidence.'

'That I wished to do away with myself?'

'I feared they had taken you, but the . . . usual storeroom was empty,' he muttered to himself. 'Then, given your state of mind, I guessed you would go to Lily's . . . grave.'

All this time he was leading me back towards town. His arm was around me. His skin offered warmth, even if his heart did not. He half carried me into a bakery where the steam of coffee snapped my eyes open. Ivo fed me three cups of coffee and a brioche, piece by piece. Then he was dragging me back outside.

'Your eyes are still glassy,' he said, staring into my face.

'Why are you trying to save me when you were trying to kill me a few small hours ago?' I demanded, stopping short. 'The truth, now! Look at you sweating! That's pure distilled guilt, those drops on your forehead.'

'Again? Really? What can I do to make you believe me? *What?*'

'Where are we going?' I asked. 'Back to the hotel so you can finish me off in great privacy and comfort? What's your commission per corpse, Master Evil? We're not far from the hotel, are we? I recognise that bridge.'

'You do not. You never can tell one bridge from another. We are a long way from the hotel. Darling, please, I came to save you. I need to think what to do . . . most of all I must think up somewhere quiet and safe to hide you.'

I wiped my face, sticky with dried salt water. 'Somewhere quiet, safe, like a cave, for example? I don't love the way you think, Ivo.'

He held out my *moretta* mask, with a gesture that said *Be silent, for I cannot bear your voice any more. And hide your face.*

I liked none of those ideas, so I dashed the *moretta* to the ground with an angry hand. He picked it up and pocketed it. Our word-war ploughed its bitter path in front of one of the alcoves I had seen all over Venice. They held paintings or sculptures of the Madonna. These niches were always decorated with fresh flowers and sometimes a candle. Even in the poorest parts of town, the Venetians offered such luxuries to their Madonnas.

Well, to be sure I myself was not feeling vastly holy in that moment. Yet I crossed myself in front of this painted Madonna, who, truth to tell, did not look down on us with much tenderness.

'Well then, my Lady,' I said. 'How about a prayer for Lily? Who has drowned. Blessed art Thou and all such. So why, for the love of little baby Jesus, can You not perform a miracle for Lily? Surely what one bad Venetian boy has done, the Mother of all Goodness can undo in a heartbeat? Perhaps You in Your great holiness can bring her back from the dead, Missis God!'

'You don't understand how these *capitelli* work!' Ivo growled. 'The *capitelli* exist because the Virgin *already* answered someone's prayer – someone who was caught in a deadly storm or in the grip of a mortal illness. In the moment of desperation, that person promised to build a *capitello* in Her honour if the Madonna would help. So there's no point in asking *this* Madonna to save Lily. She's already accomplished Her miracle and saved someone else.'

'No wonder She looks so righteous in Herself,' I said.

While Ivo and I argued backwards and forwards, I heard from time to time something that sounded like an irritable sigh and something else that sounded like a brisk *tch tch tch*. It was faintly annoying, as when some over-dressed stranger sits next to you in a carriage and makes it clear by her sniffs and sighs that you are not the class of person she hoped to be sharing a journey with. At first, I thought it was Ivo making those disapproving noises. In the end, I said, 'Would you stop it? There's no point in you carrying on as if you are the most wronged creature in the world.'

'Might say the same about you,' he retorted.

Behind me I heard a snuffle and cry that sounded exactly like a baby's. Then a deep female voice said, 'You tiresome young people. Now you've gone and woken up the Holy Infant with your quarrel. I'd only just got Him to sleep after He was owling it up all night with that Saint John the Evangelist. Face like an angel but such a bad influence!'

Ivo and I turned to the painting.

'Another talking Madonna,' Ivo muttered to himself, pale-faced.

I gave him a hard stare. *Another* Madonna? Another one of his secrets! Another thing too good for foreigners like me, a bit of hocus-pocus that Venetians kept to themselves.

'There's something down here, below Me, that might help you find the young friend that you were quarrelling so bitterly about,' the Madonna sniffed. 'A safe place for you too in the meanwhile.'

A safe place, wherever it was, sounded good to me.

'But there's nothing under the streets of Venice,' Ivo said. 'Just wooden poles and mud and then more water.'

'That is yet another case of your being very wrong, young man,' She said. 'Show Me your hands.'

Her tone was so imperious that we both immediately held them out, palms upward.

'Turn them over,' She said. 'Horrible! Whole villages of dirt under those nails! And your feet are wet and your noses running! I'll tolerate no running noses at My *capitello*. Sets such a bad example to the Holy Infant. Go and wash your hands. And bring Me a tortoiseshell crucifix. A ragamuffin stole mine. Then we shall see about that safe place and finding your friend.'

She did not say, 'Your drowned friend.'

My heart jumped with hope. If a tetchy Madonna could help us find Lily, then I would scrub my hands raw for Her.

CHAPTER TWENTY-SIX

Ivo paid a coin to a *bigolante*. The woman handed him a wooden cup to dip into one of the water buckets yoked to her shoulders. She grumbled when, instead of drinking it, we poured the water over our hands.

'I broke my back drawing that out of the well! Never heard of anything so la-di-da! Children paying to wash? You unnatural creatures!'

Leaving her laments behind us, we went to find a jeweller who might be cajoled into selling us a tortoiseshell crucifix for the only ducat I had in my pocket. Ivo muttered something about a jeweller who owed him a favour, or who at least would like to keep on the right side of him.

Bastian Olivo and *Isepo Luzzo* read the signs outside adjoining shops in the Ruga degli Orefici at Rialto. A fine tortoiseshell crucifix was bedded on a rose velvet cushion in Bastian Olivo's window.

The jeweller was a dark-skinned man with hazel eyes extravagantly lashed. He dressed like a gentleman. His wig was tightly curled. His lashes drooped lazily but I saw a glint of cruelty under them too. At the sight of Ivo, the jeweller's eyes narrowed. He tinkled a brass bell hanging by his counter.

Why? Who's he summoning? I wondered. *And that's not the face of someone who wants to keep on the right side of Ivo.*

A shadow slipped into the back of the shop behind us. For a second it hovered behind Ivo's shoulder.

'Hello, Isepo,' said Bastian Olivo.

'Shopping, are we? Running around town with unchaperoned foreign girls?' The man jabbed his fingers at Ivo's face. 'Thieving, more like. That ruby you just pocketed is the proof.'

'What ruby?'

'This one!' The hand of Isepo Luzzo reached into Ivo's pocket and pulled out a red jewel.

'You put it there!' I said indignantly. 'When you crept up behind him.'

Ivo took my hand and tugged me out of the shop. We ran until the crowd enveloped us. Finally, we paused to catch our breaths by a bridge. I gasped, 'Why did he talk to us like that? I might be someone, for all he knows. A lady of substance! I *am* a lady of substance. How dare he?'

'You have spirit, Darling,' said Ivo. 'But it's easy to have spirit when you've also got money. With money, you can buy anything. My old employer, the English Resident, bought a boy just to make him cry. His name was Eliah.'

Ivo's voice broke on the name. He fell into silence, staring down the Grand Canal.

'Eliah?' I repeated softly. '*Was* Eliah?'

'Eliah, Eliah, Eliah,' he said, his voice softer and sadder with

172

each repetition. 'It was Eliah I wanted to bring to the cave.'

'Did you want to drown him too?'

'No, Darling. To protect him. Eliah . . . I . . . loved him.'

'You *loved* someone, Ivo?'

Hearing Ivo's quiet, 'Yes. Very much' was like looking through a telescope and discovering a new land.

CHAPTER TWENTY-SEVEN

'Three years ago, I'd just started in the service of the English Resident,' Ivo explained. 'I was serving tea to the man himself and a Scottish lady who was his guest that day. I heard him tell her: "I've sent for a little slave boy from my sugar plantation in Jamaica. It's due in on the *Charming Sally*. I put out for a pretty one. Something naturally docile. It'd better be, for twenty-five gold sovereigns! It's also warranted free of disease and speaks English tolerably well. Dressed up in some Venetian popinjay nonsense, with a Honiton lace jabot, a blackamoor will serve nicely as an exotic ornament."'

I asked, 'Did the Resident actually talk like that?'

'Oh yes, and *she* was even worse, the lady. She cooed, "And such a proof of your high rank, dearest. A slave always bestows such a *comfortable* sense of luxury."'

Ivo imitated her Edinburgh accent so perfectly that I was certain he'd also trapped her words exactly in his memory.

'That Scottish lady was constantly in the *palazzo* at that time. Her pamphlets of poetry were placed on every side table.'

'What were her poems like?'

'Like her: simpering, mean and futile,' he answered.

'Eliah?' I reminded him.

'Yes, Eliah. The *Charming Sally* duly arrived in Venice. Apparently, she was not so charming in the hold where the slaves did not see daylight for forty days. Even rumpled and filthy from his journey, Eliah the sugar slave boy had the sweetest face you ever saw. His eyes were very large and luminous. And his mouth was full and tender. He was delicate of build. He spoke a strange kind of English, from the island of his birth. It was singsong, poetic. Instead of a simple "Yes" he always said, "You know it is so."

'I was in the room, sweeping out a fireplace, when the Resident made his first inspection of Eliah. He turned him around and around. He looked inside his mouth, as if he were a horse. He poked at him with the iron-tipped cane he carried everywhere. Eliah submitted tranquilly to his humiliating inspection. Finally the Resident asked Eliah, "Are you properly grateful to be here?"

' "You know it is so," replied Eliah.

' "Interesting," the Resident said. Then he brought down the cane hard on Eliah's shoulders. "Are you grateful for *that*?" '

I cried out, 'No!'

Ivo said, 'Eliah did not protest. Tears spilled out of those luminous eyes of his. I knew better than to open my mouth. But inside I raged.

'The Resident said to Eliah, "So you're wondering why I hit you, perhaps? In this household, the servants wonder if I *don't* beat them."

'For once, the dog spoke the unvarnished truth. Afterwards, as we carried wine glasses to the scullery, Eliah asked me, "What did I do so terrible? What did I say so terrible?"

'I told him, "Nothing."

'"Then I can do nothing to stop this," he said. He was right.

'Eliah looked exquisite in his miniature frock coat. The female servants universally adopted Eliah as their pet. And we loved the beautiful little pet Eliah himself had brought to Venice, a streamer-tailed hummingbird, its plumage iridescent green. Eliah had managed to keep it safe from the gang-master and other prisoners all the way from Jamaica, feeding it crumbs from his rations. In the *palazzo* it flew about freely, never far from its master unless Eliah was with the Resident, in which case the bird knew to keep a safe and discreet distance.'

'I've seen that bird! But what—?'

'Eliah was gentleness itself. He listened. He worked hard when he could have got by with charm. He would do you any little favour he could. He surprised the maids with flowers on their pillows. He'd throw his arms around me if he saw me looking downcast. First time he hugged me, I thought I'd die of shock. Then, well, it happened a lot.'

I tried to imagine Ivo receiving or giving a hug. The image did not come easily.

'But Eliah . . . he had one fault: he was clumsy. One day he dropped a soft-boiled egg while serving at high tea.

'The blue and milk-white Antonibon saucer – viciously costly, I knew – was still spinning on the polished floor. Even before it smashed, Eliah began to weep, silently but copiously. I was serving

176

at the other end of the table. I longed to run around and clean up the egg because Eliah seemed to have turned to a stone statue of a boy. He just stood there, tears falling from his big brown eyes. The Resident's guest that day was of course the Scottish lady. *She* began to rhapsodise about the quality of Eliah's tears.'

Ivo mimicked her accent again: ' "Crystal droplets! Look how they bedew his long lashes like diamonds! And the way they sidle down his little cheeks – like a streamlet in a paradisiacal garden . . ." and so on.'

'She told the Resident, "The emperors of old used to employ boys like this to cry for them. At moments when tears would adorn the occasion."

'I saw the Resident stiffen with pride at the mention of emperors. His left hand fondled the gilded buttons on his waistcoat.

'Then he beat Eliah in an absent-minded kind of way, on the shoulders and legs. For a thin man, he had fingers as fat as grubs, and he was strong.'

I interrupted, unable to bear any more of Ivo's bitter, calm voice, telling these horrors. 'The Scottish lady just *watched*?'

'With a smile. But there was another guest that day,' Ivo said. 'Elena Badoero, wife of the Doge. And she remained silent through this whole dreadful exchange and the beating. Pale with rage, the Dogaressa clutched her teacup to her breast so tightly that the porcelain fractured into a dozen pieces in her hand. That was *two* items of Antonibon china broken because of Eliah. I knew just how much he'd suffer for it. Then the Dogaressa astonished me.

177

'She rose from her chair. "A child is a *gift*," she said, "whether Venetian or foreign, whether fair-skinned or dark. A child is not a drum to beat with an iron-tipped stick. A child is not a manufactory for tears. And a child's tears are nothing to smirk at."

'"A child is *not* a gift," said the Resident. "A child is something you buy with good money. And sell for better, if you're clever. Betweentimes, you do what you please with it."

'The Dogaressa gave him a look of utter contempt and swept out of the room.'

'Fine woman herself!' I said.

Ivo nodded. 'You would think that the Resident might be distraught at offending the highest lady in Venice. But the moment the door slammed behind the Dogaressa, he and the Scottish female burst into peals of laughter.

'"Pompous old sea-cow!" said she. "You don't need *her* blessing to be an emperor in your own palace, my love! Think about those crystal tears!"

'From that day forth, whenever important guests left the *palazzo* on their journeys back to England, Eliah would be made to stand on the balcony. His work was to wave and cry his crystal tears as they were rowed away in their gondolas. You could see it in those people's faces: it made them feel as if the beautiful little boy understood their pain at leaving Venice, and that he would miss them.

'And they would go home and tell all their friends not about the splendours of Venice but about the splendours of the English Resident. It never occurred to any of them that Eliah was weeping because he would be beaten if he did not.'

178

Ivo's strange and awful tale had anchored my feet to the pavement. But I could not help noticing that the jeweller Bastian Olivo had somehow found us and was watching us intently from across the square. Ivo struck the bridge's parapet with passion, grazing his knuckles. He appeared not to notice that we had an audience.

'And so the news of the Resident's Weeping Boy came to the ears of the English Treasury, and his stipend was increased. So he could gamble more of it away at the Ridotto, and—'

'Ivo,' I said, 'the jeweller's just sent a boy off with a note. Could it be a message to the Signorina or the *badessa*? I don't think we should be here any more. You can finish telling me about Eliah later.'

Ivo did not appear to be listening. He was heart and soul with the sugar slave boy Eliah. But above us, in the crowd on the bridge, I saw the jeweller's message-boy sprinting back, accompanied by two large men.

Finally I captured Ivo's attention. His eyes followed mine to the men and the arm of the jeweller pointing us out.

'Catch that boy!' shouted Olivo. 'He stole my ruby! I'll see him convicted, and his hands cut off between the columns of the Piazzetta.'

179

CHAPTER TWENTY-EIGHT

'The best place to disappear is a crowd,' Ivo said. He dragged me by the hand into the busiest part of the seething Rialto Market. Even as the milling bodies closed around us, he did not let go. I realised I did not want him to do so.

At the market, there was as thick a knot of shoppers as any disappearing-minded person might want to get lost in. We elbowed our way through the people clustered around the stall of one of the eel-sellers in the fish market.

The fishmonger boasted, 'My eels are so cheap that you can buy them for someone you don't even like!'

But it was not the cries of the fishmonger that had drawn the crowd.

In his tray of eels, something white was thrashing – an eel with the girth of a small tree and the length of a man. Its eyes were milky white. It was eating the heads off ordinary black eels while they still lived and tossing their tails in the air.

The fishmonger insisted, 'Eat my eels and you'll have the strength of Hercules! And the refinement of a lady-in-waiting too.'

He gestured to the white eel. 'Look at my proud white beauty! My gift of the early snow! Who'll be having my finest today?'

Ivo and I pushed to the front.

The eel lifted its head and hissed at me.

'You are next,' it said. 'I ssshall drink your blood.'

The monstrous eel looked quite capable of draining every drop of goodness from my body. Those gills on the outside were like jewelled branches of coral. What kept them so red? *It must be the blood of innocent creatures, sucked from them while they still lived.*

'Could that eel be clockwork, like the dioramas at the hotel?' I asked Ivo. But, as the eel undulated in front of me like a cobra, I smelled its salty breath. It was not clockwork at all.

From their cheerfully fascinated faces, it was clear that none of the grown-up Venetians had heard the eel speak. There was just one little girl who stood statue-still and statue-pale. She hissed, 'Did you not hear that beast mouthing at you? If I were you, I'd run like rabbits! Now!'

Suddenly a heavy hand was clapped on my shoulder. The jeweller's men had caught up with us. Exchanging one stricken look, Ivo and I locked hands again. We inserted ourselves back in the crowd. Behind us came a splash and a cry: 'The monster has escaped!'

'Back to the tetchy Madonna?' I asked Ivo.

He nodded. We hurried in circuitous ways, me blessing my stars that we'd washed our hands before we met the eel and that I was with a Venetian boy with a map of the city inside his head.

*   *   *

In every canal, it seemed, the white eel with coral gills was ploughing its way in exactly the same direction as us.

'Is it following us?' I panted. 'Why?'

Lily – Lily's body – was somewhere in this green water, was it not? With creatures like this infesting it, what chance did she have? *She never had any chance,* I told myself. *She feared the water and could not swim.*

When we reached the Fondamenta della Sensa, the eel's head surged out of the water. In a second, its whole body had writhed up on to the pavement, where it moved as quickly as when it was swimming. The beast wound its tail around my right leg and began to drag me towards the canal.

Ivo seized both of my wrists and pulled with all his might. Uncoiling itself from my leg, the eel lunged at Ivo with its jaws opened wide. I felt Ivo's hands slipping from mine. The eel turned back to stare at me. Its tongue flickered. Two long teeth jutted from its jaw. I was dizzied by the milky infinity of its red-rimmed eyes.

I could not lift my feet to run, even when the eel's head approached me again. This time it nosed into the front of my dress. I could feel the jabs of its tongue flicking against my bodice.

It's listening, I realised, *eavesdropping on my heart pumping blood. But do eels have ears?* I wondered dreamily.

Ivo's face looked as blank as mine felt.

The eel withdrew its head from my bodice and sought out the crook of my elbow. Then its cold wetness made its way down to my wrist where it listened at the veins near my hand. It drew back and struck. Two of the long incisors punctured my wrist like a pair of daggers. I felt a rush of blood to the wound, but none dripped to the ground. Instead the muscles of the eel's neck showed it gulping.

'*That ye shall not do!*' A loud female voice came from somewhere behind the eel. 'Belay drinking young Humanfolk. Forthwith! Be off away, ye moon-eyed sea snake!'

A sword slammed down on the marble pavement, neatly cutting off the eel's tail, an elbow's length from its tip. The lopped tail danced briefly on the pavement and then slithered into the canal. The eel removed its jaw from my wrist and turned to face its attacker.

A young woman, with skin of rich deep brown, dark-browed and with becoming shadows deepening her berry-black eyes, lowered her sword and brandished a trident at the eel. Impossibly, she seemed to stand in the middle of the canal, where the water was surely the deepest. Her lower half was concealed beneath the water. Wet black curls cascaded either side of her high cheekbones. I glimpsed an armoured breastplate with a design of a mortar and pestle embossed upon it.

She shouted, 'Begone, Eel! Unless ye want to lose another length of yourself! I don't like to kill a fellow creature, but I shall kill ye if I'm made to, vile tube of stolen blood that ye be.'

The mouth on her! I thought. She swung her language like her sword, every parry striking home.

'Come pick on someone your own size, ye slime-snake,' she invited the eel. 'Ye have met your destiny. And it be in a pile of your own guts.'

183

Then she thrashed towards the eel in the water – not with legs, I was shocked to see, but with a scaled tail of green and grey.

'A mermaid?' I asked Ivo. 'You have them here? As well as talking eels and Madonnas? Sure I never saw that coming at all. Not a single mermaid was mentioned in all the books I read about Venice!'

Before Ivo could answer, the mermaid cried, 'Some things be too good for books, girlie!'

Then the eel was lunging at her, its massive jaws closing around her waist. The two terrible fangs left gouges that spouted bright blood. It seemed the mermaid could not survive such a loss of vital fluid, such wounds. Yet still she fought, and still she had the breath to taunt, 'Worm! Ye'll not get the bettering of *me*.'

She pinioned the eel with her trident against the wall of the canal, drew a wooden stake from the quiver on her back, and plunged it into what must have been the creature's heart, from the way it exploded with blood. The eel screamed, like a tongue of fire thrusting in my ear.

The mermaid leaned back against the wall, her chest rising and falling inside her armour. Blood streaked her face. 'Run, why don't ye?' she told us. 'This dog-hearted sea-snake won't be alone, ye know. And I see from your wrist that it's had a taste of your blood already, girl.'

'How can you fight another one, wounded as you are?' I asked.

Half of me wanted to run as far away as possible from any patch of water where another white eel might be lurking. The other half of me felt responsible for the wounded mermaid. She'd saved my life.

She said kindly, 'Ah truly, do not belay here. I don't have the bowels to save ye twice.'

It was at that moment that the second eel struck. It bit deep into her deepest wound, the one that gushed blood from her waist. Then it dragged her under the water.

She did not emerge again.

Ivo took my arm. 'She wanted us to run,' he said. 'She should not die for nothing.'

We ran until we had to stop, stitches in our sides, the breath tearing out of us. I had no idea where we were. Ivo had pulled a handkerchief from his pocket and was wrapping it tightly around my wrist when Giacomo appeared, gnawing a sausage.

'Where have you been, sweetest heart?' he asked me. 'Everyone is looking for you. The Signorina and Aldo Momesso were just here, asking all sorts of questions. They had a jeweller chappie with them too. Says Ivo—'

'What did you tell them?' I asked.

'Oh,' he said, 'just that I was pining hopelessly for a glimpse of your lovely self. They gave me such a shaking.'

'Stop flirting!' I said. 'And get your face out of that sausage. We are on the run, Giacomo. We are hunted like beasts.'

Ivo said, 'The Madonna said she would help us.'

'Our Lady spoke to you?' gasped Giacomo. 'Is she very beautiful?'

'I suppose so.'

'Then by all means let us go to her!'

'First,' I said. 'There is something I need to get rid of. Turn your backs. Yes, that means you, Giacomo.'

I lifted my skirt and untied my hooped petticoat, stepping out of it without regret. I left it there, like a dying jellyfish on a beach. My dress sagged against my legs but at least I could lift it high and run.

CHAPTER TWENTY-NINE

As we pounded through the streets, there was just enough ice-grey in the sky to sharpen the silhouettes of the chimneys. Bales of greasy-coloured clouds pressed themselves down on the city.

'You took your time,' sniffed the Madonna. 'Your hands must have been *very* dirty. And now you smell of fish. Moreover, I don't see any tortoiseshell crucifix.'

'A *worthy* crucifix . . . was unavailable. The thing is,' said Ivo, 'there's not much time—'

'And who is this new boy?' She pointed to Giacomo. 'I invited no extra boy. He has a naughty look about him.'

'Giacomo Casanova at Your service. Usually ladies like this naughty look very much indeed.'

'Please!' I urged. 'We must hurry! What are You for, if not saving innocent young people? Being the Madonna and all? And Your body is at least in one piece unlike the other bits of saints all over Venice so. Show us Your strength!'

'Of course I am in one piece. I was carried up to heaven whole, because of My great purity,' retorted the Madonna.

'Yet *we* shall be in several pieces if you don't help us now!' said Ivo.

'Very well,' sniffed the Madonna. 'I cannot have your dismemberment besmirching My conscience.'

'What's that, Your Loveliness?' asked Giacomo.

'She'll feel guilty if we get chopped up,' I said. 'Or eaten and drunk by eels, and so on.'

The Signorina's voice rattled through the air. From no more than one small street away, she rapped, 'I hold you accountable, Bastian. If you've let them escape, I'll find another jeweller. There are plenty who would be happy for a profitable side-line.'

The Madonna nodded at us curtly. And then folded Her hands at Her breast.

'You're *praying* for us now?' I cried. 'That's all You're going to do?'

It started with a quiet creaking. Then Her niche began to free itself from the surrounding bricks in a splatter of dust. Finally the whole structure revolved into the hollow space behind.

'In you get,' she told us. 'Into the crack. Yes, you'll fit. And be quiet. The Holy Infant is only halfway through His nap.'

Darkness loomed in front of us. Behind us – no more than a few paces now – Bastian Olivo's voice shouted, 'There they are!' Aldo Momesso's unmistakeable growl followed, 'I'll flay them myself with a nail file, slowly. Never mind the butcher!'

The door wailed, groaned, screeched and stuttered its way open, wide enough for us to squeeze through – first Ivo, then Giacomo, then me.

Behind us, the door sealed itself closed, as if it had never opened.

CHAPTER THIRTY

There was nothing to be done but start climbing down endless mossy marble stairs lit by occasional candles perched on gilded scallop shells. At first the light was too dim – and the staircase too long and steep – for us to make out what lay below us. But we could *hear* something – a female voice, deep and throaty, crooning a song. The voice invaded me like waves rolling across a dark lake. The sound was savage and yet also sweet. I could not understand the words, and I felt a grand craving to do so. In fact there had never been a language I longed to master as much as this one.

With every step, the air grew warmer, with a smell of fresh fish and the sea – yet perfumed.

'It's what pearls would smell like,' Giacomo purred, 'if pearls had a scent.'

We emerged into a cavern with gilded vaulting that closely resembled the ceiling of the Basilica di San Marco. Then I bumped into Giacomo, for he had suddenly stopped. He was pointing. I saw what he saw: a mermaid – twice the size of any sensible human female. The face of this giantess seemed to be

189

carved out of the same dark fire as the one who had fought the eel, her features luminous and dangerous. Unlike the smaller mermaid's, her black hair was shot through with bolts of white. Her brown eyes, woven around with lines fine as spider silk, were liquid with sorrow. Her elegant bare shoulders sagged, casting shadows on breasts that were barely covered by two yellow starfish.

The mermaid noted our arrival soberly, a quiet murmur of surprise in her own mysterious tongue.

Would she hate us, I wondered, *if she knew her young kinswoman has just given her life for mine?* Perhaps she already knew and that accounted for the sadness that hung from her. As well as a whale's size, she had a whale's dignity. Her grief seemed profound and vast in proportion.

'It's sorry we are,' I blurted. 'I —'

The brown eyes blinked with surprise. In Venetian, she asked, 'Ye see me? Ye hear me?'

'And what a pleasure it is, *sweetest* heart,' fluted Giacomo. Ivo kicked him.

The mermaid looked at us appraisingly. 'Ye all be more than children. Twelve years, mayhap thirteen? At that that age, Humanfolk fail to see or hear our kind, or any magical creatures — unless those Humanfolk be especially gifted. So ye three must be exceptionally gifted. Or are ye instead very backward for your ages?'

'We are not at all backward so,' I said.

In a tone deep and rushy like night waves, she asked, 'So Our Lady upstairs be sending me young Humanfolk now? Why?'

190

'I . . . we . . . don't know why the Madonna did it,' I ventured, 'except to slip us out of sight of some bad people who wish us harm.'

Her eyes swept over me. 'Cower not in yon shadows,' she ordered. Stepping forward, I glimpsed the smaller mermaid who'd saved me. She lay on a floating leaf-shaped platform, her face still and the eel-wounds around her middle bound with red-smeared bandages. Her breastplate was gone, and she too wore starfish where it had been.

Was the larger mermaid her mother? Or more likely, given her size and evident age, her great-grandmother?

I did not have time to ask.

For there, in a corner lit by four tall candles, was Lily.

Lily's silent, still body.

Lily lay on her side on a tall heap of dried seaweed. Her body was inserted into a girl-sized pocket of woven greenery. It did not cover her shoulder, which was embossed with the mark of a cross. It must have been the one the *badessa* made her carry round the cloister. Her eyes were closed, and there was not a single tiny flicker of her mauve lids. I laid a trembling hand on Lily's shoulder and stroked it gently. Her skin was cool as water.

'So ye know our Sorrowful Lily then?' asked the mermaid.

'What do you mean *your* Sorrowful Lily?' I asked, more rudely than was prudent, because a bone-clenching thought had just struck me. I lifted an edge of the seaweed pocket, half expecting to see Lily had grown a tail – or had suffered one to be forced on her – and was now a mermaid. She had not. Her slender limbs were intact. I breathed more easily.

'How do you know her name?' asked Ivo.

'From it being carved in her arm,' was the answer.

'Do you have a name yourself, sweetest lady?' Giacomo asked her.

'No. Not in Humantongue. Ye shall not forget me, nevertheless, I suspect.'

While they spoke, I lifted Lily's left hand and saw the letters painfully scratched into the underside of her wrist. The wound was old. She'd hidden it from me. *Why?*

As I stroked her hand, from Lily's skin arose the scent of every herb I'd ever heard of and many I had not. She smelled like a dictionary of spices. But she lay limp as death.

'She's died,' I wailed.

'Avast with the requiems! Mourning is premature,' said the mermaid. 'Yon maid has not nearly finished living yet.'

'But Lily looks quite comprehensively dead to me so!' I whimpered. 'And she's *not* a maid. I mean she worked as one, but that is not all she is . . . was.' I was not vastly ashamed of my tears. 'If she's alive, then why does she not move a muscle?'

'There be a terrible lot of fight in the *girl*, maid being a form of speech only, as in maiden, an unmarried young female,' answered the mermaid. 'I assume that marriage has not been among Sorrowful Lily's misadventures so far? It seems that she wriggled and scraped her body through reef and canal before I found her. While I sang her to sleep, I let her rave some about her secret sacred ties to a mad mother until she'd wept a sea of tears. They needed to come out. Now she must sleep till the damage be healed. 'Tis the way of things.'

Ivo echoed uncertainly, 'The way of things?'

I was thinking, *Did the Signorina speak true? Lily had a mother? A mad one? Did she know her mad mother? Why did Lily keep secrets from me?*

'My granddaughter Incubina also sleeps to heal.' The mermaid pointed to the mermaid who'd rescued us from the eel. Relief coursed through me like liquid lightning. My gaze returned to Lily. Her face was considerably plumper and in better colour than when I'd last seen her.

The mermaid looked at us critically. 'Yet ye be paler than three winter moons yourselves. And ye, Red-Hair, be damaged in the arm. Give it here.'

I knelt by the edge of the water and let the mermaid remove Ivo's stained handkerchief.

'Vampire Eel bite,' said the mermaid, recoiling. She pointed to a gargoyle implanted in the wall. From the grimacing stone fish's mouth gushed a clear liquid. ''Tis sweet water. Wash yourself.'

'Does this mean I'm a vampire too – now I'm bitten?' My voice came out too high, too thin.

'No. Your blood be in its blood. Ye'd be in extra peril were ye to meet that particular worm again. For it has likely enjoyed the taste of ye and would know your scent anywhere.'

After I had rinsed off my own dried blood, the mermaid summoned me back with a silent gesture. She spat on the wound and dressed it with a strip of dry seaweed.

'Now 'tis time for ye to be telling your stories. Why are ye here? 'Tis clear ye be in bad trouble with bad creatures.'

I wanted to ask her to speak some more Mermaid to me. I was sure I could pick it up fierce fast. But I did not dare. And I was feeling foolish for misunderstanding her use of the word 'maid'. In fact, I rather liked the idea of being a maiden.

'Why are we here?' I echoed. 'I would say that it has to do with three sisters from Sicily who all go by the name of Magoghe, who are at the bottom of many great evils, except perhaps the Eels. As far as we know.'

'Humanfolk, be they? These Magoghe? Not witches nor wraiths nor trolls or the like?'

'They are inhuman in their cruelty,' said Ivo, 'but I believe that they are people.'

'Yon boy be nursing some deathsome story of his own,' observed the mermaid, 'and it do gnaw at his innards.'

I found myself nodding, and wondering – even hoping – that she in her grandness and wisdom would be able to extract Ivo's secrets where I had failed: first and foremost being the true fate of my poor Uncle Red.

'I be interested in these Sicilian ladies,' said the mermaid. 'Given that all our Venice's other enemies – sideways of the Eels – be presently vanquished. The ghost of Bajamonte Tiepolo lies in chains at the bottom of the sea, and the Frenchified Wolves of Luprio hide their blood-stained snouts in Siberia and the History Half-Man still bides his time . . . Aye, 'tis too much coincidence that the Eels do suddenly infest our shores when these Sicilian females be bent on doing harm. Details, stripling!'

194

She delivered a fierce look to Ivo. He licked his lips and glanced at me nervously. 'The way it works,' he said, 'is almost elegant. Sister One, the Signorina, lures Englishmen and women to the Hotel of What You Want. She promises that they can avoid foreign food and foreign discomforts, while still seeing the world by way of cunning little dolls' houses set in the window awnings, full of tiny lifelike contraptions. Meanwhile—'

Ivo licked his lips again. I'd seen nervous cats do that, when guilty of some crime in the kitchen.

Now, I thought, *comes the part that concerns Uncle Red.*

He continued quietly, 'Every so often, the Signorina chooses a guest. She administers increasing doses of a drug that fills their minds with wretchedness. Their diaries are spied on until they provide clear evidence of hopeless melancholy . . .'

His voice trailed away.

I thought, *Sure he's doing so much sighing now that we'll need to buy him an extra set of lungs. But it's too late now for sighing.*

'Continue,' ordered the mermaid.

'Eventually a final dose is administered. No one can survive it. Sometimes . . . I help . . . them along, with a pillow. When there is no hope. To be merciful.'

'To be merciful?' The mermaid's voice was thick with doubt and disgust.

I was having a big argument with some tears that wanted to visit my cheeks. In my mind's eye, I saw the Signorina measuring the drops into Uncle Red's cup. I saw my guardian shipwrecked in his spirits, slumped on his bed. I saw Ivo holding a pillow over his handsome face.

Ivo's voice grew even quieter now. *Yet,* I thought, *he's determined to drain his soul of its abominable secrets.*

'When the doctor comes to assess the cause of death, we . . . arrange it . . . so that he sees a pink froth in their mouths. It is soap. We show him the victims' diaries. He records the deaths as suicide by drowning. Then their bodies are taken to a locked storeroom next door to Chamber Seven – the dying room, the Signorina calls that one – and in that place they are stripped and then dropped down a greased chute to the watergate. Meanwhile, the butcher is sent for.'

'Chamber Seven. The dying room,' I said. 'Where you put *me, after Uncle Red died in it*?'

'This be abysmally bad, boy! 'Tis horror beyond horror,' said the mermaid.

'No,' said Ivo. 'Actually it is at this point that the real horror begins.'

He cast a desperate glance at Lily, her hair streaming in black rivulets over her scarred back. 'Perhaps the worst of it,' he said, 'is that I personally conducted Lily into this business. I made her part of it. I taught her how to be a murderess.'

Then he looked at me.

'*Lily* killed my Uncle Red?' I screamed.

CHAPTER THIRTY-ONE

At the back of my neck, the little hairs tautened. Ivo was, I guessed, but one or two years older than me. Yet how much evil had he dabbled in? Sincerely, he had more than dabbled. He had waded in knee-deep, dragging Lily with him. I had no doubt of that. Ivo had forced this evil on her somehow.

'Belay mumbling, stripling,' the mermaid told him. 'Ye have brought us this far. What happens to those murdered creatures at the watergate?'

Ivo sighed out the sweet air of the cavern as if he did not deserve its goodness inside him. A growing part of me agreed with that opinion.

If he made Lily murder Uncle Red, then he murdered a piece of Lily too.

'There's a wedge of stone down by the watergate. That is where the butcher puts their heads. As the bodies lack a beating heart, he must tilt them at an angle, so the blood drains out of the vein he opens in their necks. He inserts a glass tube there so that it flows out smoothly.'

I asked, 'And that is what they did to Uncle Red?'

197

'I have to assume so,' said Ivo, gazing at a point just over my shoulder. 'Though in his case I saw nothing. Usually I take the drained corpses by boat to the Anatomy School in the middle of the night. The clerk there is Magoghe sister Number Two. The medical students pay her to learn by watching real corpses being dissected by a Doctor Ichthor. He's so eaten up by his own private miseries that he never notices that some of the corpses he cuts up are the very same English guests whose death certificates he's recently written.

'After they've earned the Anatomy School those fees, then the remains are stripped of certain pieces – usually arms, legs, skulls. I row those bones – wrapped up in a basket – to Murano, where I deliver them to Saint Teresa's Convent of the Barefoot Carmelites. Where Lily grew up. And what happens next is the business of Sister Number Three, the *badessa*.'

He threw a fearful glance at Lily's prone form.

Giacomo whispered, 'I swear by my heart and soul, I never heard anything worse.'

'Look at the face on Ivo,' I said. 'There is worse still.'

Ivo continued in his flat, quiet voice, 'At the convent, the bones are rubbed with dirt and fat, beaten with hammers, scratched with little knives until they look ancient. The choicest bits are given to the jewellers to set into golden reliquaries – as if they were the relics of thousand-year-old saints. Then the reliquaries are rowed out by night in a small boat to the galleys arriving from the Holy Land. They are taken aboard and brought back into Venice in triumph, as if they had journeyed all the way here from Jerusalem. I know because I sometimes row that small boat.'

'Uncle Red?' I asked. 'Did you take bits of him to a galley?'

'No, Darling, I've been so honest about . . . the rest . . . that you must believe me when I say I don't know. After I took him to the storeroom, I saw nothing more. I did not remove his clothes – usually one of my tasks.'

'Even the women?' I asked.

He hung his head.

'And Lily?' I asked.

'I swear that your guardian was her first experience of the secret workings of the hotel. She was . . . as shocked as you are now. It was my job to trick her into assisting . . . me. *She didn't hurt him.* I gave her little tasks to help his death seem like a suicide. She did not understand what she was doing from one second to the next. And then – *you* arrived. And the story took a different road.'

A silence fell in the cavern.

I could not think about the fate of Uncle Red's poor body. My thoughts tiptoed towards it, and then ran away to hide. Instead, I pictured Ivo's lonely figure rowing an unlighted boat in the black water of the lagoon with his grisly cargo aboard. I saw Lily staring at Uncle Red's dead face. No wonder she'd not wanted to tell me what happened. She must have feared my hatred, my fury. But all I felt was pity.

The mermaid said, 'So the only truthful thing about all those famous relics from Saint Teresa is that the bones are from foreign parts. Parts of *Englishmen*, they are. Not the wishing bones of saints at all. Yet the Venetians set such store by them.'

'It's easy to fool an innocent human,' I said, staring at Ivo, 'if you are a devious article yourself.'

199

'Belay,' said the mermaid. ''Tis more to this. There must be a Beast-caller at work, summoning those Eels to Venice. Which means there is devilishly Baddened Magic afoot here.' She gave Ivo another of those looks. 'Have ye spilled everything, stripling?'

'What *is* Baddened Magic?' Ivo asked. 'Everyone talks of it – even the Madonna – and no one explains it.'

'All magic is born good, but it can be corrupted or inflamed,' the mermaid said. 'Ye could think of Baddened Magic as magic gone mad.'

'But if the Magoghe sisters had magic,' I observed, 'would they not have Badmagicked themselves up some money without working so hard, so sneakily and so horribly to get it?'

'Perhaps. But Baddened Magic be not easily controlled by Humanfolk. They *think* they can manage it, if they have the cleverness to summon it. But those who call up Baddened Magic never understand that Baddened Magic be far stronger than bad Humanfolk. 'Tis like pulling a great shark into a small fishing boat. Sometimes the great fish capsizes the boat, and everyone dies.' She turned again to Ivo. 'Can you swear on the life of yon poor maid' – she pointed to Lily – 'that you never noticed anything supernatural or otherworldly about that Signorina, that *badessa* or that anatomy clerk?'

Ivo said, 'There was a headless Flayed Man who came alive at midnight in the Anatomy School. Alina Magoghe was shocked as we were. And angry.'

The mermaid sighed. 'Indeed. Now . . . 'tis never a strength that makes Humanfolk go to the bad. 'Tis always a heinous weakness. What do we know about the cravings of these women?'

200

Ivo explained the anatomy clerk's inhuman coldness. 'Even her sisters avoid her.' He spoke of the Signorina and the romantic disappointment that had led to her desire to hurt Englishmen and women.

I told the mermaid all about the *badessa*'s cruelty to Lily, her greed for roast goose, the starving and beating of orphans and the babies left to die.

The mermaid rose high in the water, lashing her tail. 'Cruelty to Venetian babies? Venetian childer? That *badessa* shall smell Hell! I shall tattoo teardrops on her cheeks!'

I hoped that Lily, even so profoundly unconscious, could hear this.

'But why be these Sicilian sisters in Venice?' persisted the mermaid. 'Did the creatures come here for love of the place?'

Ivo answered, 'I've worked out they must have washed up here after the plague hit Siracusa back in 1729. Like so many others. They gave themselves a new surname and set up in their different trades, each perfectly suited to the temperament of the sister in question. They found ready-made local villains like Aldo Momesso to work with. Not to mention the English Resident, who turns a blind eye to the disappearance of his countrymen and women, doubtless for a fee to fuel his gambling fever.'

I felt a grudging tingle of respect for Ivo. Whatever else he had done, he had been vigilant and collected a creditable spread of facts.

'Sicilians,' mused the mermaid. 'Who called themselves Magoghe almost exactly like the evil seagulls who are on the side of bad whenever badness comes to Venice.'

201

Lily had said, *'I hate those big gulls. They are always laughing at us.'*

'Yet I do insist – I smell Baddened Magic here,' said the mermaid. 'Ye have forgotten something, surely.'

Ivo said, 'Baddened Magic explains the strange awful weather? Or is that really because of Saint Lucy's stolen foot?'

'Well, that theft at least is not down to the *badessa*,' I said. 'Lily told me she was after searching every crevice of the convent for that foot and never found it. But what of your . . . colleagues . . . the missing mermaids from Miracoli? Is that part of it?' I asked, remembering the story the newsboys cried out in the street.

''Tis a difficult time for our little sisters at Miracoli.' The mermaid's face softened with sympathy. 'They be at that tricky wrigglesome age, only a few centuries old, not quite sure if they be girls or women. 'Twill take a few more decades or even centuries before they be fit for service. I've great hopes for the one known as Lussa. And in the meantime, what's the use of being young and female if ye cannot behave abominably, scandalously, unreasonably and excessively from time to time?'

'No use at all,' Giacomo agreed.

'I see it now. The Magoghes will have tempted the Miracoli mermaids with tales of Sicily and marzipan cake and sweet buns with lemon ices inside, the scent of the orange groves. Those flitty girls wanted to stretch their tails and dive through the waves of far blue seas, to itch their scales on African sands . . .'

My heart leapt as Lily stirred in her deep sleep, turned over and began to suck her thumb. She released a sigh that could break a stone heart.

But a sigh means she's alive, I told myself. *The dead have finished sighing. Haven't they?*

'The shipwrecked maid will be waking soon,' said the mermaid. 'Shame ye young people shall not be here to see it.'

'Don't make me leave Lily again,' I pleaded.

''Tis not for your personal convenience that I despatch ye!' thundered the mermaid.

'But Lily must not wake up alone. She's been too much alone. At all the worst times. '

The mermaid crossed her vast arms. 'There be more at stake here than your tender heart.'

PART NINE

Under Venice

CHAPTER THIRTY-TWO

That night, the waves had cared nothing for me, for my kicking, my fighting, my screams. Those waves had pulled me out of the cave where Ivo had lied to me that I'd be safe.

I kept praying to Saint Lucy, even as I tumbled through the foam. *I am Sorrowful Lily,* I told her. *Please save me. Sorrowful as my life is, I find I want to live it. And I swear if you save me, I shall find your foot and return it to you.*

Till my last conscious moment, I prayed to her. But, after that one time, she never answered me again.

I did not know that Saint Lucy had a certain unusual colleague at her bidding or that she'd have skin of a rich deep brown, fins, a tail and all the storms of the sea in her voice. Or that she'd be the size of a small whale, yet graceful with it.

I'd grown up with rumours of such creatures. Of course I had. Where else would mermaids dwell but Venice? But I believed I was dreaming, even when the huge mermaid took me in her arms and lifted me up to the water's silken surface. Her strength was more animal than human. Her smell was of salt water and churches. She brushed the mud from my face, saying, 'Another young maid taken by the sea. Fair wrecked, she be. Yet she breathes, so the fishes have fed her some air. She must be alive for a reason.'

I certainly could not have guessed that the mermaid would carry me to a cavern under the House of the Spirits and that she would lay me on a pallet of shredded seaweed, softer than a bird's breast.

I was torn, bruised and something woolly packed the inside of my head. Waterfalls of pain rippled through my limbs. Sometimes I shivered uncontrollably; sometimes I was unable even to blink.

The mermaid tended my injuries with salves and bandages. Despite her size and her strangeness, I felt the bond of femaleness with my saviour. Her appearance was terrifying, yet she could not mean me ill as she had saved me. She seemed to carry centuries of age in her luminous skin. There were old barnacles and oysters crusting her tail. Yet her eyes were fresh and young.

Every time I roused myself from my stupor, the mermaid would feed me pieces of a salty bread-like substance. 'Sle-e-ep,' she said. 'Then ye shall heal.'

And so I drifted in and out of consciousness. In one dream, I entered a candle-lit convent, where I knelt in front of a veiled woman who said she was my mother. I hugged her knees, but she was cold as stone. When I rose and lifted her veil, there was only a marble head of an emaciated madwoman grinning like a skull.

'Are my secret sacred ties to you? To stone?' I cried. 'To madness?'

Then I saw an arched cavern tiled in tiny golden mosaics, shimmering like those inside the Basilica di San Marco. In my dreamy state, I thought I heard the voices of Darling, Giacomo and Ivo.

But that all seemed to be part of a dream in which I thrashed like a fly in an intricate spider's web.

PART TEN

Murano

CHAPTER THIRTY-THREE

'Where must we go?' I asked, still holding Lily's lifeless hand.

'Murano,' the mermaid answered. 'Bad Humanfolk be a human battle to fight. But a land-witch might help ye, for a price. I have heard tell of one on Murano who cures the lovesick and curses neighbours who empty slop buckets out of their windows.'

'The Murano witch with the black cats?' asked Giacomo. 'She's the one who cured *me*. When I couldn't talk!'

'*You* couldn't talk?' I stared at him. 'That seems . . . vastly unlikely.'

Giacomo, of course, loved to be centre of attention. He took up his raconteuring pose, one knee elegantly tucked behind the other. 'My dear lady,' he told the mermaid, 'my mother brought me into the light of this world on the second day of April 1725. Yet I remember absolutely nothing until I was eight. Before that, I lived with no feelings, words or memories. I just stood mutely, with my mouth gaping open, bleeding profusely from my nose.

'My mother, Zanetta, is an actress. She travels around the courts of Europe, entertaining kings. Why should she bother with a little idiot son back in Venice? Even when she was at home, she never spoke to me. I suppose she thought I'd die soon so there was no point bothering with me. She consigned me to the care of my grandmother, Marzia.'

His own mother. I thought. *No wonder he loves the attention of ladies now.*

Giacomo continued, 'However, when I was exactly eight years and four months old, I suddenly woke up from my long, bloody sleep, and it was the witch on the island of Murano who woke me!'

He paused for dramatic effect.

'On that day my Grandma Marzia washed me, dressed me and took me on a gondola to Murano. She led me into a shabby dark hovel with tall windows filled with all the trappings of witchery from floor to ceiling. A young woman was sitting on a straw mattress, a black cat in her arms. A dozen other cats prowled to and fro. I guessed straight away that she was a witch. *That was the first time I ever had a conscious thought.* It was like lightning in my head! But, as always, I stood mute and motionless. Grandma Marzia quickly handed the witch a silver ducat.'

'A whole ducat?' asked Ivo. 'She must have *really* loved you, your grandmother.'

Giacomo nodded. 'The young woman opened a big wooden chest, picked me up and put me inside. She shut the lid and locked it. I lay listening to strange noises outside: cries, singing, laughing, weeping.

'Finally, the witch opened the lid. Light flooded into my dull eyes. The witch laid me tenderly on a straw mattress. I gazed at the ceiling above me, painted with stars and saints and angels.

I could hear the strange tick of a clock and another, softer thumping. Raising my head, I saw that I was surrounded by beating hearts in buckets.'

'Hearts in buckets. A sure sign of a witch,' said the mermaid. 'Surer than broomsticks.'

'But it does not sound like a *good* witch so,' I worried.

Giacomo continued, 'The witch sprinkled herbs into her fire. She wafted a sheet over the perfumed smoke until it was saturated with the scent. Then she folded me into it, said spells over me, and gave me five delicious little cakes. She told me that the nosebleeds would stop, but only if I told *no one* what had happened – if I ever in my life dared to reveal her secret then all the blood would flood out of my body in a great red wave and I would die.'

'You're telling us now,' I reminded him.

'I'll take that risk,' Giacomo said grandly.

He continued, 'From that day forth, I began to develop a functioning brain, a memory and a sense of being a human. Within a month, I could read and write. I began to speak. The nosebleeds stopped.'

Ivo asked, 'You really think that's the reason why you can talk? Because some cat-crazed female shut you in box and gave you cake?'

You don't need to be scornful, I thought. *Or perhaps you do.*

'Was it a masquerade my grandmother staged for me? Is that what you mean?' Giacomo furrowed his brow. 'I'll never know, but if it was, it was created out of love, and that love saved me.'

Ivo's face closed.

'I'm sure that same witch can help us now,' concluded Giacomo.

'Belay there, stripling,' the mermaid said. 'She took your granddam's ducat, her witch-price. A witch for hire has a shark's brutal greed. But her enchantment worked on ye, which means ye gave her a portion of your soul. That land-witch will always have some power over ye. It be not safe for ye to visit her now. That task be for this sad-faced boy, and the red-haired maid, be they willing.'

'More than willing myself,' I said. 'Though I cannot speak for *him*.'

The mermaid gazed at Ivo, the dark eyes judging. ''Tis a task that will take courage and long trousers,' she said.

'Could you draw a map, Giacomo, of the way to the witch's house?' Ivo said stiffly. 'Thank you. Are you coming, Miss Dearworthy?'

'What?' I said. 'So now that you've finally revealed yourself as one of Uncle Red's murderers, you go all "Miss Dearworthy" on me?'

Giacomo changed the subject. 'Is the Signorina still lurking up in the street? With her henchmen?'

'We've been here a long time,' I reminded him. 'They'll have given us up for lost.'

Giacomo waved us goodbye at the foot of the stairs. 'I'll look after our dearest girl,' he promised. Lily sighed profoundly again. Her eyes did not open.

The mermaid said, 'Before ye parlay, remember to ask her witch-price for helping. Agree, whatever it is. I see from your

216

clothes, girl, that coin be not a problem for ye. Ye must offer money before anything, for the exact service you require. Do not consent to any enchantment of yourselves, no matter how pretty. And be wary lest she help herself to a part of your souls.'

Upstairs, we had only to touch the door and it revolved to allow us out. The tetchy Madonna was in repose, as if She were just a painting. I crossed myself in front of Her anyway and sketched a curtsey.

It had been morning when we entered the cavern. Now the low winter light crowded down and the air was stuffed with evening humidity. Ivo and I spoke not a word as he led me to the hotel boat and rowed the twenty minutes to Murano. As the brooding island grew closer and larger, I could not help thinking that it was the home of Lily's deadly enemy, the *badessa*.

At least, I told myself, *we're not going anywhere near that desperate article.*

CHAPTER THIRTY-FOUR

The *calle* outside the witch's house stank of cats with very bad manners. Indeed, sitting in the doorway was a cat with the very worst manners I had encountered in all its race.

This Murano cat, black as boiled ink, stood up on its crooked legs and berated us. But it didn't do so in the manner of the kitchen cats at the Young Ladies' Academy. It yowled in words. It said, 'Goodbye! Should you rabid son and daughter of flea-bitten French sailors have actual business with my mistress, I doubt if it will make us money. *Fish* costs money.'

'You,' I told him, 'should grow a brush on the end of your tongue for cleaning the dirt that comes out of your mouth.'

Another black cat nosed around the door, adding, 'What na-a-a-asty red hair that girlie has! Not even a Venetian red.'

A third cat leered from the doorway, 'Come in, why don't you? Something for everyone in here.'

As we crossed the threshold, my eyes fell on dozens of glass buckets, each holding a beating heart, just as Giacomo had described. They floated in a clear liquid, some the size of human hearts; others had been taken – I hated to think how – from smaller creatures like puppies or sparrows. But Giacomo had not mentioned a carved black clock, with human bones for hands, which ticked badly out of time with the hearts. He had not spoken of skulls that hung from their own long hair from the ceiling or of the bundles of more bones tied in bunches with black ribbons, and long rustling strings of dried seahorses looking like shrivelled mermaids in miniature. I imagined what the far-from-miniature mermaid would say about these garlands of murdered sea creatures, full sure it would not be pretty.

Ivo said, 'In Venice, seahorses are supposed to bring luck. And' – he blushed – 'mother's milk to the breast.'

Not these ones, I thought. Everything was upside down here; everything good had been translated into its evil twin. Even the many portraits of saints looked uncomfortable. Their alarmed eyes and raised fingers seemed to warn of ungodly dangers. *Saints?* I looked up and saw stars and angels painted on the ceiling.

'Ivo,' I said, 'this place is a *church*. Or the remains of ruined one. A witch in a church – isn't that all kinds of wrong?'

It occurred to me that years had passed since this witch had cured Giacomo. Had she fallen into bad ways or bad company in the meanwhile?

We pushed our way through ropes of human hair. Some were plaited. Above the long plaits hung clumps of shorter, coarser hair, men's hair. One clump was as violently red and curly as my own.

Uncle Red had hair like that, I thought.

Ivo pointed to a glass bottle in which some small

219

mint-and-brown frogs leapt about vigorously. 'Peruvian poison arrow frogs. Deadly.'

How did he know that? I moved away, wanting air between me and Ivo. A little coil of mistrust began to twist in my stomach again. I was alone on the island of Lily's *badessa*. With Ivo. I glanced at his hands – the ones that had slid from mine when the Vampíre Eel lunged.

My heart beat frantically while my eyes roamed around the room.

In one corner, I was startled to see a small girl tied to a chair. A vein in her wrist was slit; her blood dripped slowly into a glass jar. As we approached, she disappeared into a green vapour.

And suddenly there was the witch herself, sitting on a stool. I took in the dark, terrifying beauty etched into the cheekbones and slanted eyes on her. She must have been sitting there all the time: it was as if she'd only just *allowed* us to see her. Surely that was magic so. *Was it Baddened Magic?*

She was drawing an ivory comb through her long tresses, which were black as mole fur. As she combed it, she sang to herself in a dialect even I could not work out. It brought into that Venetian room the burning heat and spices and even the sands of Africa. Around her waist hung a dagger shaped like a scimitar. Its blade glinted like an icicle in the firelight. I tried to shrug off the drowsiness brought on by watching the witch's comb pass rhythmically through her hair.

I knew I was meant to give her something, but I could not remember what it was.

She was singing not to us but to a glass bowl in which swam – or rather undulated – a small white creature that seemed to be

220

nearly all tail. The creature repeatedly threw itself against the side of the bowl, evidently furious. Even at its tiny size, it seemed dangerous as a wounded lion. Yet gradually, the little monster too succumbed to the witch's hypnotic crooning. It stilled, its head raised as if on an invisible string.

The witch showed no sign of having noticed us, absorbed in the creature and the combing of her long locks.

I glanced back at the bowl and could have sworn that the creature, and the bowl, had grown by a hand's span. *How could—?*

I whispered to Ivo, 'This woman is beautiful. Aren't good witches supposed to be ugly as toads?'

Ivo said, 'Good or bad, witches can change their appearances when they want to.'

I looked back at the creature in the bowl. I was full sure it had grown yet again. Something flashed red at the side of its neck.

I said, 'She must be a Beast-caller. Remember, the mermaid spoke of such.'

'I hear every word,' said the witch in her rich voice. 'I hear what you whisper and also what's in your heads.'

She pointed to me. 'Come here, Irish,' she commanded. 'Irish who lost her mama and papa in a carriage accident, give me your hand.'

How did she know I was Irish? Or what had happened to my parents? My ankles were gripped as if by invisible pincers which dragged them forward, one by one. It was easier to give in. I felt dreamy and unafraid. I even held out my hand to her.

Her fingers rasped like bark against my skin. She traced the

221

pale pink lines in my palm. Suddenly she dropped my hand as if it were made of hot glass. 'M,' she spat. 'M for the Madonna. You are beloved of the Madonna. You are no good to me.'

I thought that the tetchy Madonna had not been excessively loving towards me. In fact, disapproval seemed to be Her main emotion in my regard.

The witch spat. 'Fie on your Madonna.'

The pictures of saints on the wall swung backwards and forward on their hooks, uneasily. Then they spun on their ribbons so that they faced the wall.

I withdrew a step. That was as far as my feet would consent to take me. 'In fact we came to . . . ask for your help,' I said. The words did not come easily, and I heard them as if they were not my own.

Ivo spoke disjointedly. 'We need . . . could use—'

I remembered what I should have asked her before anything – her witch-price. If we did not pay her for what *we* wanted, she'd exact her own price in something more dangerous than money. I wanted to ask now, but my tongue hung limply in my mouth, unable to rouse itself.

'What cannot be used, must be abused,' the witch crooned to herself. 'And then sold for profit. I can guess where there's a market for it.'

She reached out and tugged at my braid. With my hair in her hand, she began to talk to the creature in her bowl. It replied to her in a stream of bubbles.

'Your hair has a lovely blood-red vitality, my dear,' she said. 'Let me comb it, my sweetum.'

Again my betraying feet carried me a step closer to her. I stood like a statue as she loosened my curls and then fanned the hair out down my back.

She combed and combed. Ivo's eyes grew dim as he watched each long pass of the comb through my hair.

The witch held up her comb. She mouthed some noises over it. Tendrils of my hair unwound from the spokes of the comb and lifted into the air. Then one of them flew over to Ivo, inching through the air like a worm. It curled into a tight spiral and then darted like an arrow into his ear.

He shrieked in agony.

'The Irish girl's hair,' said the witch, 'is slithering through the chambers of the Venetian boy's ear. It will find the narrow entrance and push into his brain. There, when I order it to do so, it will tie a knot around his brain. And when I feel like it, I shall tighten it, and he shall not believe the excruciation.'

She waved the comb in a circular fashion. 'That wraps it round thoroughly.'

She drew the comb up into the air. The colour fell out of Ivo's face like a stoup of water emptying. He clutched the side of his head where the thread of hair had gone in. Then he fell to the ground, retching.

His cry of pain emptied the enchantment out of me. I ran to him and lifted his head. I put my little finger in his ear, trying to find the hair and pull it out. 'Why?' I asked the witch. 'Why be so cruel to a boy you don't even know? Who never hurt a fly?'

I stopped myself there. Ivo had hurt much more than a fly.

And by then the witch had lifted her comb again and this time she wound my hair around my face like a mummy's bandages, till all I could see, all I could breathe, was redness.

At my neck it, it tightened. The witch said, 'Now, where are my manners? Let me introduce myself. My name is Aleesia. Aleesia Magoghe. Did you sweetums think you were dealing with just *three* sisters from Sicily?'

PART ELEVEN

Under Venice

CHAPTER THIRTY-FIVE

Finally, after unknown days or hours, I lifted my head and saw the mermaid.

'Be ye awake at last, maid? From your face, I believe ye can see me?'

'Should I not?'

'Just unusual at your age, for ye be older than a child? Or mayhap ye have experienced more than a child should.'

'I can explain that,' I said boldly. 'There are nasty goings-on at a convent on Murano where they make false relics of antique saints that Venetians pay rare fortunes to buy . . .'

'Do ye think I do not know that?'

I did not quite like the red light in her eyes or the way she towered above the edge of the pool by my seaweed pallet. If she knew about the murder manufactory at the hotel, then perhaps she knew I had been part of it. Had she saved me from the sea just to hand down a grim punishment? Then I saw another smaller mermaid, wounded at the waist, lying on a floating pallet. *What had happened? Might I be held responsible for this crime too?*

I backed away on my haunches, slithering on the golden tiles.

My eyes darted to a staircase lit by candles flickering in golden sconces. *Where did those stairs go?* I saw my clothes folded neatly at the end of my strange bed and knelt in my chemise to put them on.

'Do not contemplate the notion of leaving. It be not my work to let ye escape, girl,' said the mermaid. 'When the sea delivers an orphan to me, well, I be obliged to find the correct use for her. There always be something to her. The sea knows. What be ye good for, maid?'

'Do you mean, what can I do?'

She nodded.

Should I say I am good for setting fire to convents?

Assisting at murders of innocent Englishmen?

And that reminded me. I whispered, 'Ivo! Darling! My friends must think that I am dead!'

I had used that word 'friends' quite naturally. A smile lifted the corners of my mouth.

'They do not. This Ivo and this Darling have been here while ye lay in the sleep of recovery. It be they who informed me of certain grim matters a-brewing in Venice. I sent them to parlay with a land-witch on Murano. Reputed good, but now I begin to nurse some doubts. 'Tis a worrisome long time since they left.'

'A witch?'

'Aye,' said the mermaid, 'your friend Giacomo told them to seek help from that witch, who had cured him of being silent and stupid and bleeding from the nose like a fountain.'

'*Giacomo* was *silent*? Did he go with them?'

'I sent him back to his grandmama. It be not safe for that stripling to attend a witch who will surely have some hold over his soul.' She said darkly, 'And it be on his head if *his* witch turned out to be a bad one.'

Suddenly the mermaid was less human and more animal. Her size seemed to swell, and the gesture she now made with her hand was like a panther's paw making a kill. If Giacomo had been there then, I felt she might have inflicted a deathly violence upon him.

'My spies say that the boy and girl never left Murano,' the mermaid said. 'That be the strange thing.'

'What spies?'

'The good black-headed gulls – not the vile grey-backed ones. And various *Incogniti* – they being grown up but not-yet-grown-stupid Humanfolk who can see mermaids and who help the city in her times of danger. Most Humanfolk cannot even conceive of us, let alone see us, not past thirteen years of age. Ye and your friends be clearly something out of the ordinary.'

'Out of the ordinary,' I echoed.

'I be coming to the conclusion that 'tis the fact that none of ye have secret sacred ties of your own. Orphans. Or good as. 'Tis the *lack* of love that defines ye and brings ye together – certainly yourself, the Red Irish and the grim-faced boy. And I be not sure if the stripling Giacomo be so soaked in love as he gives forth to be. The unloved be the bravest souls, 'tis true.'

I did not need to ask her who the grim-faced boy was. But I protested, 'Darling has known love.'

She sighed, 'Yet 'twas taken from her, twice over. My search be constant for heroes, and it seems that they be getting younger. Our old *Incogniti* be so few now. Yet what kind of work be at hand, that requires unloved *childer* to take it on?'

229

PART TWELVE

Murano

CHAPTER THIRTY-SIX

A fourth sister! Why had we not even considered that possibility?

But three is always the fatal number, I thought. *Of bears, of trolls, of evil sisters. And clever, brave young people are supposed to win against them.*

Then I realised, *Yet we are four, too! Me, Lily, Giacomo and Ivo. If Ivo is truly one of us.*

The witch's hard fingers tied us in rope. She rolled us in canvas that reeked of rotting fish. She was as strong as a lion, lifting us easily and binding us to a trolley.

The mermaid was right, I thought. *To be sure this is Baddened Magic and no doubting it.*

'Not so clever after all, are we, my sweetums?' gloated the witch. She let out a laugh like the caw of a seagull who has killed and rejoices in ripping the heart out of some helpless creature.

'Run and tell the *badessa* at Saint Teresa,' she ordered a cat, 'that for the right price she can have a pair of small saints-in-waiting. A boy saint and a girl saint.'

233

In Lily's mouth, the name of the *badessa* had been fearsome enough. To hear the witch saying it in that familiar way made my spine prickle.

Through my hair, I heard the light of patter of cat claws on stone, disappearing into the distance.

The witch sang quietly to herself as she eased the trolley out of the door and slammed it behind her. 'Guard my treasures well,' she told the remaining cats.

'But of course, mistress,' yowled one cat. 'With my life.'

'With all nine of your lives,' she snapped.

'You already took one, when you needed catgut for a Charm Cello,' the cat reminded her in a surly voice.

'So I did,' the witch said without regret.

I heard paws drumming again on the stone outside.

'Mistress,' called the cat. 'Your sister will pay an additional ten ducats apiece for these items, and twenty for a loan of what's in the bowl.'

'Mean as ever,' the witch grumbled. But she raised the trolley's handle so we tilted almost upside down. The blood rushed to my head. I could feel Ivo's body beside mine, but I didn't want to add to the terrible pain in his head by whispering anything into his ear. In my mind's eye I saw the filament of my red hair wrapped around his brain.

I saw our situation with a horrible clarity. Little as they apparently liked each other, the four Magoghe sisters all helped one another. They passed bodies around, rifling them each for their own desires – revenge, money, bones. Lily had presented a difficulty to the *badessa,* so she'd been given to the Signorina to

234

deal with. The *badessa*'s goose grease oiled the chute in the hotel. Now the witch and the *badessa* would settle the Signorina's problems – Ivo and myself. No one would know what happened to us behind the convent's walls. No evidence would never lead to the Signorina's door.

'For the love of little baby Jesus. Isn't it just diabolically clever?' I whispered to myself.

I noticed a rip in the canvas near my face. I forced my teeth through my hair and into the slit. My tongue cringed at the salty-sweet-bitter taste of dead fish and the roughness of the fabric. Little by little I tore away at the canvas, using both teeth and tongue, until the tear opened up in front of my left eye. The evening sky flooded in, and suddenly the shapes of buildings were looming above me.

Then the witch was brought up short, rumbling our bones. It seemed she'd paused to find out what was detaining the attention of a crowd of people who were laughing and shouting.

Above me, visible through my slit of canvas, was a wooden stall taller than a man, with a striped canvas front and a stage the length of a child's arm. A wooden puppet in a fisherman's costume peered over the ledge at me.

I took my chance and screamed, 'Help!'

A corner of the striped canvas lifted, and the human puppeteer peered out. He shouted, 'There's a young lady in trouble down there!'

'Tell everyone!' I begged, but my voice was muffled by my hair and the canvas.

People in the crowd were starting to murmur. 'What young lady? Where did that yelping come from?'

The witch jerked the trolley up again, forcing her way through the puppeteer's audience. A few minutes later, she paused again, rapping on a wooden door in a great fortress of a wall.

It was opened promptly by a woman whose face closely resembled the Signorina's in its beauty and its cruelty. This could only be Lily's enemy, and therefore mine, the *badessa*.

The witch saluted the *badessa* without smiling. 'Here they are, Arabella, your bothersome young sweetums.'

The *badessa* did not ask her sister in. The witch slit the ropes and canvas with a dagger chained to her belt and tipped us inside the door. We landed on a cold stone floor. My hair fell away from my face at last and I saw walls towering above us.

'And the *other* matter?' the witch asked, holding out her hand.

'Twenty ducats, Aleesia,' said the *badessa* coldly, 'is a high price. The thing in the bowl is tiny, insignificant. I could strangle it myself.'

'Why do you always belittle my skills? All three of you, always carping, criticising. Yet where would you be without me? The twenty ducats are for the *growing*,' said the witch, 'as well as the lending.'

Scowling, the *badessa* counted the coins into her sister's hand.

'Nice doing business with you,' said the witch. 'I'm off to grow a revenge rose for a jilted bridegroom. *Enjoy.*'

The *badessa* turned to me and Ivo, who lay curled in silent agony on the ground. 'I guessed it must be you two,' she said. 'My sister Anna shall be gratified to hear of this.'

She muttered to herself, 'If *anything* can gratify that sour-faced sow.'

A dozen nuns in brown habits stood behind the *badessa*. I searched their faces for kindness or regret. I saw none.

'What shall you do to us?' I asked the *badessa*.

'Think of your worst nightmares,' she replied. 'And they'll be pleasant dreams compared.'

I wanted to spit in her eye. My heart was so full of bitterness I'd be sure to poison her. But my mouth was dry with fear.

Six nuns surrounded each of us, lifting us by our legs, shoulders and middles. They carried us to a vaulted room that smelled like a rose garden.

It was bare, apart from six stone tombs as grand as Egyptian sarcophagi, two large barrels on gridirons over embers and an array of curious leather flasks. Two tombs stood open, their immense stone lids pushed aside. The *badessa* pointed to the barrels, from each of which two leather tubes emerged like the antennae of a fat cockroach.

'Full of olive oil,' she said, 'about to become holy.'

'How?' I asked. The tombs were empty apart from a dense scattering of dried rose petals.

'I was hoping you'd ask that.' She smiled. 'Some saintly flesh, they say, never rots, even in the grave. It stays sweet and whole. And even if saints are but dry bones, perfumed oil still flows from their remains. Oil from *young* martyrs smells particularly sweet.'

'Martyrs?' I asked.

'Martyrs are those who die the most agonising deaths. Martyrs' Oil is worth more,' she said, 'than any other kind. And sometimes my famous Martyrs' Oil has the perfume of delicious truth about it.'

237

The nuns lowered me into one of the stone coffins. I stole a look at Ivo. His body drooped, unresisting in the hands of his captors. His eyes were open, but his face was blank. The hair had destroyed his brain – my own hair. I was as good as alone. I longed for just one feeling glance from him. I envied him his merciful distance from what was happening.

I struggled like a python, writhing and biting, and clinging to my captors when they tried to drop me on to my bed of dried roses.

My back hit the bottom of the tomb with painful force. A stone pillow raised my head.

The *badessa* leaned over to tell me, 'Drowning in oil is said to be a gentle death, less harsh than choking on sea water – slower, sweeter, longer.'

'Such a connoisseur of murder you are so,' I said.

'As an extra kindness to you, the oil's at the same temperature as your blood. The feeling of drowning will be subtle, not shocking. That is why your heads are elevated: so that you will watch your death coming for as long as possible.'

Playing for time, I told her, 'You're the woman for knowing everything about oil, are you not? Swallowing all those greasy geese roasted in their own fat! All the while feeding your poor orphans on almost nothing and making them work their thin fingers to the bone. This is not a convent. This is a charnel house. Why, all the writers in the world – even the writers of *Ireland* – could not make up something so bad and sad and evil as you have manufactured here for your pleasure. There's nothing worse within the four walls of the world.'

'Lovely speech.' The *badessa* applauded. 'Do amuse yourself with conversation while I start filling the tomb. By the time my orphans come to gather the oil enriched with your tears and the oozings of your dead bodies – well, *you* won't be saying anything any more.'

There's no appealing to a woman who makes an art of murder, I realised. *Isn't it making her all the happier to hear my lamenting so?*

But there were other women in the room. *Perhaps I could convince them?* I said, 'You're already damned ten times over, you desperate article. But now you're about to turn twelve innocent nuns into murderesses too.'

I saw one nun stiffen; another loosed a terrified tear, which she hastily wiped away.

'Lily told me how you made these poor women kill babies with starvation and cold. You've stolen these nuns from God their Bridegroom. Will He be wanting them in heaven after what they've done down here?'

The nuns were silent. Their faces had hardened. I'd painted too horrible a picture – they hated me for it. There would be no help from them now. And it was my fault. My tongue always went too far.

To the last, it had gone too far.

'Close them up!' the *badessa* ordered. Still wordless, but grunting now with effort, the nuns heaved the slabs over us. Darkness sheathed me, and the smell of cold stone filled my nostrils. My eyes searched out two pinpoints of light. One came from a hole above me, near the top of the sarcophagus. The other was near my feet. I thought, *That'll be for draining out the oil when it's infused with the essence of my corpse.*

Even as I watched, that hole was swiftly sealed with a sturdy plug of cork. There must have been a third hole too, for the leather tube feeding from the barrel of oil. A slow trickle by my foot told me that the *badessa* had released the tap of the barrel. Quiet nun footsteps proceeded to the door, which was then closed. To the *badessa*, we were already dead. She did not bother herself with any final remarks.

Ivo found his voice again then.

It was a quiet voice, aching with strain.

It said, 'Darling, I need to talk to you.'

CHAPTER THIRTY-SEVEN

So, while we died, we talked.

We talked of things that had happened since I came to Venice and those that had happened before I'd ever seen the place. Scraps of thoughts, tiny memories, old wounds, little pieces of our childhoods, all inconsequential. Our voices echoed hollowly through the stone troughs, floating out of the holes above our heads and meeting in the dank air of the crypt.

Yet I knew in my core that this was not what Ivo meant by needing to talk.

Silence fell suddenly between us.

'What are you thinking about?' I asked Ivo. 'Is my . . . hair still giving you pain at all?'

'It was working loose while the trolley bounced over the cobbles. When the witch dropped us on the floor, it finally fell out. But never mind that, now. Lily is what I am thinking about. I cannot stop. I have this vision of her, with her face – her crumpled sad eyes open – under water, buffeted through the canals with her hair flowing behind her. She always feared water would kill her. Will she ever really wake up? I don't think so. The old mermaid has ancient powers, but can she bring a girl back from drowning? She pretended Lily would live so as to give us heart for this mission . . . which we've failed at anyway.'

'You saw Lily sigh and turn, did you not? I don't love to hear you say she's . . . gone. Even now, I do not love it,' I said.

'Lily's death is on me, as much as your guardian's is. The cave was my idea. It was an innocent idea, but it was deadly to Lily. Even before then, at the hotel, I betrayed her. I tricked her and taught her do things that it was not in her nature to do.'

'Was it in *your* nature to do those things?'

'It had become so. Because of what happened when I worked for the English Resident. Darling, can I tell you what I've told no one else?'

I wanted to say, 'Isn't it as safe as the grave with me here?' but this was not the time for playing with words. Ivo seemed more troubled about Lily and the English Resident than he was about his own imminent death. I did not want to make it any harder for him. I said, 'I would love to understand you, so I would.'

I did not add, 'Even if it's the last thing I do.'

But I thought it.

Ivo paused while a gush of oil washed over him. I heard it swilling around the stone. The backs of my own knees were soaked, and the rose petals were floating, tickling my skin. I breathed in their perfume. From the sound of the gushing, Ivo's tomb seemed to be filling faster than mine. He said, 'The English Resident fancies himself a dashing kind of spy. Yet he's had precious little to spy on in Venice. The whole city's devoted to the pursuit of pleasure, not power.'

242

'Is this the time to talk politics, Ivo?'

'Yes. The Venetians have yet to understand it – only outsiders like the Resident do. Yet still the man tried and tries to make something of the nothing that is his posting here. I saw some papers . . . he was corresponding with the Pretender who plots to steal the British throne – he takes money from both sides in the murderous diplomatic game. He must enjoy that, double-crossing them all.'

'You're telling state secrets to a dead girl,' I told him, impatiently.

'I must tell them to someone.'

'I am not just *someone* so!' Ridiculous as the notion was, I wanted Ivo to speak sadly and tenderly of what we were sharing in our deaths. Did we not, at this moment, have some secret sacred ties of our own?

Instead, he said, 'The English Resident sells information and ideas to anyone who would buy them – even Sicilians trying to steal Saint Lucy. Now, do you remember Eliah, the sugar slave boy from Jamaica – the boy who waved people goodbye?'

I had always known that there was more to hear about Eliah. *Now*, I thought, *I'll hear the hurting core of Ivo's bitterness, at last, when it's already too late to melt that dark thing that holds the key to his heart.*

'There came a day when Eliah enraged the Resident by dropping a dish of butter on the floor,' Ivo said. 'It wasn't his fault. A maid had just slammed a door very loudly in the next room.

'It was not a good day to make a mistake. The Resident was thin-skinned and dangerous from a ruinous night at the gambling

243

tables. He was on the hunt for someone to blame for how sordid he felt. So he took up his new cane with a little silver dagger at its tip and began to beat Eliah. Slowly at first, but with his usual skill. Then faster, and deeper.'

'What did you do?'

'I,' said Ivo, 'was made to stand and watch, like the other servants. The Resident liked us to watch.'

So many the terrible things Ivo has seen, I thought. *And done.*

'The beating went on and on. Eliah's green hummingbird darted at the Resident's head, trying to peck his eyes. But nothing would distract the monster. Only when he realised that Eliah had fainted did the Resident stop. He had Eliah carried away by two footmen, to a boat store by the canal. He went off to the Ridotto to gamble and dig for more information to sell to any spy who'd buy it.

'The maids, the cook and me – we all rushed to the door of the boat store. Eliah had woken up. He pleaded for help. But the door was locked. A footman told us that the Resident had pocketed the key. The hummingbird threw itself against the door again and again until it dropped, unconscious. Its little heart beat still, so the maid took it into her apron, promising to take care of it. I seized a poker from the kitchen fireplace and prised the door off its hinges. I gathered Eliah in my arms and ran with him to the Apothecary of the Golden Hercules in Santa Fosca, a man known to have a drop of kindness. I tested it sorely when I walked in with a stolen slave child in my arms.

'I laid Eliah on the counter. I said, "This is my brother. That is, he has become my brother."

'The apothecary examined Eliah's injuries with horror. He said it would take Venetian Treacle to save his life. He warned me that Treacle was expensive, seven *lire* a pound, because it has seventy ingredients including vipers from Monselice.'

'Ugh!'

'But the apothecary looked at the unconscious boy bleeding on his counter, and said, "You say he's your brother. So this boy is now a Venetian, like us. We cannot let him die."'

'I told him I had some savings. He promised that whatever I could give him would be sufficient. When I came back the next day, Eliah was still living. He lay on a pallet at the corner of the apothecary's back office. But he could not speak.'

'He lives even now?'

'If you can call it living. He's like a terrified animal. He cannot bear the sight of people, except for me and the apothecary. He still does not talk. Nor does he cry. Most of my wages go to the apothecary for Eliah's board and food. Eliah has been trained to sort the herbs and spices . . . But the apothecary's kindness may not last if Saint Lucy is stolen and *all* the secret sacred ties are broken. The prophecy says that Venetian will turn against Venetian, and blood will flow. When I die here, Eliah will have no one to protect or provide for him.'

'When *we* die here,' I reminded him. While Ivo wove this story from the past, the future was closing in on us, liquidly, far too fast. 'And the Resident?'

'He tried to beat Eliah's whereabouts out of me. The last time he did it, I was crouching in a corner while he struck at me. He said, one word with each thrash, "Do . . . you . . . think . . . I . . . bought . . .

it . . . just . . . for . . . decoration? I haven't got my money's worth out of the blackamoor yet. Someone has to pay. It can be you."

'Now I believe that, after he'd had his fun with Eliah, he'd planned to sell the boy's bones to his friends the Magoghe sisters. Of course I did not know about those women or their *operation* back then.'

'Eliah's bones are white like yours and mine,' I said.

'So he could easily have been fashioned into a boy saint's relics,' Ivo agreed. 'Worth a lot. Which is probably why the Resident kept beating me.'

'How is it that he didn't kill you?'

'I think his heart wasn't in it. He didn't enjoy beating me the way he did Eliah. When his arm grew tired, the Resident said that I deserved to be turned out on the streets. But he had a better idea: the Hotel of What You Want, where they wanted a boy with immaculate English. I had few hopes of it – I knew that it would be the nastiest place he could find to send me.'

'So why did you let him?'

'I needed new work immediately. I had Eliah's medicines and keep to pay for.'

'But why *there*?'

'I was trapped. The Resident would give me a bad character reference if I applied for work anywhere else. '

'And you couldn't leave Venice because of Eliah.'

'And there was another reason to stay. Until I met Signorina Magoghe, I thought I could find no one who would hate the English as much as I did. On my first day at the hotel, I found myself telling her all kinds of things about the Resident. She offered me glass after glass of a spicy green juice to drink. It had an odd, smoky taste, but each glass seemed more delicious than the last.'

'She was drugging you?'

'Of course. Then she said she'd help me save the poor sugar slave boy from Jamaica. She even knew his name. She tried to trick me into telling her Eliah's whereabouts. Fortunately I still had the wherewithal to keep *that* from her.

'She said, "You cannot touch the Resident. But you *can* avenge Eliah on other English people here. As often as your heart desires."

'When she said that, I thought she meant petty revenges, like dropping their valises in the canal. Or spitting in their tea. I had no idea how deadly her revenges would be . . . not until the first time I was tricked into helping Aldo Momesso finish off an old baronet with a pillow. Like Lily, I was in too deep before I knew what I was doing. Then suddenly I was complicit. From innocence to guilt, Darling, it is – was – just one small blind step.'

Would I not have taken that small blind step myself, if I were trapped as he was? As Lily was?

Ivo said, 'And then . . . unlike Lily . . . I confess that each time I . . . quietened . . . one of the Signorina's victims, I persuaded myself that I saw the face of the Resident under every pillow I held down. After I'd done it a few times, I got to thinking that the Hotel of What You Want was the only kind of place for a . . . monster like myself. Please don't hate me, Darling.'

'You were set a trap, Ivo. I cannot hate you.'

'If I'd only met *you,* before it was too late, I'd never have wanted to hurt anyone, English or Irish, again.'

247

'If only you'd met me,' I whispered.

'If only I had,' he repeated, hollowly.

After that, for a while, there was just the noise of oil trickling slowly, and of our own last precious breaths.

'It's the end, isn't it?' I asked Ivo, when the oil had covered my legs and belly and was making its way around my shoulders. My hair dragged in the liquid, pulling my head back against the stone pillow.

My mind went back to the Young Ladies' Academy, the dark cupboard in the spidery attic that Esmeralda Sweeney used to shut me in. There, too, had been helplessness and suffocation. I had screamed up there, wept and pleaded. No one had heard my cries. Hadn't I wished to be dead with the grass growing over me rather than live through that torture a moment longer? But I had lived. Now that seemed less likely.

I beat my hands against the lid. I knew it was hopeless. The lid weighed five times what I did. My blind fingers encountered something leathery and complicated in shape. I explored it gingerly with the tip of one finger, drawing back suddenly when I realised what was fastened there.

'I know where Saint Lucy's foot is,' I said.

I heard Ivo spit out a mouthful of oil. 'What?'

'It's been here all the time,' I said, 'tied inside the sarcophagus. No wonder Lily couldn't find it.'

A muffled gurgling answered me.

A mystery solved and yet the solution will be known to no one, I thought, *except the evil and the dead.*

'I can see no way out of this,' Ivo gasped.

'I was vastly pleased to know you,' I said.

'In spite of what I did—'

'In spite . . .' My words trailed off into bubbles. Thick coarse oil was invading my mouth and starting to enter my nostrils.

Ivo was dying his own death, silently, sealed in his own guilt and misery. I could not reach him.

My second-last thought was, *Now, at least I know I can trust Ivo. He'll be as murdered as I am in a moment.* And my next thought was, *I know how Lily must have felt, drowning in that cave.*

Lonely, is how she must have felt. I was lonely too. I cried out, 'Ivo, I wish I was in there with you, that we could be together in the end.'

There was a noise outside, a shuffling rasp. The *badessa*'s henchwomen, I guessed, coming to make sure we had died.

From Ivo, there was nothing. Either he disliked the image of me beside him in his tomb, or he was dead already.

I wanted Lily to be there to comfort me as I lay dying. I wanted her infinite eyes looking at me with that hungry affection she always showed me. So I sent my mind to dwell on Lily, peacefully asleep in the mermaid cavern. Lily would wake. Lily would live, even though I would not.

Meanwhile, I held on to Saint Lucy's severed foot, and fancied, in the wildness of my death, that I felt a strange warmth flowing from her papery toes.

PART THIRTEEN

Under Venice

CHAPTER THIRTY-EIGHT

I grew hot under the mermaid's long appraising glance. Then she continued, 'Among the *Incogniti*, there be a puppeteer on Murano who saw a woman reputed a witch, with a young maid in trouble, tied to a trolley.'

'Darling?' I asked.

'Could be. When the puppeteer noticed the girl, the witch took off at a trot in the direction of some convent or other. I know nothing more, except that something be not right on Murano.'

Suddenly I knew exactly where Ivo and Darling were and how much danger they were in. My mind's eye went straight to the convent, picturing the *badessa's* smile of triumph. That smile told me just what she'd want to do with them, where she'd hide them, how slowly she would dispose of them.

When I shared my fears, the mermaid asked, 'Inside a stone tomb? Covered with oil? Humanfolk will die like that.'

How much did this gloomy mermaid care if Humanfolk died?

A voice rang down the stairwell. 'Anyone home?' called Giacomo, pelting down the steps. I was glad I'd been able to put on my dress. In his hand he carried a handbill with Ivo's likeness printed on it. I saw the words *RUBY THIEF!* beneath it.

On seeing me, he dropped it. 'Lily! You've woken up at last! My poor battered angel, what you've suffered! Why that stricken face, my *sweetest* heart?' He looked deep into my eyes.

I cannot lie, is what I cannot do. Being called 'my poor battered angel' and 'my *sweetest* heart' by Giacomo Casanova was extremely pleasant. But stronger even than that pleasure was the ugly thought of what might right now be befalling Darling and Ivo at the convent.

'My guess is,' I said sternly, 'that your beloved witch has sold Ivo and Darling to the *badessa*. The world's never known a creature like her for malice.'

'Ye have done poorly, stripling, by your friends,' said the mermaid.

Giacomo groaned, burying his face in his hands.

'Guilt is a luxury we've no time for,' I said, stumbling to my feet. My legs, unused to my weight, wilted under me like broken stalks of wheat. 'Darling and Ivo need *saving*.'

'This will be dangerous, Lily,' said Giacomo, rushing to hold me up. 'It would be madness for you, of all people, to go near that place after what that woman did to you there.'

He kissed the top of my head tenderly.

The mermaid said, 'Fondling one girl will not save another. We'll *all* go to Murano. And we must hurry, for the tide be on the turn.'

'You'll help us, then?' I asked her.

'My enemies be those who would bring danger or disgrace to the city. Your enemies would seem to be my enemies,' she said.

254

'I be tipped to your side by that. But I be not here to serve ye personally. Now I must rouse my granddaughter Incubina.'

She pointed to the wounded mermaid, who still lay sleeping. But I noticed that her bandages were clean of blood now and that her skin was rosy. The large mermaid swam to her side, whispered at length in her ear. Incubina stretched, yawned, opened her brown eyes wide and slipped into the water.

We were out of the cave in minutes, skimming the surface of the water into an icy dawn. Giacomo and I crouched in a gondola, propelled from under the water by the strong arms of the mermaids. Giacomo's fingers encircled my wrist, warm as a living bracelet.

Strapped to each of our backs was a stout sword for helping to prise open the sarcophagi – or defending ourselves.

'Pirates dropped them,' the mermaid had explained, thrusting them into our hands.

'For why did they drop them?' I asked.

She said, unsmiling, 'Ye tickle a naked pirate with the points of a trident and he'll do almost anything ye want.'

Incubina added, 'And sometimes things ye'd rather he didn't.'

Minutes later, we were at Murano. My courage had not travelled as fast as my body, which shuddered at the sight of the island where I'd endured so many different kinds of pain.

At the convent, I let Giacomo lift me so that I could scrabble to the fork of the tree that clung to its tall wall. A thick branch almost invited us along it. Dropping down into the courtyard, I sniffed for the smell of goose-fat and roasted meat. It was there, as always, faint but rich and full of menace. The courtyard was empty. The corridor of the cloister was also deserted. With relief, I detected the sounds of hymn-singing in the church next door. With my finger on my lips, I led Giacomo to the vaulted room where the sarcophagi were kept. It was as empty of nuns as I could have hoped. A faint gurgling came from inside the sarcophagi. Oil was trickling out of the holes into the basins where it was collected before putting into the flasks.

'No!' I cried.

'What a heavenly smell, like a young lady's bathwater—'

'Stop it, Giacomo!' I whispered. 'Ivo and Darling are in those coffins. Maybe they're silent because their mouths and noses have filled with oil and they are drowned.'

The corners of his lips dropped. He pushed his sword under the rim of the first sarcophagus and threw the weight of his body on the hilt. I ripped away the tubes and used oil to smooth the passage of my blade along the rim. Slowly, painfully, the lid began to ease to one side. Then Giacomo pushed too hard and his sword slid into the dark space inside.

'No!' I cried. 'You'll decapitate her!'

But Ivo was the sole occupant of the first tomb. Limp and mute, he was a heart-hurting sight, ghostly pale and green from the oil. His hands shook. His head made little jerking motions. He pointed frantically at the other sarcophagus. The oil was hovering around his mouth. His lips were slick and swollen.

'Dar . . . w . . . ing!' he gurgled indistinctly.

Darling did not make it easy for us.

She'd say it herself, Reader: she was a fierce one for the struggling. She'd struggled at her Young Ladies' Academy,

256

friendless and teased. She'd struggled in Venice to uncover the horrible truth about her guardian. She struggled simply because she was my friend and had got caught up in my war with the *badessa* and her sisters. Darling Dearworthy was a fighter, is what she was. But sometimes she seemed to make fighting her job, when occasionally she'd be better off accepting that she would be looked after.

So when we lifted the lid of her sarcophagus, Darling shrank away from me, screaming, 'Ivo! Is he alive?'

'I'm here,' he said, and she accepted his arms to pull her out. Then she sputtered, 'My spectacles! Fallen off! I cannot leave without my spectacles.'

I reached into the coffin. My hand groped blindly through the swarthy oil, warm from Darling's body. Eventually my fingers closed around the delicate structure of metal and glass. I lifted the spectacles, only for them to jump out of my hands, slippery as a frog.

'Come, Darling,' I urged. 'We shall get you another pair.'

Darling was in no state to be argued with. Her red hair was damp like the feathers of a newly hatched bird, she sat stubbornly on the edge of the tomb. 'My spectacles!' she whispered. 'There is no life for me without them.'

She groped in the oil until she found them. I wiped them on my skirt and placed them on her nose. I urged, 'The *badessa* could find us at any moment. Can we go now, please?'

'Momentarily,' Darling said thickly. She reached back into the sarcophagus, pausing to belch a grown-up portion of oil. Her hands scrabbled under the lid of the tomb.

257

'Now!' she announced, carefully extracting a small, tattered object from under the lid. As she did so, a bell began to ring in the distance. I knew where the noise came from: the *badessa's* office. I saw a fine wire leading away from the sarcophagus lid and through a hole in the wall.

It must go all the way to her desk.

Whatever Darling had pulled off the underside of that lid was something the *badessa* did not want to lose.

'Lily,' Darling croaked, 'I'll wager a saint's ransom that this is the lost foot of your Saint Lucy.'

CHAPTER THIRTY-NINE

The mermaids were waiting at the quay, bracing their tails to hold the gondola in place.

'Speed!' Incubina called. 'Remember the tide.'

It was then that the *badessa* charged out of the convent, yards behind us. 'You will not get away so easily, Eulalia!' she screamed, her beautiful features contorted with fury. But as her voice scoured the linings of my ears, she tripped over her long habit and sprawled on the ground.

'Watch us!' I called over my shoulder. Reader, you may commend my brave words, but I was still too frightened to laugh at the sight of her struggling to get up, spitting with rage.

'I'm watching,' she shouted. 'I'll watch you till the end, Eulalia. And I shall watch that end.'

The mermaid's face rose from the water. 'Let's be off, striplings!' she urged. The *badessa* showed no surprise at the sight of the mermaid. Then I realised, *The* badessa *is an adult, and cannot see her*.

At the quay, Ivo helped us into the gondola.

We were only yards from the shore when the mermaid uttered

a loud oath. The water boiled up on the lagoon side of the boat. Coarse white scales rippled above the water, and a mighty force lifted the gondola and turned it over, delivering me, Darling, Giacomo and Ivo into the cold water. My whole body sank below the waves.

Strong hands closed around my shoulders, pulling my head out of the turbulent sea. 'There you are, Lily!' said Giacomo triumphantly.

I saw Darling's streaming head rise, her spectacles firmly in place. Ivo had one arm around her, the other looped over the side of the gondola.

There came the awful sound of hissing amid the splashing and the swearing of the mermaid. The head of a vast white Eel lurched up out of the water. Now the whole lagoon looked like a witch's cauldron and the creature was a wicked ladle whipping up white waves.

From the shore, the *badessa's* laughter rang out.

The mermaid righted the gondola. Then Incubina hoisted me above the waterline and I hauled myself inelegantly into the boat, declining Giacomo's help. Ivo was as politely as possible pushing Darling up out of the water, his hands awkward around her skirts. She tumbled into the gondola and reached back to help him.

Lastly, Giacomo climbed in, just as Incubina struck the Eel a mighty blow on its head. It seemed to render the creature senseless. Then we were scything through the waves away from the creature faster than a sled on ice. The *badessa* let out a howl of frustration.

'Did you recognise that animal?' Ivo asked Darling.

Darling said, 'The witch was singing to a *miniature* of it in a bowl, and it grew. In front of our eyes!'

Ivo nodded. 'It must have kept growing while we were . . . talking . . . in the sarcophagi. Remember, the *badessa* paid her sister twenty ducats "for the growing".'

'The witch is another sister?' I cried. 'Four of them? No!'

Giacomo blanched white. Ivo exchanged a long look with Darling – Ivo, who never looked anyone in the eye.

What did they talk of all that time, in the face of death? I hunched my shoulders over a strange sore feeling in my chest, thinking of the intimacies they might have exchanged. Darling was supposed to be *my* friend, not his.

Smiling, Darling held up the tattered foot to show the mermaids. 'Who would be the winner if it came to a fight between four finagling sisters and a genuine saint? You see, Saint Lucy will owe us a favour when we take this back to her. And not just a smattering of pleasant weather so.'

We all looked at the small, damaged foot. The skin was like paper, translucent with oil. The bones glowed white inside.

'Yon *badessa* thieved the foot of the saint?' said the mermaid. 'It do begin to hang together now.'

'You know the prophecy?' I asked.

The mermaid said, 'The one whereby if Saint Lucy is lost to us, Venice will lose all her colour? Aye. And what follows too – that without colour there will be a great rending and tearing of the secret sacred ties between Venetians. Then shall it be all over for this city, bar the screaming and the killing.'

Incubina said, ''Tis clear as day-old jellyfish! These sisters be

261

the very Siracusan villains who set out to steal Saint Lucy! Starting with the foot. Damn their dog-faced faces!'

I said hopefully, 'There are always guards now around the church where the rest of Saint Lucy's body lies.'

The mermaid said, 'I wager the sisters have made sure these latest guards are from Murano. Just think of all those foolish Humanfolk who went to that witch for spells and potions and cures . . . now Baddened Magic holds their souls in thrall. They shall act at her will. Even Giacomo sent Darling and Ivo to almost certain death at the witch's hands, because the stripling's had a taste of her enchantment.'

Darling said, 'Perhaps Saint Lucy actually *wants* to be stolen and go back to Siracusa? She was born there. She might even be in on the plot.'

'She is a *saint!*' I said. 'She doesn't plot. She doesn't work with murderesses. Have a little faith.'

Darling flinched, her shoulders drawing in. The strange thing was that *Ivo* flinched too. Since when were his muscles working in time with hers?

'Leave her alone,' said Ivo, leaving me silent with fury.

'Would the Madonna help us protect Saint Lucy, Lily?' asked Giacomo loudly, interrupting the awkward silence.

 **CHAPTER FORTY**

Mid-morning at a capitello in northern Cannaregio

'Me – joining forces with *mermaids*! Imagine!' the Madonna sniffed. 'They come from the sea, like Venus, that wicked pagan goddess of love! Why would I be parlaying with such creatures? To save a *Sicilian* saint? Too many favours here. And not enough praying on bended knee with eyes downcast.'

'But are not mermaids among God's marvels?' I suggested. 'Like elephants and dragons, both mentioned in the Bible, rare strange as they are.'

'And,' said Darling, 'are You not the *Mother* of all sea-creatures including mermaids Yourself so?'

Giacomo added, 'And mermaids must be particularly beloved daughters in Venice, where it is all about the water, no?'

'Maybe there are *some* good things about *some* mermaids,' conceded the Madonna, shifting the Infant higher on Her hip. 'Venetian mermaids, anyway. The two below have been known to commit brave acts against enemies of their city.'

I said, 'And this city You protect – can you imagine her without colour, awash with hate and violence instead of bound by loving secret sacred ties?'

'That prophecy has always sounded more magical than Godly to Me. Venetians are altogether too superstitious. The Holy Infant has an uneasy relationship with prophecy in general—'

Darling cajoled, 'Can You be taking the risk so? If the Sicilian sisters succeed in stealing Saint Lucy, all those glorious Venetian paintings of You . . . would they not be fading away to dusty pencil sketches . . .?'

'Saint Lucy!' said the Madonna. 'There are Venetians who . . . honour her *almost over Myself*! That's how mad they are for colour! Why don't you go to *her* and see if *she* can deal with these monsters from her native place?'

'Well, we've thought of that, of course,' I admitted. 'But Saint Lucy's rare frail, unlike Yourself. Her skin is all papery. Her fingers are like rolled-up wafers. She's already lost a foot.'

'The truth is,' said the Madonna shrewdly, 'that you don't want to use your Saint Lucy as bait for the Siracusan women. Because they might snatch her? Am I wrong?'

We looked at our feet.

'Saint Lucy is too precious?' she grumbled. 'The *Madonna*, however, you will risk against a savage enemy?'

There was a brief but pointful silence.

'We-e-ell,' said the Madonna, kissing the Holy Infant's head. 'Let Me think on it. I am not your woman for instant action. I am more for graceful contemplation. I shall pray for guidance.'

'As quickly as possible, if You please!' I couldn't restrain myself.

'As *gracefully* as possible. Meanwhile, what of your own endeavours? Have you really exhausted your own talents so fast?

You've proved good at saving one another, but what of a whole city? A whole people?'

Then the Madonna's tone softened. 'My sons, my daughters, the first step must be to find your ways forward inside yourselves, in the usual slow, painful, human way.'

It was as subtle as a sigh and undetectable by the naked eye, but suddenly she was just a painting again.

CHAPTER FORTY-ONE

'Inside ourselves?' said Darling.

'What talents?' I asked sadly. 'We failed even with Our Lady—'

'I'll get Her back on side. Never fear! Bringing ladies round is my speciality,' Giacomo declared. 'I love me a challenging female. I shall turn Her with my charm—'

'Turn Her stomach perhaps,' said Ivo.

I snapped, 'And what do you know about charm, Ivo? Ever tried it? No. About frightening innocent people to death, yes, you know a great deal. About getting so-called friends mischance-ily drowned in caves, plenty.'

Ivo bit his lower lip hard. Darling put a hand on my arm. 'Ivo may not be much of a charmer, but when we were in the tombs I found out he rescued a slave boy called Eliah from a deadly beating. He still pays the child's keep from his own wages.'

Ivo slashed the air with his fist. 'The others don't need to know about that, Darling. I told you only because I thought we were dying.'

'They are not "*the others*". We are all "us" now so.' Darling turned to me. 'There's an apothecary who shelters the boy. Poor creature cannot cry or talk.'

For why has Darling kept this a secret from me until now? An acid taste flowed into my mouth. Did she and Ivo share other secrets? I asked, 'I suppose you've tried a prayer to Saint Drogo? He's patron saint of mutes.'

'Sarcasm is not appropriate, Lily,' said Darling. Perhaps I imagined it, but it seemed that she moved a little closer to Ivo. 'The Madonna said we had to look inside ourselves. What is inside us but our hearts? Inside Ivo's heart, you find Eliah.'

Ivo's blush was fierce, but he did not object when Darling said, 'I insist we go to the Golden Hercules right now to meet Eliah for ourselves.'

The Golden Hercules at Santa Fosca! That was where I'd seen Ivo disappearing all those times when I spied on him. My stomach tightened. It was so much simpler to hate Ivo.

Darling pointed to yet another handbill with Ivo's name and likeness, nailed to a wall. 'Ivo, you shall wear my mask, lest anyone call you out for a jewel thief.'

'The *moretta*'s a *girl*'s mask,' Ivo protested. But he took it anyway. The mask button that had been in Darling's mouth disappeared between Ivo's lips. Reader, I did not like the thought.

I walked at her right, and Ivo stubbornly kept pace at her left. But only I dared to take her arm, I was pleased to see. Giacomo walked behind, refining his persuasions. He crowed, 'The Madonna shall shortly swoon at my luscious words. The thing is to *dazzle*!'

The three of us ignored him all the way to the Golden Hercules.

'Oh, it's closed,' lamented Darling. But Ivo produced his own key and let us inside.

267

'Don't be afraid, Eliah,' he called softly, taking off the mask.

A beautiful dark face peered around a doorway. The boy was trembling so hard that his outline blurred. He pointed to us and looked at Ivo questioningly. When Darling took a step towards him, her hand outstretched, he ran back into the room from which he had appeared.

'He'll be hiding under his blankets. He's afraid of everyone now,' said Ivo. 'He used to be so full of joy. I don't know what to do for him.'

Darling touched Ivo's shoulder. 'You've done so much already.'

She actually touched him. The way she touched me, without embarrassment or hesitation. She said, 'The mermaid will help him talk again. She brought Lily back to us, after all.'

She disappeared into the darkened room where Eliah hid. Ivo and I stood in stiff silence, he staring at the ceiling, me at the floor.

Five minutes later, Darling and Eliah emerged. The boy was holding her hand and looking at her with adoration. And Ivo gazed at them both, as if his eyes owned them. As if he owned Darling Dearworthy, my only and best friend. It was not long since I'd tried to save her life by offering myself up as a nun. Had she forgotten?

But now it was as if Darling and Ivo were a family, with the boy as their beloved child.

There was no place for me in this family.

So I could not but hate it.

CHAPTER FORTY-TWO

Without any sign of life, the Madonna allowed the niche to swing round and let us in.

'So Her Upstairs be leaving ye to your own devices? Such as they be?' The mermaid's eyes seemed to judge those devices as poor. 'And who be this manikin betimes?' she asked. 'With the huge eyes?'

Ivo's tongue was tied, so Darling explained, concluding, 'Have you anything that opens up throats and eyes? This boy needs to talk and cry. Urgently so.'

Eliah was gazing at the mermaid with fascination, his thumb in his mouth. She said, 'Our salves and unguents be good for actual woundings to the body. This child be needing something altogether different. 'Twill take some pondering on. We must spin his dreams to find what needs to be culled. Incubina!'

The younger mermaid swam forward from the shadows. She said, 'We be waiting to hear how ye striplings plan to proceed. But in the meantime, I've despatched two *Incogniti* to put a bit of backbone into guarding the entrances to Saint Lucy's church.'

'Who?' asked Darling.

I explained, 'Gifted humans who help Venice in her troubles. People who are able to see mermaids even when they are older than thirteen. Grown people cannot, normally.'

'I would like to meet some of them, these *Incogniti!*' Darling said.

'Ye already have,' said the mermaid. 'Yon puppeteer from Murano be one.'

Incubina directed Eliah to the same seaweed pallet I'd occupied during my long sleep. He lay with his eyes glassily fixed on Incubina and his thumb in his mouth. With her elbows above the water, the mermaid sang softly to the boy, occasionally stopping to exclaim, 'No! That be wronger than a butterfly in a slaughterhouse!' Then she rolled her hands, as if balling up yarn, and snipped the air with her fingers.

'Dream-culling,' said the grander mermaid. 'And young Eliah be not the only one of ye young folks who needs some nightmares culled.'

'What if they're not nightmares?' asked Ivo. 'What if they are things that really happened?'

'Eliah be not asleep, ye'll notice. Incubina culls the *living* nightmares, his memories. It may not seem so, but the child works as hard as she does.'

Indeed, Eliah's face contorted with pain from time to time. It was hurtful to see how his little fists clenched.

'Please don't make him recall too much, too clearly,' Ivo said. 'Some of his memories . . . no one should have to remember things like that.'

'Unless he does so,' said the mermaid, 'his mind will scamper

270

round those darknesses, in circles. He must remember before he can cry. He must cry before he can talk.'

'Poor creature so,' said Darling. 'Now I'm going back to the hotel. I need to collect my valuables. There is going to be a war. War is expensive and my money's all we've got.'

I said, 'No, it's too dangerous for you there. By now, the Signorina must be aware that her witch sister delivered you and Ivo to the *badessa* for drowning in oil.'

'That's exactly what will keep me safe. The Signorina must pretend she knows nothing of that plot. She won't dare to put a move on me so, not in a hotel full of English guests all worked up about Uncle Red. Meanwhile I shall make myself very visible to those guests and endear myself to them mightily.'

'Which will annoy the Signorina mightily,' I said,

'Don't eat anything or drink anything you're given,' Ivo urged. 'The Signorina will poison you again as soon as look at you.'

'I can keep an eye on her,' Giacomo said. 'The Signorina has no idea of what I know. I'll bring you food, Darling. I'll test it before you swallow a mouthful.'

'Ivo, Sorrowful Lily,' the mermaid said. 'Night has fallen. Ye must sleep. Yet it be not healthful for Humanfolk to spend too much time in this cavern. I've seen striplings grow scales and even the beginnings of fins if they sleep down here more than a few days. Ivo cannot be seen on the streets until his name be cleared from the slander of jewel-theft. We have a safe place for ye. An apothecary by the name of the Two Tousled Mermaids. Moreover, it's but four bridges west from the hotel and ye can see the church where Saint Lucy sleeps from there and be our eyes and ears on it.'

With one long look at Eliah, Ivo started walking towards the stairs. I followed him, unwillingly. Giacomo offered Darling his arm, and a smile that I wished had come in my direction.

Upstairs, the Madonna was busy in still, graceful contemplation. She did not speak to us. But I thought the Holy Infant winked at me.

As we approached the Two Tousled Mermaids, the door swung open. There was no living soul inside, however. Its shelves were lined with white and blue china jars that bore unrecognisable names. Everything else was stored in painted boxes. The merchandise inside them was advertised in ribbons of ivory silk that coiled and uncoiled like flags in a sweet breeze.

HELP FOR HURT MINDS was written on one ribbon.

Pots to Put Thoughts That Are Too Painful to Hold, said another.

Slippers for Feet That Just Cannot Go On, rippled a pink ribbon.

Sealing Wax for Secrets That Want to Come Out.

Holes in the Ground for the Humiliated.

Tether's End Extenders.

While we were examining these signs, a door opened and a pleasant rush of warm air drew us to a staircase. A ribbon beckoned, *Rest for Tired Limbs*. Suddenly, mine felt as heavy as a pair of iron pipes.

Upstairs we found two clean straw pallets. I watched without comment as Ivo drew his pallet to the corner of the room furthest from mine.

I thought, *Are you afraid of my watching you dream, Ivo?*

272

I insisted on taking the first watch. My thoughts were too dark for sleep. The moon presented a cheerless sliver that seemed only to intensify the blackness of the night. I rested my elbow on the window sill, looking at the unlit church where Saint Lucy rested, while I listened to Ivo pretending to breathe evenly.

I had grown up sleeping in a dormitory full of nightmaring orphans, both boys and girls. But suddenly, to be alone with just one boy, Ivo, made me acutely aware of my own breathing. Was it too loud? Too quick? Could he sense that I was listening to him? Was he silently smiling to himself in that cold way he had – at my discomposure?

Darling, I knew, would have handled this without embarrassment. She'd have tossed Ivo some spicy Irish good night. And when it was her turn, she would have slept like a cat, comfortable in her bird-light bones and dreaming righteously.

Ivo's breathing finally slipped into the irregular rhythms of unfeigned sleep. I pressed my forehead against the window. There was no movement at the church for the next two hours. When the third hour struck, I roused Ivo for his watch.

He reported nothing when he woke me two hours later with a tap on my foot.

Two hours' sleep were not enough. My eyes soon wearied of gazing at an empty church in the dark. The guards were visible, alert and still. I saw a man hiding in the shadows – I guessed he was one of the *Incogniti* because he looked straight at my window and saluted me with a smile. Perhaps he was that puppeteer from Murano who had tried to help Darling? I smiled back, waving. He placed his fingers on his lips and withdrew to the shadows.

By the time the next hour tolled, my arms and knees had grown stiff and sore. I pulled my pallet to the sill so I could rest for a few minutes.

Would it have made any difference if I had managed to stay awake?

When I woke, I did not at first notice anything different, except that the moon had waned. It was that especially dark time before dawn.

I felt guilty. But then again, I had always felt guilty since Mr Dearworthy's death. Every pleasure – even saving Darling from the sarcophagus – had been dirtily tinged by knowing my complicity in leaving her alone in the world. My dozing off added but a little to my burden of guilt. Ivo was still sleeping and had not noticed my dereliction of duty. I might yet get away with it.

It was only when I saw my grey face in a shard of mirror on the wall, and my grey hand, and my grey eyes, that I began to feel something was gravely wrong. Outside the window, the town was painted in a thousand shades of grey and thirty more of silver. The water rippled in the cold light of the ball of mercury that was the pale dawning sun. A depression fell over me like a black crow swooping. Tears pooled in my eyes, which looked as sad as sorry in the dim mirror.

Wasn't I madly arrogant to think that I might cease to be Sorrowful Lily, that Darling might befriend me after what I did to her Uncle Red? For why would Giacomo bother with a drab girl like me? Drab in looks, drab in spirits, is what I am. Drab as a rat. I deserve Ivo's scorn.

I stared into my reflection. Grey, I decided, suited me. It suited

274

my crumpled eyes, my thin face. Grey was my colour, the colour of lonely. It was never my destiny to be part of some kind of happy, friendly, confident, colourful *something*, with Darling, with Giacomo. I glanced out of the window. The dismal state of my soul seemed to have rendered the vivid stones of Venice as grey as my thoughts.

Then I understood.

While I'd been wrapped in neglectful sleep, the body of Saint Lucy had been kidnapped from her church.

It was not just Sorrowful Lily who had turned grey. Venice had lost her colour. Left in my mischancy hands, that was my city's fate, just as you, Reader, knew it would be.

Without colour, I thought, *who are we? What is our town? Is there any point to her? Who will bother with her now? Venice will sink into a new Dark Age without visitors to pay for their pleasure here.*

The same would go for me. I, who had vowed revenge on the *badessa*, now knew again the cold certainty of hopelessness. She would find me and drag me back to the convent. There I would die, slowly or quickly, whatever she preferred. The Magoghe sisters would harvest my bones. They might as well. I was the mad daughter of a mad mother. No good would come of me. I stood as if turned to stone, gazing at my grey face in the dismal glass. I already felt halfway to dead. Perhaps more than halfway.

A scream broke the grey silence outside. And then another scream, low and desperate. I heard a man cursing, then a blow that could only be a hand slammed on someone else's flesh. An orchestra of violent noises tuned up and broke into a dissonant rage.

I knew at once – as you must have guessed, Reader – that

these were the ugly sounds of Venice's secret sacred ties being severed: Venetians screaming at one another, children being slapped, glass being smashed, oaths being sworn.

Hearing a dull thud outside, I opened the window and leaned out. A man lay on the flagstones beneath me, the street darkening with a halo of his blood. Two Vampire Eels slid from the canal and buried their heads in the spreading pool.

The man's blood, the Eels, even the coral-like gills that grew behind their ears – all were black and white. And somehow this was more horrifying than the real colours of life and death.

Ivo joined me at the window. A grey Ivo, with grey hair, grey eyes and a grey expression on his face. In the window's reflection, our two faces were briefly twinned, until he looked away.

'It's happened, hasn't it?' he said.

The Eels looked up with interest.

'They heard you,' I whispered.

The white creatures abandoned their prey and headed towards the Two Tousled Mermaids, and us.

PART FOURTEEN

Venice in Black and White

CHAPTER FORTY-THREE

29 October 1739

It was not quite dawn. Everything outside my window glowered a dismal pearly grey. Not a familiar Irish grey, which is always tinged with a little green, but a grey that looked like a sore absence of hope. That soreness made me think of Ivo, and I wondered what he and Lily had talked about between their watches at the Two Tousled Mermaids.

The newsboys shouted down the streets of San Felice, 'Saint Lucy gone! Three guards bludgeoned outside the church! Bloody family strife breaks out all over the city.'

I leapt out of my bed and ran down in my wrapper to claim an *avviso*.

My newsboy held it out to me in silence. He was listening to a woman a few yards away threatening her little daughter with a raised hand. The child answered her back and was slapped. I recoiled, only to bump into a pair of twins pulling each other by the ears and swearing horribly.

LUCY'S BODY STOLEN! was the headline on my *avviso*. And now the first light of dawn was revealing to me and everyone with eyes that the terrible prophecy was nothing fanciful and nothing more than the truth.

I gazed down the Calle della Racchetta. Venice was drained of colour. She was no longer the city of terracotta browns, jade greens, ochre yellows, rich, plummy reds and strawberry-icing pink. She was a pen-and-black-ink sketch of herself. And, without her colour, four-fifths of her beauty had been lost. Her picturesque alleys loomed like black ravines. Her canals slumped like swamps.

And the sounds of conflict were everywhere – the shouting, screaming, and punching. *Venetian against Venetian*, I thought. *Is that not the most sorrowful sound in the world?*

A small girl tugged the sash of my wrapper. 'Lucky foreigner! Can't you take me away with you? My mother's dead to me and my father hates me.'

'I am sorry,' I told her. 'How are you knowing I'm not Venetian?'

'S'obvious. No one is hissing or spitting at you. No one wants to beat you. You never had any secret sacred ties to lose.'

Being loved has become a danger, I thought. *The world is upside down.*

The girl's shoulders dropped. Tears fell. I had to brace my heart to tell her, 'I'm not leaving Venice, not just yet.'

'Then you are mad,' she sobbed, running off. 'The place is doomed.'

I tucked myself into a doorway to read the *avviso* properly.

Saint Lucy's kidnappers had struck in the dead of night. A diamond earring, found at the scene, had apparently been used to cut a panel in the glass tomb. The saint's fragile body had been wrenched out. The guards had been put under some kind of intoxication. Dazed and stumbling, they remembered nothing of what had happened.

'That's because they were weak witch-enchanted fools from Murano!' I said aloud. 'What of the *Incogniti* that the mermaid had sent to guard the guards?'

The next paragraph gave me my answer: the bodies of a puppeteer from Murano and a bookseller had been found bludgeoned to death just outside the church. I remembered the puppeteer's concerned eye on me as the witch wheeled me and Ivo to our fate. His message to the mermaids had saved us. And now he was dead.

The means of the kidnappers' escape was the most audacious of all. There had always been a galleon moored at the quay by the two columns of the Piazzetta. It was kept fully armed and manned in case any threat should present itself to Venice. It seemed that the saint-nappers had somehow drugged the sailors aboard and thrown their unconscious bodies into the water. Six drowned sailors had been recovered from different parts of the Grand Canal.

The *avviso* carried the report of a young light-boy who had been standing on Rialto Bridge in the early hours after escorting a nobleman home from the Ridotto. He beheld the strange sight of the ghostly galleon, lit with yellow lanterns, being rowed down the Grand Canal by oars that appeared to move on their own. The body of poor Saint Lucy – recognisable by her silver mask and papery fingers – was carefully tied up inside a cage and fastened to the prow like the most fragile of figureheads. She did not struggle but wept audibly through her mask

The light-boy had run to the *Signori di Notte*. But by that time the galleon had disappeared.

'Too late,' I said aloud. 'Lily, Ivo, what of you? Were you not supposed to be keeping watch?'

Did the Signori di Notte *arrest Ivo for jewel theft? Did something happen to them there at the Two Tousled Mermaids?*

The Two Tousled Mermaids! I knew it was near the church of Saint Lucy, and that was just four bridges west of the hotel. I did not know Venice, but I knew east and west from the sulky light of the sky.

An iced wind sulked around my ears as I hurried along the streets. The waves in the canals trundled grumpily into clots of foam. Everywhere I passed, I witnessed distress and chaos. Venice was like a graveyard, haunted by angry ghosts.

For the Venetians, it wasn't worth talking except to shout. Now that the secret sacred ties were broken, there was no limit of decency to the insults shrieked across the narrow streets. I heard aunts called ugly witches and fathers called monsters and children called devils. The air was empty of the usual delicious smells of anchovies, cheese and polenta. No one's mother was cooking – they didn't care to nourish their families. Instead they used their frying pans to clash together like cymbals, threatening to put someone's head in between next time.

People clustered at the doors of every church I passed. Poking my head inside San Felice and San Leonardo, I saw that colour and peace still reigned. Mothers sat praying, with their arms around their children.

Only in churches, I thought, *are the secret sacred ties of Venice safe. But for how long?*

When I reached the Two Tousled Mermaids, I found the front door smashed. Inside was littered with broken bottles and limp ribbons torn in half. Behind the counter, a staircase was also covered with broken glass and a salty-smelling slime. I crunched up the stairs apprehensively.

The room was empty. I found two pallets, wet and stinking. Someone or something had befouled them. I could only hope that Lily and Ivo were long gone by then, back safe with the mermaids.

Safe with the mermaids was where I needed to be too. But – I cursed myself for it – I had rushed out of the hotel in my wrapper and nightdress, without gathering my valuables and my coins.

It was purely my fault, but I'd need to go back there one more time.

'The last time,' I told myself aloud. 'The very last time ever.'

Giacomo was waiting for me outside the hotel, his face taut with worry and the red imprint of a hand on his face.

'Where have you been? Look! My own grandmother slapped me!' he said. 'And for you, Darling, there are worse things than slaps if you don't escape from this place. If the Magoghe sisters have taken Saint Lucy's body, and they suspect that we know something about it—'

'Don't I know it!' I told him.

'You must eat breakfast as usual, in the full public eye,' he said. 'So as not to raise suspicion.'

283

'Yes. Then I'll tell the Signorina that I'm expected at the lawyers' office.'

The Signorina was nowhere to be seen. But the guests at the Hotel of What You Want were already milling around reception, demanding discounted bills and refunds for their disappointing grey accommodation. Now monochrome, even the dioramas failed to charm.

In the dining room, Mrs Sprigge held up a handbill, whining, 'To cap it all, now we discover that the hotel employed a *jewel thief*! Is this not *our* Ivo Peruch? My pearls are not safe!'

I longed to defend him, but that would only draw attention.

It was hard to force down grey bread. Butter without its sunshine colour tasted like slick mud. Meanwhile rumours flew around the grey breakfast tables of the Hotel of What You Want. The English guests traded snippets of information. The Honourable Lownton Fishcold told us that the Grand Council had met in emergency session, each of the fifteen hundred senators jostling to voice his suspicions about who might have stolen the body of Saint Lucy and the colour out of Venice. It had come to blows there too.

The latest *avvisi* were delivered as I ate. They reported that the Council of Ten had ordered all known Sicilians rounded up. The three Inquisitors were questioning them. I felt a pity for those innocent merchants and refugees, treated as the enemy while the true perpetrators went entirely unmolested. It was clear that not one of the other hotel guests had the least idea that their hostess was a Sicilian. Of course, the English could not tell a Sicilian accent from a Venetian one. And, by virtue of their positions, the Magoghe sisters kept themselves isolated from anyone who might detect their true origin.

I could not stop myself. 'But the Council of Ten did not think to arrest any *women*, did they?'

Miss Mullvein eyed me reprovingly. 'How could *women* be potent in these evil matters?'

I sighed.

Up in my room, Giacomo helped me tuck coins into my hems and the threading of my chemise – not neglecting to admire my slender ankles and how well my violet-blue dress, now of course grey, fitted to my shape. I knotted Saint Lucy's little foot into my sleeve again.

It's all that's left of her, I thought sadly. *It's more valuable than all my gold.*

Giacomo laced and buttoned me into a second dress, this time for Lily. It would be a green one – if the colour ever came back to Venice.

We agreed not to leave together. Giacomo set himself to cheering his English ladies with a quick tune on his violin.

Just as I entered the reception hall, the Signorina glided to the desk. *Where has she been?* Guests milled around her, complaining. Over their heads, she gave me a look that made me feel like a flea in the grip of tweezers. *Why is the Signorina still here if the sisters have Saint Lucy in their clutches? Why, except to take care of all loose ends like myself?*

'How agreeable,' she lied, 'to have you back among us, Miss Dearworthy, after all! We thought we had seen the last of you . . . after what you said.'

I said, 'I've not yet made up my mind to stay here. Did you know that the suites at the Sturion are larger than these and cost but eight *lire* a day? And I don't give a fig for your silly dioramas. Sure there are better backdrops in Punch and Judy puppet stalls in Dublin! At least they are in colour! Unlike your gloomy hotel, Signorina Magoghe.'

The English guests nodded sympathetically, almost as if they understood my rapid flow of Italian. But that, of course, was impossible.

The Signorina grinned at me, hatred suffusing every feature. I knew she was measuring my bones with her eyes.

But she could not stop me leaving.

CHAPTER FORTY-FOUR

In the mermaid cavern Lily and Ivo sat listlessly on mossy rocks. They gave me the barest of greetings. Their clothes were torn and their knuckles scraped raw. 'We had to climb over a roof to escape an Eel,' said Lily. I didn't have the heart to ask what had gone wrong with their watch on the church. From the way they hung their heads, it was clear they felt responsible.

Despite the greyness of their expressions, Lily's and Ivo's skins and clothes had colour. My own dresses had resumed their violet-blues and greens as soon as I ran down the steps. The mermaids' tails still glowed with colour under the gilded arches – a relief to my eyes that were heavy with too much grey.

Incubina had patrolled the canals to see for herself what was happening. ''Tis a matter of urgent desperation to restore colour to Venice. Something that *saturates* be needed,' she said. 'Something to soak through the bones of this place and bring back her true, loving nature. Something beautiful. Something strong . . .'

'Perfume? Magical essences? Can they be found? I could pay,' I offered, and began to unburden my clothes of their treasures, and to shed the outer layer of my garments. I handed the green dress to Lily.

Giacomo had just arrived, still carrying his fiddle. He asked, 'How about *music*?'

He explained how his music had cheered the grey spirits of the English ladies at the hotel. He lifted the violin to his shoulder now and played a few sweet notes.

'Aaah,' sighed Incubina. 'That would charm the petticoats off a duchess.'

Giacomo looked thoughtful. And the music was indeed halfway to charming my own petticoat off, teasing, probing and tickling as it did.

'Enough, Giacomo! Mercy me!' I said.

The older mermaid said, ''Tis true that music enters into places and people without permission. Ye don't even need to look it in the eyes. Music gets inside ye anyway. It passes by the brain and conveniently goes straight to the heart. Mayhap music can do the same to this most feminine of cities? Make Venice fall back in love with herself? Remember why she's so precious?'

'Even without Saint Lucy?' Lily asked.

Giacomo said, 'Violins do most definitely make humans fall in love, dearest possible ladies. I have . . . seen it done.'

The mermaid mused, 'If we could but add some magic to yon instrument . . .'

'What about mermaid hair?' Lily said. 'Surely that's rare magical? If Giacomo strings the violin with your hair . . .?'

This idea was not received charmingly. The mermaids shuffled in the water, touching their dark curls anxiously. Giacomo stepped forward, smiling hugely. 'For *me*, sweetest hearts? Won't you do it for me? Or are mermaids, as the legends say, actually without hearts? Tell me it's not so!'

The mermaids' hands flew back to their hair.

'If you won't do it willingly, I despair of you as vastly vain creatures!' I said hotly. 'Venetians are dying like flies out there and you are afraid for your hair-dos. Here, I shall set an example for you.'

I raked through my own curls and yanked out a painful clutch of hairs. Then I stepped forward, giving the mermaids a look over the rim of my glasses.

'If ye put it like that,' mumbled Incubina. She reached up to her head and plucked a single black hair, holding it aloft for the other mermaid to see.

The older mermaid pulled a bouquet of hairs from her head, both black and white. 'Can ye re-string the instrument?' she asked Giacomo.

He took their hairs as if he were harvesting roses. He grasped each mermaid's hand and bowed over it in the courtly Venetian manner, lowering his head to kiss it but withholding his lips at the last moment. Then he sat cross-legged on the ground and began to slacken the strings of his fiddle. Deftly, he plaited the mermaid hairs into thickish threads.

As he laced the new strings into the violin, I held my breath, waiting to hear what kind of noise would come out of a violin strung with the hair of ancient mermaids.

Giacomo lifted the instrument to his shoulder. An eerie sigh eased into the cavern. It was more like the cry of a gentle seabird than the sound of a violin. There was a breathiness to it, like the swell of a calm sea. Giacomo looked at his instrument with surprise. He tried the next string. This one throbbed – wine-red blood, intimate, warm, alive. The third string's sound danced around the gold mosaics of the cavern, reflecting light in a shower of sparkles.

Lily whispered a word that sounded like, 'Sbarlusso'.

Eliah's lips fluttered into a smile.

The fourth note was darker, moodier, creeping around corners, making me shiver. I guessed, 'Blue for the water, wine-red for blood, yellow for the sun, purple-black for shadow. The colours of the rainbow.'

The mermaid said, 'If ye can play all the colours together, this instrument could paint out all the unhappiness.'

'Can my violin really be . . . such a paint box?' asked Giacomo.

Lily said, 'Think of the blue of an eye that winks at you flirtatiously, the shadow at the nape of a lady's neck when she bends to kiss you, the yellow of a satin ribbon, the pink of . . . your favourite . . . crab soup with russet-coloured nutmeg grated into it—'

'Ah,' said Giacomo, setting the violin under his chin. 'Now you are talking.'

Different sounds came out of the violin. Sounds that purely lifted your heart and placed it on a velvet cushion. The mermaids flapped their hands over their breasts. And so did I, my skin all stippled with goose-pimples of pleasure, and my heart bubbling like hot chocolate.

'Am I good at this? Or am I *exquisitely* good at this?' crowed Giacomo.

290

'Look at Eliah,' said Lily suddenly.

Tears lay on the boy's cheeks. I hated to think of the Scottish lady's words, but she'd been right. Eliah's tears had the quality of crystal.

'The music has unlocked them,' I said. 'At last.'

'I must stay with him,' said Ivo. 'He will need to talk.'

'First he must weep. Ye cannot cry his tears for yon nipper,' said the mermaid. 'Instead, go out and make this a place worth his feelings waking up in.'

CHAPTER FORTY-FIVE

The moon swam high and greasy-looking in a lifeless kind of darkness. The four of us nestled on cushions in a gondola that the mermaids had liberated from its mooring.

My gaze was drawn up to that cold and empty moon, bleached of any gold or silver. I wanted to see what lurked behind Ivo's eyes, but he wore my mask. We could not afford for him to be recognised.

Rowing through the dark water was like pulling through old cooking oil thickened by the scales of fried fish. From out on the streets, we could hear the voices of Venetians cursing one another, their running feet, their screams of rage.

The mermaid gave our gondola one final push, and cautioned, 'Fear not. This is good magic. Even Vampire Eels, be there any still lurking, will be quietened by this music.'

She slipped under the water. We were on our own.

Ivo rose and began to row, the oar sinking silkily into the ink-black canal. As we entered the Misericordia, Giacomo stood up, fixed his eyes on Lily's, and began to play.

The music started slow and haunting, but gradually grew

wilder and freer. The sound amplified, as if Giacomo was lifting ten, then twenty, then a thousand elbows in unison.

Mermaid hair must have given it that power, I thought. And like the grander mermaid herself, the power of the music was almost frightening. My heart lolloped about in my chest. I felt my mouth loosening and my eyes grew moist.

My heart was not the only one touched – no, *rifled* – by the music. Couples walking by the canal – arguing furiously – paused as they heard us and began to kiss one another so passionately that I had to turn away. People threw open their windows to listen and then draped their arms around one another, caressing one another's hair and shoulders.

On the Fondamenta della Misericordia, a rat dropped the apple core he was gnawing. At eye-level to us in the boat, he stared at Giacomo and rose and danced with his paws raised high. Then he kissed his right paw to us three times, with the left one on his heart.

'Beautiful is what this is,' sighed Lily. 'The music, the people, the love. Even the creatures.'

Her hair rippled over her shoulders and her eyes shone. Lily, I suddenly realised, had never in her life had any actual fun. *When all this is over*, I promised her silently, *fun will be handed to you in buckets. I'll make full sure of it.*

Giacomo kept playing, stroking every filament of beauty and magic out of the mermaid-hair strings. The music trickled like honey and sucked like the north wind, jiggled like a cat about to pounce. It surged like a tide and dripped like honey. It hovered like a hawk in mid-air, and it looped, chuckling like a dove. It whispered like the hem of a silk dress trailing along a cold marble floor, and it roared like ten thousand rejoicing angels.

We passed under a bridge. The bricks suddenly acquired a warm glow of gold, as if lit by a candle. Then the sail of a nearby boat blossomed into a rich russet.

'It's working!' I whispered. 'The music's making colour.'

'Love turns everything to colour,' purred Giacomo, and Ivo forgot to scowl.

The colour never really went away, I thought. It must have just shrunk back inside itself when Saint Lucy was taken. Now it was coaxed back into the moonlight, where it shook itself off and waxed fierce bright. All around us, the moon showed the walls blushing into their old faded pinks or freshening into greens and mustards. Inside the houses, glass-flowered chandeliers bloomed like meadows.

'Haven't you just gone and done it, Giacomo?' I cried.

It was only at dawn that we returned to the cavern, tucking our heads down and scraping our backs on the entrance tunnel. We had rowed and played down the Rio Marin, the Rio Novo, the Rio di Noale and all the tiny back canals of the city, some too small for any but dialect names.

The city was alight with colour, glowing where the dawn light touched it. Our faces, meanwhile, were drained chalk-white with exhaustion.

The mermaid had been out in the canals and already knew the joyful news. 'Exquisitely done!' she said. 'Her Upstairs did indeed send me the right striplings for this work.'

'Eliah?' was Ivo's only word.

'When the music could no longer be heard, his tears stopped. He be sleeping now, and so should ye. Just a few hours, mind, for fear of fins growing.'

We laid ourselves down on soft pallets of dried seaweed. I fell into a deep sleep, dreaming of loving pink faces at windows and a blaze of colour, like fire, running up a flag. But somewhere along the way, my dreams grew darker. Suddenly I saw Venice's newly vivid facades cracking like a too-thin glaze on a clay pot. I saw the colour leaching out of the walls again and cormorants settling on grey chimneys, spreading their wings like black bats. The big bad seagulls cawed over and over again, 'No Saint Lucy! No colour!'

And I heard the *badessa* speaking in the same cruel tones she'd used when I lay in the sarcophagus. She said, 'Heart against no-heart always loses. Heart is vulnerable. Heart makes colour but not armour. Heart leaves you weak. Heart fails. *Hate* makes you strong.'

The shock of hearing her voice again jostled me into a miserable wakefulness. I stared up at the gilded ceiling of the cave. Its shine had not faded. But the mermaids were protected by their ancient magic. Outside the cavern, Venice was still vulnerable.

Are we, I wondered, *really the right striplings for this job of saving Venice?*

I lay sleepless and restless until the others finally awoke.

'Is the colour holding?' was my first question.

'From water level, it does,' the mermaid said. But one of the small, good seagulls had flown into the cavern with a worrying report.

'Some of the roofs be reverting to grey,' said the mermaid. 'And the grey be spreading.'

'Temporary, was it?' I lamented.

'We must hope it holds until those Sicilian women be made to give Saint Lucy back, to stop murdering the English, making fake saints, terrorising Venetian childer and Beast-calling Vampire Eels.'

'What if they don't actually *want* to do any of those things?' I asked.

'That's why we must prepare for war,' said Incubina.

We were laying out our arms in a walled garden above the cavern. It was not grandly impressive, our armoury. We had our rusty swords and a couple of asthmatic arquebuses that the mermaids had rescued from a wreck. The kickback from those guns was so powerful that Lily and I were laid flat when we tried to discharge them.

'It matters not overmuch if ye can't aim,' the mermaid was saying. 'In the main, we require ye to make a terrible lot of noise with the guns. 'Twill discourage the enemy, when we find those horrors of women, making them believe our troop far larger than 'tis. Just practise until ye learn not to shoot each other in the vital parts. That'll be fine enough.'

'It will so,' I agreed.

So there were Ivo and Giacomo and Lily and myself cleaning the rust out of the guns when a small papery lady flew into the middle of our preparations. She hovered above us like a moth.

'Pardon the silver mask,' she said. 'I don't want my face to frighten anyone. It has somewhat . . . deteriorated . . . in the last thousand years.'

Giacomo was the first to recover. He said, 'Don't speak so of your beauty, Saint Lucy. You are radiant in our eyes!'

You would flirt with a stone, Giacomo, I thought. *Or a bit of a moss on a stone.*

'Saint Lucy,' asked Lily, 'where have you come from?'

'Where? The furthest corner of the lagoon,' she said. 'Far beyond the shores of Venice.'

'You might be glad of this,' I told the saint. From my sleeve, where it was still knotted, I pulled her tiny foot.

'Why, thank you, my dear,' she said, taking it from me with a kiss on each cheek. The kiss of a saint proved a fine feathery thing. My eyes began to tingle, as if with the beginnings of happy tears.

The saint said, 'I'll just tuck this into my robe until there's some peace and quiet to get myself re-jointed. Meanwhile, are you the little lady who made me the big vow from the midst of a watery danger?'

'That was me,' said Lily quietly. She told us, 'I vowed that if Saint Lucy saved me from drowning, then I would return her foot. It was Darling who actually found it, of course.'

Something was bothering me. I started rubbing my eyes behind my spectacles, finally taking them off and squinting at the sky.

'I can see!' I squealed. 'Clearly! Without the spectacles.'

'But of course, my dear,' said Saint Lucy. 'All my warriors must have clear sight and clear consciences. You know my song,

297

I'm sure.' She warbled, *'Lucida lucent, lucesci Lucia Luce; Lux mea lucescat Lucia luce tua.'*

I translated from the Latin into Italian, 'Lights of Lightness, Lucy the Light; Let Your Light light My Light.'

'Speaking of light,' said Lily, 'would you like to see a gilded cavern and meet some warrior mermaids?'

'Why wouldn't I?' answered Saint Lucy.

CHAPTER FORTY-SIX

'I love this city,' Saint Lucy whispered through her mask. 'So I rather *encouraged* that prophecy that Venice would suffer if I was taken away. Perhaps that wasn't too saintly of me? Then the Magoghe sisters contrived to turn the prophecy into reality, something I'd never counted on – unwisely and dangerously, as it turned out.'

She was hovering comfortably above the water. The mermaids had uttered not a word since the saint floated down the stairs after us into the cavern. Their eyes were round and their hair seemed suffused with shocked energy, floating restlessly over their shoulders. I guessed they'd never had a saint in their cavern before. Eliah's eyes, meanwhile, were glistening with frank and happy wonder.

'But it turned out that the prophecy is true anyway,' said Giacomo. 'So you've nothing to reproach yourself about, Your Loveliness.'

'Or perhaps,' mused the saint, 'the Venetians believed in the prophecy so much that they have *made* it true ... certainly they've acted in a most bloodthirsty manner since I was taken, clearly *believing* that their secret sacred ties were broken. What happened to their own good sense? Why was their love for one another not strong enough?'

She sighed deeply, and little flakes of skin flew off her neck.

The mermaid said, 'Indeed Humanfolk cannot resist a prophecy. Yet they might have shown a spoonful of restraint and resisted tearing at one another's throats the moment the colour went. Instead, they forgot themselves.'

Saint Lucy said, 'But I cannot judge the Venetians too harshly. I've seen it so often over the centuries – when human beings, even good ones, believe in *anything* fanatically, then sense and decency are the first things sacrificed.'

'So,' I asked, 'you are back for good, Saint Lucy? Did you not slightly quite wish to go back to Sicily, where you were born? Isn't that where your *own* secret sacred ties are?'

'Five centuries I've lived in Venice now,' the saint said. 'I'm loved here – *very* loved. The Venetians adore saints more than anyone. And eyesight – my speciality – is the favourite of their five senses.'

'So that's why you came back?' I asked.

'Not entirely. First of all, I was not righteously taken. The fact that my kidnappers were women from my very own Siracusa – well, it did not endear me to the idea of going back there. Then I began to worry that no Siracusan in Venice would be safe. So many pious souls have already died fighting for me over the centuries – I can't bear for anyone else to be killed in my name. And it would be so unfair. Apart from those sisters, all the Siracusans here are innocent, having simply fled earthquake and plague on our own island. Those Sicilian *victims* should have received compassion and help. It seems to me that the Venetians did not behave like good Christians towards those refugees. The Sicilians arrived with nothing and were treated to nothing but contempt and suspicion. Indeed, it seems likely that this very behaviour might have hardened the hearts of four young sisters fleeing Siracusa for their very lives twenty years ago.'

The mermaid nodded. 'Also giving those females reasons to seek revenge, now they have money and power to carry out their desire for it.'

'Are you after looking for *excuses* for the Magoghe sisters?' I could not keep the outrage out of my voice. 'That money and power you speak of – wasn't it beaten out of orphans or robbed from the English guests they murdered and dismembered for profit so?'

'Not excuses, dear,' said the saint. 'But reasons. They are different things.'

'How did you escape?' I asked.

'I was lying upon the table where the sisters planned to have me dismembered if Siracusa could not afford the vast price they wanted for my body. If that happened, their great idea was to sell pieces of me to every cathedral in Europe. Outside, in the water, I could hear my guards – some young mermaids from Miracoli – arguing among themselves. On my right, I could see the surgeon's instruments ready. On my left, through a porthole, I noticed that some colour was creeping back into the grey city. How I rejoiced! Even without me, someone had contrived to bring the colour back to Venice. It gave me heart to finish that work and make it

301

last. And I wished to meet the brave and brilliant souls who defied the prophecy.'

All four of us blushed in unison. I'd been called plenty of things in my short life, chiefly by Esmeralda Sweeney. 'Brave' and 'brilliant' had never been among them.

'The sisters didn't know a saint cannot be bound with mortal chains,' the saint continued. 'So I slipped out of mine. I was gathering my strength for the necessary act of levitation – one of the blessings of sainthood – when the leader of the Miracoli mermaids – she goes by the name of Lussa – swam up to me, her lovely face burdened with trouble. So I asked, "Are you sure you chose the right side here? Are you still enjoying yourselves now you've made your point and had your little adventure?"

'Lussa hung her head and sobbed a bit and said that they were sorry for running off. They all missed their Madonna and their beautiful church. Lussa told me that they were planning to escape the Siracusan women and return to Miracoli as soon as possible. She said they wouldn't leave me behind.'

'Sense at last!' said the mermaid. 'Silly young flitwits.'

'Lussa distracted our guards with some shameless flirting. I rose from the table and floated out of a porthole. I waited in a low cloud until the Miracoli mermaids could slip away. Obviously, they knew of their sisters in this cavern, so they guided me here on their way home. I believe they are presently remounting their marble platform at Miracoli, snug as once-upon-a-time.'

I couldn't help clapping my hands. Ever since I'd read about them in the *avvisi*, I'd felt something like kinship with those misbehaving mermaids. I felt as if I understood them very well, and their flight from confinement. Had I not departed from the Young Ladies' Academy in a spirit of wildness too?

'What about the sisters from Siracusa?' Ivo asked. 'Can you help us get rid of them from Venice?'

'And the Vampire Eels,' I added, 'while you are about it. One of the sisters is a witch who Beast-called them to Venice. She grew at least one to a frightful size.'

Saint Lucy stroked her silver nose. 'In Sicily, Vampire Eels have plenty of pirates to prey upon and so perform the duty of cleansing the ocean. In these present times, I take it, there are no significant problems with pirates in Venice?'

'None,' said Lily firmly.

'Well, then the Eels shall be *encouraged* back to Sicily. Where Eels are needed and may gain dignity from good work. I shall talk to them,' promised the saint. 'Take me to the place where the frightful Eel presently dwells.'

Ivo asked, 'Can you not do so from the safety of this place? With saintly thoughts? You can't show yourself to the Siracusans! They'll just have the Eel snatch you back. This time you'll be taken far away and guarded by nastier things than the Miracoli mermaids.'

I took up his cause: 'You'll be in danger from the moment you are seen so.'

'Seeing isn't having,' Saint Lucy said tranquilly.

Our party travelled in two boats, accompanied by mermaids. The saint sat quietly in the prow of the boat Giacomo shared with Lily, whose anxious face, averted from the water, broke my heart. And I sat by Ivo.

I kept making my old gesture of pushing my spectacles up my nose, only to find that I had no need of them. I found it hard to look at Ivo without the twin shields of glass between us. But Lily stared over at my naked face. 'You are even more yourself without the spectacles,' she said.

Her look was unreadable. I wondered, *Does she mean that's a good thing?*

Our eyes darted back and forth, looking for suspicious ripples in the water.

We needn't have stared so hard. The head of the vast Eel began to lift out of the water as soon as we approached the Murano shore. All four of us raised our rusty arquebuses.

'Don't look at it,' warned the mermaid. 'Such beasts are like the Flayed Man. Your fear will make it grow larger and stronger.'

'Then how can we aim?' I asked.

Saint Lucy said, 'There will be no war on a Beast-called creature. It's not its fault. Kindly move yourselves all into the second boat, young people, while I attend to this.'

'You're so fragile!' I protested. 'Just skin and bone—'

'Leave me. Leave us,' she said quietly.

Giacomo and Lily clambered into our boat. Ivo rolled an anchor out into the water. The boat with the saint aboard jolted gently towards the Murano shore. The saint sat calmly with her hands folded. She began to pray in a strange accent. We could not catch the exact words, but we could taste their sunburnt foreignness in the breeze.

'Sicilian,' I realised. 'Amazing how different it sounds when *she* speaks it.'

At first the Eel merely raised its head out of the water and shrieked back, like a gull that fights another over a fish. But then it lunged, picking up the saint in its jaws. I heard the faint, sickening sounds of rupture. The saint's ribs, miraculously preserved over all her years of arduous travel, were breaking.

Then I caught sight of Lily's face, fixed with terror and intent on the churning water.

'Lily!' I screamed. 'It is *not* foredoomed that you shall drown.'

But the distance between us was so much greater than it had been even when she lay unconscious in the cavern. Lily's mind had gone to a place I could not follow.

PART FIFTEEN

The Lagoon

CHAPTER FORTY-SEVEN

This is the start of drowning, I thought.

Dimly, I heard Darling scream at the Eel, 'Do you even realise what you are doing? This is a saint who does nothing but love and bring light.'

As if through a mist, I heard Giacomo wheedle, 'Do you really want to go down in history as the beast who destroyed Venice's loveliest saint?'

In answer, the Eel plunged its tail in and out of the water, sending fierce waves to crash against our boat.

Now it's happening.

Then Saint Lucy called out to the Eel, 'You are not doing this because you want to. A witch has put you under an enchantment of Baddened Magic. You've turned into a monster with no mind of your own. Inside, you are ashamed of your acts. It's not too late to stop.'

There was a sudden stillness and then the Eel gently lowered the saint's body into the water and drew back in a way that seemed almost respectful. Saint Lucy began, nevertheless, to sink.

Should that not be me? I thought. *Well, it shall be soon.*

Ivo dropped his weapon and leapt into the water.

'No!' Darling whispered. 'The witch still has sway with that Eel! It will kill him.'

But the Eel did nothing more than nudge the saint's unconscious body towards Ivo, who pulled her carefully back to the boat. Her eyes opened, and her hands flew to where her ribs must have pained her horribly.

'I shall survive,' she told Ivo. 'What would have happened if a young warrior like you had been around in 303? I might not have become a saint!'

The Eel watched in silence. And we watched the Eel. From the torn expression in its red-rimmed white eyes, the witch was still battling for dominance over the creature's soul.

'It could go either way with yon white worm now,' said the mermaid, raising her trident.

The sea wants me, I thought. *The Eel will deliver me.* I felt myself drawn towards the edge of the boat. The waves made a dark opening for my body, just the right size. Darling seized my hand. 'Stop it, Lily!'

Saint Lucy began to sing a hymn in her quavering sweet voice.

The Eel lifted its head and howled horribly.

'Fear not. It is saying farewell, in the only way it knows,' said Saint Lucy. 'Young people! Show polite and wave goodbye nicely to the Eel.'

The waves closed over the hole they had made for me.

Not yet, I thought.

The Eel sank beneath the water, a light stain in the blue-grey. We watched a trail of bubbles heading south. It was joined by other, smaller trails.

Darling said, 'Eels leaving Venice in their dozens!'

'But there are still four horrible creatures from Siracusa to get rid of,' said Giacomo.

'They are humans, young people. This means they are your problem to solve,' said the saint. 'Even the witch is just a human who has dabbled in Baddened Magic. She's a clever practitioner but not clever enough, I am sure, to defeat four stout souls like you. Stretch yourselves to fit the situation. By stretching, we grow taller. And straighter. Just as by being in the sea you learn to swim.'

She looked straight at me.

CHAPTER FORTY-EIGHT

Belatedly, Saint Lucy's church was swarming with guards who had not been enchanted by the Murano witch. Giacomo was obliged to distract them by breaking a Gothic window at a nearby *palazzo* with an expertly thrown stone.

When the guards rushed off to investigate the tinkling glass, we escorted Saint Lucy back in.

'Thank you, my dears,' she said, settling comfortably in her tomb.

'Imagine the *avvisi* tomorrow!' laughed Darling, back in the mermaids' cavern. 'Saint Lucy and the colour restored! Mermaids back at Miracoli too!'

'Do you really think the Magoghes will let Saint Lucy be?' Ivo flushed. 'Apart from us, no one knows their crimes. They'll be back at the convent, the hotel, the Anatomy School and the island, plotting their next move, starting with those who just thwarted their plans. Do you think that they'll leave us unpunished?'

Darling said, 'And in the eyes of the law, sure isn't Ivo still a ruby thief, with a price on his head?'

'Well, let's not wait here for trouble to come,' Giacomo said.

'Let's take trouble straight to the Magoghes. If we strike first, at least we'll dazzle them with the element of surprise.'

Ivo said, 'We must pick them off, *one by one*, before they even know what's happening.'

Incubina nodded. 'We keep cages here in the cavern for miscreants. A little shabby, as not needed for a few centuries.'

'Shabby is good,' Darling said. 'Don't you think so, Lily? Lily? Where are you?'

Underwater, I thought, *drowning in guilt. Not only did I let your Uncle Red die, but I also fell asleep on my watch.*

'Starting with which sister?' asked Ivo.

'I vote for the witch,' said Giacomo. 'So she can't call any more beasts.'

'How about a witch curse for her?' asked Incubina. 'I adore a good curse with blood and guts and curlicues about shrivelled livers and mangled kidneys.'

Darling said, 'That sounds something purely wonderful to me.'

'Incubina!' said the larger mermaid. 'We practise *Righteous* and not Baddened Magic here.'

Incubina persisted, 'A *Righteous* curse lasts three days but everyone has an Evil Hour in their day. And if the curse meets with the witch at her Evil Hour . . . 'twould be twice as potent.'

The larger mermaid bristled, her dark curls crackling with indignation. 'Who appointed ye the soothsayer in this cavern, Incubina? And wherefore did ye discover all this darkness?'

'The *Book of Baddened Magic*,' said Incubina. 'In the library.' She pointed back to the dark passages that led out of the cavern.

'So we can distract her with a fat witch-price,' said Darling,

313

beginning to unpick some coins from her hem. 'Then we find out when her Evil Hour is. We can lay a *Middling* Righteous witch curse on her – nothing actually killing. I'll do the cursing. I'll even enjoy it. I usually do.'

I knew she was thinking of Esmeralda Sweeney at the Young Ladies' Academy.

'Not you, Irish,' said the mermaid. 'Remember how the witch enchanted ye with her hair-combing? The only one among you the witch has not met be Lily . . .'

Seeing me flinch, Darling said, 'Mercy me! Poor Lily cannot! I'll be fine as fivepence this time—'

'I shall go too,' said Giacomo and Ivo in one voice.

'No, ye don't!' Incubina said. 'Ye're both sitting this one out, striplings! Ye be not safe around that witch. And ye'd make your friend unsafe too.'

The mermaid said, 'Lily, ye must go and face all your fears. For they will not stop facing ye just because ye turn your back on them.'

'Ye'll be needing this,' said Incubina, handing me a damp roll of parchment. 'The curse, 'tis.' She added a fine golden net, folded. 'And this may prove useful for—'

Giacomo interrupted, 'How will this cavern feel with four evil sisters in it?'

'Let's not be counting our vultures till they be hatched,' advised the mermaid.

CHAPTER FORTY-NINE

Ivo rowed me through the entrance of the cavern. The sun shone now but the cold persisted. After all, Saint Lucy's foot had not yet been properly refastened. Floes of ice jostled in the thickened water. I tried to stare straight ahead and not down.

The faster Ivo rowed, the more shards of blue ice clamoured against the side of the boat. I offered to take the second pair of oars, and he smiled gratefully. *I don't deserve that smile,* I thought, *for the ways and sheer number of times I have doubted him. It must have hurt rare sorely each time he saw the suspicion in my eyes.*

'Look!' said Ivo. 'It's joining up.' He pointed to the thin crust of ice glittering all the way to Murano. Halfway across the lagoon, the boat lurched to a halt with a groaning of wood. The ice crowded in around us. Ivo's left oar refused to be pulled out of the frozen water. In fact, it stood up on its own.

'I'll walk,' I told him.

'No!' he said. 'How will you know where the ice is thick enough to take your weight? Lily, there's *water* under it.'

'If I take off my cloak and shoes, I'll weigh even less. I'll run so fast that I won't *need* to know,' I said, kicking off a shoe.

'I . . . forbid it!' said Ivo.

'By what manner of means have you the right to forbid *me* anything?' I demanded, shedding my cloak and shoes.

'But I cannot come with you,' said Ivo. 'The ice will not bear my weight.'

'And here's me not even thinking that you should,' I said, climbing out of the boat. *That's what Darling would say*, I thought. *I'm bringing her courage along.* Agonising cold greeted my bare foot, as if I'd stepped upon an upturned knife. I refused to cry out. Ivo handed me the curse and the net.

The first stretch of ice held my feet easily, but within a few yards my right foot plummeted through to the ankle. Cold water gripped my toes as if it did not want to let go.

Now it begins, I thought. *If I am to drown, let it be quickly this time.*

'Keep running!' cried Ivo. 'Don't sink!'

Imagining Darling beside me all the way, I ran like a gazelle until I reached the shore of Murano. Ivo was just a dark shape in a boat in the sea of ice behind me. He raised his hand in a salute. 'Hurry!' he called. 'The tide is rising. The cavern entrance will fill up and we won't be able to get in. I give it two hours. That's all you've got.'

The churches of Murano began to toll then and did not stop until they had done so ten times.

*   *   *

316

Reader, can you guess how I hated to be on Murano again? My footsteps dragged along the narrow *fondamenta* towards the witch's chapel, just a few hundred paces from the Convent of Saint Teresa.

A black cat guarded the hovel. It demanded, 'And have you brought the anchovies, you ugly trifle?'

'Err . . . I brought *money*, a fine witch-price,' I said, shaking my velvet purse. It was mostly full of stones, but at the top were three gold coins Darling had unpicked from her hem.

'Money!' scoffed the black beast. 'What good is that to a cat? I cannot play with it. I cannot kill it slowly. I cannot eat it. A cat-price is different from a witch-price. An anchovy, for example, I can roll on my tongue . . .' His expression grew dreamy.

'I'm here to pay your mistress for a spell,' I lied. 'I don't have any anchovies.'

'Well, that was fatal silly of you, to turn up without one,' said the cat threateningly. 'Given that you must get past *me* before you may parley with *her*. Go away and get me an anchovy. Anyway, my mistress is out.'

'Now, my fine Fur Prince,' I wheedled, 'might I not go inside and wait? It's cold out here, and I don't have your handsome pelt to keep me warm.'

'Anchovy. Now. Or be off, you filthy fleabite.' If that cat could have whistled, it would have done so then, with impudence.

'The mouth on you!' I said reprovingly. 'For shame.'

The cat asked, 'What are you hiding behind your back?'

'Nothing,' I said.

'I wager it's an anchovy. Don't tease me. Cats have no sense of humour.'

'It's not an anchovy,' I said, taking a step back. 'But it's something rare nice, is what it is. However, as you're not interested . . .'

I made to walk away.

The cat could not bear it. He strutted right up to me. And when he was under my nose, I threw the net over him and tied its ends.

'Whaaat!' the cat shouted, rolling over and over inside the net. 'It smells of mermaid in here!'

'How would you know?' I asked.

'I tasted a bit of mermaid recently,' he admitted. 'A wounded one washed up, almost killed by a Vampire Eel, it seemed. It tasted like—'

'You ate mermaid? Then you are doomed, which is not the greatest pity in the world,' I told him. 'Unless you help me.'

'You are a friend of Fishwomen?' the cat moaned. 'That's the end of me, then. My mistress will have my liver. She's a hate on mermaids. She had some flighty ones from—'

'Miracoli,' I said. 'They couldn't stand the Sicilian sisters any more and flitted off home.'

The cat mumbled something incomprehensible but decidedly wretched. I carried him inside the witch's house. 'Now, tell me your witch's Evil Hour,' I demanded.

'Do you think cat time is the same as witch time?' he whined. 'I've not the remotest idea what her Evil Hour is. Mine, obviously, is this minute.'

I did not love to be inside that room. Everything that Darling had described to me now came to life, rare unpleasantly. The black clock with human hand bones still ticked; the hearts were beating fast and delicately in their buckets. I pushed my way through the strings of dried seahorses and ropes of hair hung from the ceiling. I wrenched down a hank of what could only be poor Mr Dearworthy's hair, so exactly like Darling's own. I did not want any part of him to stay in that evil place. I stuffed it into my sleeve.

Presently we shall bury it, I thought, *decently*.

'Tell . . . me . . . her . . . Evil . . . Hour!' I said to the cat, shaking it hard inside the net with each word.

'Or what?' said the cat. Even curled upside down, with his nose buried in his tail, he still acted like the winner in this battle of wills. 'You're not going to hurt me,' he sneered knowingly and rightly. 'All females have a soft spot for cats. And what human with any heart whatsoever could hurt a beast in a net?'

Reader, I let him go. What else could I do? He was right.

He tumbled, licked one paw nonchalantly, and marched off. It was then that I noticed the little green girl crouched in a corner, muttering, 'I know I know I know I know I know.'

'What do you know?' I asked her.

'I know the witch's Evil Hour.'

'What is it?'

'Will you help me escape if I tell you? I'm trapped here till someone releases me. My stepmother poisoned me and sold my soul to the witch.'

319

Two pieces of good luck in one, I thought. *A chance to save this poor girl and deal with the witch.*

I asked, 'Would you like to learn a curse that would weaken the witch? And would rid you of her, if uttered in her Evil Hour?'

'There's nothing I would like better,' the girl replied.

'Can you read?' I asked.

'Of course. I can write too.' She floated up to the steamy window and wrote *10.12* with her finger. The numbers dripped, yet I could read them quite clearly.

'That is her Evil Hour? Twelve minutes past ten. That must be any minute now.'

The girl nodded. 'Now give me that curse.'

I handed her the roll of parchment. She began rehearsing, whispering its words under her breath. Righteous and Middling it might be but I considered myself fortunate to hear just snatches of them. I'd not be even happy to record them here. Just be imagining the worst wish you wish you'd never heard, the one that'd drown your nose in tears, put your world in bits and rip your feelings apart. Then think it ten times eviller, and that's not even as bad as the curse Incubina had written.

It ended, '*And be thou, slinking and sneaksome as thou art,*

Captured, bound and caged by this curse's darkest art.'

There was a flurry of blackness in the air. The witch stood beside me, her bony hands on my neck. Her shriek rent the air. The curse was working on her, but not fast enough. Her face with crumpled with pain but her fingers still throttled the breath out of me.

'What's good for black-mouthed cats is good for witches,' said the green girl, pointing at the net in my hand.

I threw it over the witch, who immediately curled up inside it, limp as a wet spider. I commenced worrying if it was strong enough to hold her. And how was I to drag a full-grown woman over the thin ice?

Then, in front of my eyes, the witch disappeared from inside the net.

'Escaped!' I mourned. 'I succeed at nothing!'

'Ah no,' said the green girl, grinning. 'Now the witch'll be with whomever made the net. That's how a gold net works with a human, though not with a cat. I have seen it before. I saw so many things while I was a prisoner here . . .'

'Then the mermaids have the witch!' I rejoiced.

'And I shall be in my father's arms in five minutes.' The girl smiled and curtseyed, making me feel like an old lady. The greenness of her skin was rapidly melting into a lovely shade of peaches-and-cream.

I followed the girl out of the door. Waving gaily, she disappeared into the maze of little streets. The air had warmed slightly with the coming of the evening and waves were once more slapping against the shore when we reached it. Ivo was approaching in the boat. Before he started to row me back, he took my blue feet into his hands and rubbed them until they were red again. Then he laced up my boots and settled his cloak around my shoulders.

Shouts came from behind us. Men in black cloaks stood in a gondola, being rowed towards us by two oarsmen. 'Stop! In the name of the law! We've reason to believe that the jewel thief Ivo Peruch is aboard that boat. In the name of the Doge, stop, and hand him over!'

The colour drained from Ivo's face.

'Row, Ivo!' I shrieked at him.

CHAPTER FIFTY

Ivo rowed like one of those candle-powered figurines in the hotel's dioramas. His arms flailed into a blur. The fading light was on our side, as was a rising wind that lifted the waves around us. We could not see the men, and nor could they see us as we disappeared in troughs. Their big boat, however, sliced through the ice floes without difficulty. Ivo veered ours suddenly to the right so that we nearly collided with a buoy.

'That's not the right way,' I shouted.

'We . . . cannot . . . lead . . . them . . . to the cavern,' he panted. 'I'll circle behind the buoy so they don't see us. Then I'll dash into the entrance behind their backs.' He glanced at me sharply. 'Lily, stop looking at the water. Don't let it eat you alive. We're not done yet.'

The men raced towards Murano, shouting angrily, 'Where is he?'

We shot inside the opening, gliding on top of ice, then scuffing the surface of the water all the way to the cavern.

The first thing I saw there was an iron cage hanging from the ceiling. It was full of gagged, furious witch. And there was Darling too, putting her arms around me, saying, 'Sure you're a little wonder – look what you did!'

'What about the other three?' Giacomo asked. I noticed he kept his back carefully to the witch. 'We need to harvest those ladies quickly, before they get suspicious about this one's disappearance.'

'Do you know what?' I said. 'I've a great desire to push each of those sisters down the goose-greased chute at the Hotel of What You Want. Straight into a golden net and so here to the cavern.'

Darling hugged me. 'That's a better face on you now,' she said. 'Where did you go? Welcome back!'

Ivo said, 'That storeroom's a good place. We'll be out of the sight of the guests. But we cannot handle three sisters at once. And there's Momesso to deal with too.'

'How about one at a time?' I asked. 'We have this in our favour: none of those sisters likes or trusts the others. We can use that to separate them.'

'Yes!' said Ivo. 'It's Thursday. The Signorina attends her usual tea party with the English Resident. She's always away between two and five. Momesso always takes advantage of her absence to see to his own sordid errands. I can do the Signorina's handwriting. So I'll row to Murano and give a note to a lamp-boy to deliver to the *badessa*, summoning her to the storeroom at the hotel for an urgent secret meeting at half past two . . . something about a new piece of incompetence by the witch—'

'Eels in the hotel plumbing,' Darling suggested.

'Then I'll row back into Venice with a note from the Signorina for Alina the anatomy clerk – inviting her for cakes and tea at

3 p.m. That'll drive Alina Magoghe wild with curiosity, because none of her sisters ever want anything to do with her.'

I said, 'While you're doing that, Darling and I shall already be at the hotel, hiding behind the door when the women enter the storeroom. It's only a few steps to the chute. I've a copy of the key. But how can we get up there without being seen? The guests will ruin it all if they catch sight of us.'

Ivo said, 'It doesn't take much to get past those dullards. Giacomo can distract them with some of his nonsense.'

Darling shot him a look. Her Uncle Red had been among the people Ivo dismissed so contemptuously.

But Giacomo was enthusiastic. 'Once you girls are safely upstairs, I'll wait down in the *sotopòrtego* with that pretty gold net ready at the bottom of the chute.'

Ivo said, 'And by the time you've netted the *badessa* and the anatomy clerk, the Signorina will be on her way back.'

'And what of the notorious jewel thief, Ivo Peruch?' Darling asked. 'You're already a wanted man. And what if they also accuse you of kidnapping the Resident's so-called property, the slave-boy Eliah?'

Eliah shrank back on his pallet at the mention of the Resident's name.

I continued. 'What happens if the *Signori di Notte* snatch you from the boat and clamp you in irons? You put the whole plan at risk.'

'I'll go masked. I'll keep to the boat and the servants' entrances.'

The mermaids had stayed silent through all these discussions. But now we turned to them. I, for one, was rare eager for their blessing.

'I be sure that almost nothing can go wrong with such fine plans,' said the large mermaid.

'Indeed,' I said. But, Reader, why then did we four look so pale in that moment? We looked less like a group of young people off to trounce evil women and more like pirates' hostages, about to walk the plank in shark-infested waters.

'Anna!' called the *badessa*. 'Yes! Aleesia must be punished! Whenever she flexes her claws, it's *we* who come off worst.'

We listened to her panting up the stairs, our hearts in our throats.

But it all worked beautifully in a blur of busy seconds. As soon as she opened the door, Darling and I shoved the *badessa* towards the hole. I had the pleasure of pushing my enemy down the goose-greased chute, shouting, 'See you in the mermaid cavern!'

'You! Eulal—' The *badessa's* shocked face was the last thing we saw as she slithered downwards. Then it was our turn to be badly surprised. From below, there came a thump, a scream and a splash. Giacomo cried out too, something I could not make out. Then we heard his footsteps running.

Giacomo rushed into the room so fast we had to stop him falling down the chute himself. 'She's too heavy. She tore straight through the net and rolled into the canal.'

He held up a ragged nest of gold. 'And now the net is destroyed!'

I reached the window in time to see the *badessa's* head disappearing beneath the water.

'Can we drown all three of them like that?' I asked. But even as I said it, the hairs were rising at the back of my neck. The drowning of the *badessa* was an accident. But if we did the same to the other sisters, well, then we would be as bad as they were. I had never planned to be a murderess, not even of murderesses. I did not like the feeling.

Darling buried her face in my shoulder, and I felt her shaking with tears. 'It's not a relief, it turns out,' she gasped. 'It feels *worse* than being killed by her in a tomb full of oil.'

'Sweetest hearts, do not repine,' urged Giacomo. 'The mermaids shall understand we had no choice. It's all working a bit differently to the plan, but still working beautifully!'

Then, suddenly, it wasn't working at all.

The *badessa* moved surprisingly fast and silently for such a solid woman whose clothes were weighed down with water. She was pulling a dagger from her pocket as she stormed into the storeroom.

'Did you think Sicilians cannot swim?' she screamed. 'Did you believe it would be so easy to get rid of me?'

Behind her, I saw one of the black lionesses twitching in the corridor. Two more padded into the doorway, so there was one beast for each of us.

It was me the *badessa* grabbed first, holding the knife to my throat. 'You are going to die anyway,' she told me. 'But here's a little luxury. You may choose which of your two fine friends will live. Miss Dearworthy or Master Casanova? I'll spare one of them to walk free, on the condition of secrecy of course. And they would be too ashamed, of living when the other died, to ever betray the truth. So. You choose. See how generous I am.'

'She's lying,' I cried. 'She'll divide us and kill us all, one at a time, is what she'll do!'

The room fell silent but for the sound of breathing. My eyes blurred with tears. The *badessa* tutted. 'You can't decide whom to spare? Just say farewell to both of them then. The maggots shall eat the meat off their bones. And then we shall use the bones for *saintly* purposes.'

'That is the worst of you,' I said bitterly. 'You are so cold-blooded that you'll kill just to make money out of cheating the innocent church-goers of Venice. You have a stone for a heart, a stone for brains, a stone for a soul, is what you have.'

'If those numb-witted priests in Venice wish to contribute to the coffers of Saint Teresa . . .' the *badessa* began to boast.

While I distracted her, Darling moved an inch closer, as did Giacomo. *But where is Ivo?* I wondered. *Safe, that's where he is. He did not put himself in the same rooms as any of the sisters. He gave himself all the easy jobs.*

'What of those Venetians,' the *badessa* continued, 'who whine to saints as a lazy shortcut to getting what they want, instead of doing their own hard work? Do they deserve real saints' bones to wish on? You, Venetian girl, orphan girl, mad girl, daughter of a madwoman, lowest of the low in the whole world, why do I even waste time talking to you? A Venetian who's afraid of water! What could be more useless?'

'Was my mother really mad?' I demanded. 'Or did your nastiness drive her to thinking she was so?'

'As it happens, your mother's only problem was that she was too beautiful, too much beloved of her parents. Her brother wanted her portion of their father's will. He slandered her sanity and had her confined at our convent.'

'So I was not left at the wheel like the other babies? I was born *in* the convent! *That's* how you knew who my mother was!'

'I was happy to help the brother, for a handsome consideration.'

'Let me guess. Did you tell your sisters about that money? Or did you keep it all to yourself?' I asked.

'Why should I share? It was *my* plan. And it was not the first time I'd taken care of an inconvenient noble girl. I even gave the brother useful advice on how to persuade the family that their daughter was lost to them anyway, for her wits were gone, and that burial in a convent was the only way to save the family's reputation from the taint of madness and the disgrace of a baby born out of wedlock.'

'So she really was with child?' Darling asked.

'That she was. A young man of good family loved her and wanted to marry her. The thought of another heir is what drove her brother over the edge. Shocked by her brother's cruelty, pining for the man she loved – your mother was so delicate. I broke her. There are certain ways that a young woman may distress herself into an *apparently* maddened state. Things become worse when you deprive her of liberty, clothes, company, warmth . . . it also helps to tell her that she's mad at every opportunity.'

'As you did with Lily,' Darling said. 'There's no madness in Lily's blood. Her face tells the truth of her: she's from a noble family. There is great heart in her; that's why she's suffered so.'

329

'What happened to my mother?' I asked, my voice raw.

'She had a difficult birth,' said the *badessa*. 'We left her alone with her animal cries. The next day we found she'd bled to death. Yet you were stubbornly living, mewling in her arms.'

Into my mind came the memory of my seven-year-old self, cradling the dying baby I tried to rescue from the cloister.

'That was murder,' Darling said flatly. 'Nothing less. Babies, mothers, you didn't care who died under your rule. But you couldn't kill everyone. Lily still has family,' she insisted. 'We'll not be wanting to know her mother's brother, may he wither and burn. But Lily has a *father* and *grandparents* who are surely decent people who should know the truth.'

'Do you really think I'm about to give you particulars and addresses? Anyway, they know nothing of her. The brother told his parents that the baby died too, and that it was better that way. For *him*, it truly was. He'd set a trap for me: no one could prove whose brat you were, he said. So I lost my monthly stipend from him.' She turned back to me. 'Which did not encourage me to love you, Eulalia. Your mother did a bad thing: even in death, she cost me money. You have been raised solely to recompense me.'

'Bred like a beaten dog, not a child,' I said. 'But even beaten dogs find their dignity in the end. They bite.'

I twisted and sank my teeth into the *badessa*'s wrist. At the *badessa*'s scream of rage and pain, the three lionesses roared like sooty fires, advancing on us.

'My sister's pets are angry,' said the *badessa*, not for one second letting go of me. 'And hungry. They've only ever *pretended* to be made of stone. My sister Aleesia Beast-called them from Africa.

She charged me a fortune. So I've seen to it that they've not had a decent meal since.'

'Run!' I screamed to Giacomo and Darling, the *badessa*'s dagger back at my throat. 'The witch can't control the Baddened Magic in those cats. It's *your believing in them* that's bringing them to life. Like the Flayed Man.'

I tried hard not to believe in the lionesses, though their breath was warming the room. By a vast effort of will, I imagined the closest lioness stiff and stony. She became so. Giacomo and Lily looked away from the creatures. Another suddenly grew sleekly solid again, then the third one.

'See!' I said. 'Now be off with you! Darling! Giacomo! The other sisters will be here in seconds.'

The *badessa* sneered, 'Your friends will not run, not when they foolishly imagine they might be able to save you.'

And indeed they stood still as stalagmites in a cave.

'This is getting tedious,' said the *badessa*. 'It's not a parlour game. Need proof that I'm serious?' She tipped the blade of the dagger into my neck. I felt my warm blood begin to run.

'I . . . do . . . so . . . hate . . . it when ladies go to the bad,' said Giacomo from behind gritted teeth. He lunged towards the *badessa* and was stabbed in the left hand for thanks. He folded the wounded hand under his armpit and took a step closer. The *badessa*'s knife cut another tiny slit in my skin.

'I forbid you, Giacomo!' I whispered. 'Keep away from me. I'm done.'

Giacomo said quickly, and in his most winning way, to the *badessa*, 'Dearest lady, I am sure that deep inside you there's a well of sweetness. You really do not want to hurt orphans. It goes against nature. Even yours.'

The *badessa* said, 'Not such a deep well of sweetness. Ingenuity is more my line. Many ingenious things can happen to girls and boys whom nobody wants. Even after they're dead.'

'In general,' said Giacomo, 'I don't go unwanted. And orphans are merely young people who have not yet found someone who deserves their love.'

Now Giacomo is playing for time too, I thought. And indeed he had caught the *badessa's* interest. She smiled at him.

'So again we are speaking of mothers? When did you last see *your* mother, boy?' asked the *badessa*.

Giacomo grew suddenly pensive. 'Well, presently she may be in Warsaw or Paris or Saint Petersburg.'

'And does she always send for you when she returns to Venice?' He hung his head.

Ah, I thought, *this is for why Giacomo has such a passion for making ladies happy. The one lady who really counts has no interest in him.*

With Giacomo briefly silenced, the *badessa* began to push me over to the hole in the floor. Unlike the *badessa*, I could not swim. I would drown if I tumbled down into the water. Darling and Giacomo would never get past the *badessa* in time to save me. And meanwhile the anatomy clerk and the Signorina would be here any second to take care of them.

I pitted my whole strength against my fate, but I was losing ground inch by inch. With each shove, Giacomo and Darling crept closer, but with each step of theirs, the *badessa* made another little rip in my skin with her dagger.

This is what I deserved, I thought, *all along. For my part in Mr Dearworthy's death, I deserve to die. The only surprise is that my death does not come by water after all.*

'I shall make a bloodied colander of this girl if you don't step away,' the *badessa* growled. 'And I'll do it slowly, so I can enjoy it more.'

The last thing I heard, Reader, as I fell into darkness, was a calm, strong voice.

'I don't think so,' it said.

PART SIXTEEN

The Hotel of What You Want
San Felice, Venice

CHAPTER FIFTY-ONE

Ivo strode into the room, carrying a flour sack in one hand. He pushed past me and Giacomo, grabbed both the *badessa*'s hands and pinned them behind her, tying them neatly with the rosary he ripped off her chest. The shock was too much for the *badessa*: she let her dagger tumble to the ground. Lily, already unconscious, dropped out of her torturer's grasp and into Giacomo's arms. Ivo threw the flour sack over the *badessa*'s head and tightened the drawstring.

I noticed that his left eye was swelling into a mass of black and red blotches. 'State of you, Ivo!' I cried. 'Who did that to you?'

Then I saw that the blood was still coursing down Lily's neck. I ran to press my hand over the wound. But the blood found its way between my fingers, dripping on to the ground. 'We have to stop it!' I cried. 'She'll bleed to death.'

Ivo called out, 'Miss Mullvein, if you please!'

It was the wrong side of strange to hear Ivo uttering that name in a friendly voice. It was stranger still to see the English ladies Miss Mullvein and Miss Birthwort bustle in. 'Fear not, Miss

Dearworthy,' said Miss Mullvein. 'I am trained in field hospital procedures and have all the correct kit.'

She produced a black leather reticule. From it, Miss Mullvein drew a roll of bandages and a collection of glass bottles. Miss Birthwort added, 'I too am a nurse. In the service, we all are.'

'In the service of what?' I asked.

Miss Mullvein was busy with Lily's wounds, cleaning them and deftly sewing a few quick black stitches into her pale skin at the worst incisions.

'It's a mercy the girl's in a faint. I shall bring her round with spirit of hartshorn when I'm done. Now, as I've just been explaining to young Ivo – who came rousting through the parlour twenty minutes ago like a boy made of fury – we are all members of the Covert Cohort, having done a year-long correspondence course in clue-hunting and under-cover investigation. Then we graduated to Field Work, including Dangerous Situations and Medical Emergencies like this one.'

'What about Mrs Sprigge?' I asked. 'With all her complaints?'

'No, she's not one of us,' said Miss Mullvein. 'She really is a mean, whiney old besom of an Englishwoman.'

'Enough to make a dog bite his father,' I agreed.

Miss Mullvein finished her sewing, neatly cut the thread, applied a clean bandage and wafted a bottle under Lily's nose. Lily spluttered, opened her eyes and stared around her.

Miss Birthwort said, 'At first Ivo did not wish to hear our account of ourselves, despising us English as he evidently does. However, at last he understands. The Cohort has been investigating the Hotel of What You Want. Several lawyers contacted us, suspicious about clients who were one day enjoying a stay in Venice, the next month wretched and the third month dead *at their own hands*. Then we received a letter from a young man who had wanted to give his old teacher a decent burial. But the body had disappeared. We had many reasons to believe that there were shady goings-on here.'

'That's for why these ladies – and Mr Dearworthy – became guests at the Hotel of What You Want?' asked Lily.

Miss Mullvein said sadly, 'Gregory Dearworthy was one of our finest. He even volunteered to drink your Signorina's potion so the Hon. Fishcold – a retired apothecary – could analyse the dregs, and the effect. Gregory was confident he was strong enough to withstand the opium, as he took a powerful remedy against it every night.'

'No, he didn't,' Ivo said. 'Because we always replaced what was in the guests' own medicine flasks with more Night Mixture.'

'That is too heinous,' moaned Miss Birthwort. 'We never suspected that Gregory would fall prey to your Signorina. He told us that there was a breakthrough coming . . . He was so sure of his case that he confided his suspicions in the English Resident here.'

Ivo's face contorted at the mention of the Resident. The *badessa* laughed, an ugly caw muffled inside the flour sack.

'When I told young Ivo about the Resident,' said Miss Mullvein, 'I thought he would explode. All along there were worse crimes afoot than we ever guessed. We failed to even skim the surface.

And as for this fine young man being a jewel thief . . . *well*! A slander of the deepest dye!'

'That Resident!' I said. 'He was taking Magoghe money to turn a blind eye to the English deaths here. The Resident must have told the Signorina that Uncle Red was on her trail. So the poor man was naturally chosen as her next victim.'

Sebastian Sourcollar, Mr Bungus and the Honourable Lownton Fishcold had just appeared at the door. Miss Mullvein told them, 'I fear our first foray into practical covert work has been a failure. We must learn from these young people, who don't need theory because they are *all* practice. They had already vanquished this villainess' – she pointed to the *badessa* – 'before we arrived. All we contributed was a little first aid to young Lily.'

Miss Birthwort said, 'Gregory would never forgive us if we lost Lily! He loved this girl as much as he loved you, Miss Dearworthy. He told me you two would be dearest friends at first sight. He hoped to arrange a meeting soon. Last thing he said to me was, "They are bending her out of shape, poor preyed-on girl," he said. "So brave, so good at heart. If something happens to me, take care of Lily as if she was my own."'

'It shall be done,' I promised, putting both arms around Lily. She blushed.

Then her face darkened. 'But it's not over. The Signorina—'

'Ah,' Mr Bungus said comfortably, 'that lady's been detained already. By young Ivo, again. I myself witnessed the brave boy insisting on confronting her in the street outside this hotel. He got a nasty blow for his pains – which accounts for that black eye

340

he's got – yet it did not stop him tripping her up and rolling her skirts into a grand binding.'

Miss Mullvein said, 'She's presently tied up in my room, in fact, enjoying a diorama of old Cairo from an eye-slit in a pillowcase. For company, she has that pleasant chappie Aldo Momesso with a sharp headache and *his* head too in a stout canvas sack. And *that* was all young Ivo's work too. He took the brute unawares dipping in the wine larder – and applied a rolling pin to the back of his head.'

'Good man yourself, Ivo!' I said. 'A contusion to the head will suit Momesso handsomely and improve upon nature. Don't I wish that I'd been there too to deal him an extra buffet in the chops.'

'But the anatomy clerk is running free.' Lily said.

'In fact, no,' said Ivo. 'She came up behind me when I was tying Aldo Momesso and tried to strangle me with one of her gold necklaces.'

He pointed to a red line around his throat.

'How did you stop her?'

'I'm afraid I turned around and threw both hands at her dangling diamond earrings. And I wrenched them off . . . the hard way. There was a lot of blood and even more screaming. While her fingers were at her ears, I . . . rather . . . went for her ankles and bit them hard as I could. She fell on top of Aldo Momesso . . . in the wine larder, and I may have . . . *tapped* her on the back of the head, too, with that rolling pin.'

'For the love of little baby Jesus!' I said. 'I hope it was more than a tap.'

The Honourable Lownton Fishcold said, 'I heard some suspicious noises in the kitchen. When I entered, I found this lad bagging the head of the lady with a flour sack and tying her hands behind her back with a linen tablecloth. He explained what he was about in admirably concise terms, and I offered my room as a temporary prison.'

'Good fellow yourself,' I said.

Miss Birthwort said, 'Now, there are just a few things we don't yet understand . . .'

'That's because they involve an evil *badessa*, a Beast-calling witch in a church on Murano,' Ivo said, 'and Baddened Magic. And mermaids.'

'Our dossier for the authorities,' faltered Miss Birthwort, 'is . . . thus far . . . a masterpiece of rationality, calculation and precision. Its credibility would be fatally undermined by—'

'*Mermaids*,' I insisted. 'In a gilded cavern under Venice.'

After some strong cups of tea, and a chorus of explanations from us, the members of the Cohort were surprisingly understanding of the fact that no human over thirteen years of age could actually see or hear Venetian mermaids. Indeed, they were regretful. They absolutely agreed that our prisoners should be delivered to the cavern.

'This is Venice business now,' said Miss Birthwort quietly.

However, Mr Bungus and Mr Winchelsea helped Ivo and Giacomo carry the bound and gagged Signorina, anatomy clerk and *badessa* down to Ivo's boat. Sebastian Sourcollar and the Honourable Lownton Fishcold received them into the boat and laid them side by side between the benches. Aldo Momesso came last, and it took six of the Cohort to bundle his struggling sack into the prow. Miss Birthwort took a nasty kick to the arm. We covered the sorry four of them with canvas, so we were not forced to breathe the ugly smell of Momesso's anger.

'Thank you for your help,' I said to the Cohort, as I was learning to call them. 'We'll be sure to tell you what happens next.'

'What makes you think that we'd give up the chance to not-see some Venetian mermaids?' asked Miss Mullvein.

'We have our own boat,' said Mr Bungus, pointing to a sturdy *San Pierota* by the *fondamenta*, 'for pursuing our investigations. Members of the Cohort are fully trained in all maritime matters before being released into the field of duty.'

Miss Mullvein sprang into the *San Pierota* with the agility of a goat, saying, 'Trained, yes. But everything we've trained for years to do has been accomplished quite naturally by these talented Venetian young people and with so much more style and swashbuckle than we'd ever manage.'

'And one Irish girl,' said Ivo. 'Darling Dearworthy has done her guardian proud.'

That pinned my ears back. I stared at him until he dropped his eyes.

Ivo and Miss Mullvein rowed the hotel boat; Mr Bungus and Giacomo took the Cohort's *San Pierota*. Lily and I sat beside Ivo and Miss Mullvein, our feet resting on the bundled Magoghe sisters and our arms around one another. I noticed that Lily trailed her hand in the water with a thoughtful expression and not a smidgen of fear.

She has learned that Uncle Red cared about her, that he knew it wasn't her fault, I guessed. This knowledge starts to undo what the sisters did to her, by way of making her feel guilty, by way of making her think she was nothing and could be drowned like a rat.

We proceeded up the Rio di Noale to the cavern's lagoon-side entrance.

'Lower your heads!' shouted Giacomo and Ivo.

The Cohort showed not a single sign of fear as we shot into the mouth of the dark tunnel and then rowed through the silent gilded archways.

The final arch opened into the high glory of the cavern, where Eliah stood on tiptoe waving to us with joy.

'Who have we here?' asked the mermaid. 'Striplings, maids and a pale crew of grown Humanfolk?' She looked closely at Lily's face. 'I see at least one of my unloved childer be changing into something better.'

Incubina added, 'And look! Some bundles of badness, tied up with rope!'

In moments, four more cages were lowered from the roof and our captives hustled inside.

'The plan worked after all?' asked the mermaid.

'It took a fine new shape for itself,' I said. 'It expanded to fit.'

*   *   *

I offered to act as interpreter.

The Cohort gazed first at the Murano witch sitting sulkily in her cage. Then they cast their eyes blankly into the candle-lit water where the mermaids appeared – to us, at least – one large and grave, the other smaller and lively. Mutual salutations and compliments were exchanged, with me translating.

Miss Mullvein snapped her fingers. 'So frustrating not to be able to see these magnificent creatures or hear their voices!'

''Tis a shame,' agreed the mermaid. 'But there be a solution . . . if yon fine Humanfolk would agree to become members of the *Incogniti*.'

I explained to the Cohort, 'The *Incogniti* are a band of humans prepared to fight for Venice in the case of any enemy trying to destroy the city. Such people have the gift of seeing and hearing magical creatures. So the mermaids wonder if you might consider . . .? "*Incogniti*" means "unknown" . . .'

'Unknown, secret – covert, in other words.' Mr Bungus smiled. 'Right up our alley. Or *calle*, as you say in this marvellous town.'

'Does that mean we could really stay in Venice?' asked Miss Mullvein wistfully. 'And make ourselves actually useful? The Signorina was right about one thing – none of us has anything to keep us in England. I adore this city. I want some secret sacred ties to her!'

I was pure astonished to hear her say the words in immaculate Italian.

Miss Birthwort explained, 'We all speak the language perfectly, but we do so only when safety permits.'

345

The mermaid said, 'Tell them that *Incogniti* receive the gift of several Humanfolk lifetimes – unless they suffer themselves to be murdered by some horror or another.'

'Then let us become *Incogniti*,' cried Miss Mullvein, unflinching, when I translated. 'Horrors be damned!'

'Hear, hear!' said Mr Bungus.

'Who knows,' said Miss Birthwort, 'but there might one day be another dangerous and interesting crime to solve in Venice?'

''Tis highly likely,' said the mermaid lugubriously. 'Darling, tell them to put their left hand upon their hearts. And tell them to think of Venice as a beautiful glass city in a bottle, something they could cradle in their arms and love like kin. And tell them to swear on their lives that they will not let her sink under the onslaught of any enemy, being it human, ghostly or beastly.'

Why have I not been invited to be one of the Incogniti? *I wondered, pinch-mouthed with jealousy. Have I not done enough, risked enough? And what of Ivo and Giacomo and Lily? Why are these old English people being honoured ahead of us?*

The mermaid's deep voice reached out to my thoughts, setting them to rights. '*Jealousy be not a pretty colour on anyone, maid. Ye younger ones will have a choice to make when the time comes. Meantime, ye be but silken threads waiting to be woven into what ye shall become. Ye have been tested like Murano glass – put in the fire, pulled out, re-formed. But ye have far to go still. Perhaps ye shall be as a queen, mayhap as a hound.*'

'Oh my goodness! I never laid eyes on anything so wonderful!' breathed Miss Mullvein. As a new member of the *Incogniti*, she'd just had her first sight of the two mermaids.

Sebastian Sourcollar blushed a fierce red and Mr Bungus stuttered, 'Well I never!' For weren't the mermaids clad in nothing but a couple of starfish?

'So,' I said, partly to fill the resulting silence, 'what shall be done with the rest of our prisoners?'

'Let's be having a look at them,' said the mermaid.

The Signorina and the *badessa* had struggled out of their canvas sacks, their faces contorted with fury. The anatomy clerk's face showed no emotion whatsoever, but she stared greedily at the gold mosaics of the cavern ceilings. The Signorina and the *badessa* shrieked insults not at us but at the witch, who sprayed them with spittle as she roared, '*You* got us to this pass, sisters! *You* let the little devils escape from the tomb, Arabella! *You* failed to poison them at the hotel, Anna! Always sneering at me, but derelict yourselves, you—'

The *badessa* glared down. The mermaids were of course invisible to her, so her venom was directed at us humans. 'You must feed us! It is our right.'

'Pining for a goose drumstick, be she? Tell her to try being hungry,' the mermaid instructed me. 'Hungry as an orphan, for example.'

'We *have* been hungry!' the *badessa* shouted, when I repeated those words. 'For years, we were hungry on the streets of this city. Four young sisters, orphaned by a terrifying earthquake, turning up here, hoping for a bit of kindness. The Venetians looked at us with cold eyes. They wanted rich Grand Tourists to fleece, not beggars dusty from the rubble of Siracusa. There was no question of giving us something to eat just

347

because we were starving, nor a roof because we were cold. To be *kind* to four young girls was not the first thought in the minds of the Venetians.

'So we took our fates in our own hands. Arabella offered herself as a novice in a convent, I worked as a chambermaid in a hotel; Alina . . . cleaned the viscera of corpses in the Anatomy School; Aleesia became an apprentice to a wise woman on Murano. We were *your* ages' – she pointed at me and Lily – 'yet the Venetians never allowed us to be young.'

Then came the anatomy clerk's voice, flat and grating. 'But we were clever. We prospered in the menial work we'd been forced to take. We worked harder than the Venetians, which wasn't difficult, as they are so lazy. We worked like dogs until we were women of business, with money behind us, in positions of power over those who had once treated us like dirt.'

I said, 'As cold as that, isn't it? Because you did not vastly care for one another, did you? You never met up for the pleasure of being sisters. It was all business to you. Each sister made the others *pay* for her special, horrible services. Your only secret sacred ties were to do with hurting people and making money so.'

Ivo said, 'No affection for one another, but you found yourself some friends. The English Resident, a butcher of men, criminal jewellers. A thing like Aldo Momesso.'

The *portiere* swore under his breath.

'And they'll all go down with you,' I said. 'I see vegetables thrown by a furious crowd as you're dragged off for long years in a Venetian prison. Or worse. Doesn't Venice hangs murderesses between the columns of the Piazzetta?'

348

The mermaid raised her hand. 'No, striplings. That shall not be,' she said quietly.

'Why not?' Lily demanded.

'Her Upstairs isn't having any of that.'

CHAPTER FORTY-TWO

Hands washed, Giacomo, Lily, Ivo and I stood in front of the Madonna, alongside all the new *Incogniti*.

We listened in strained silence as She told us that She was miffed beyond all miffdom – not Her exact words – that we had disrespectfully forgotten about Her graceful contemplation as to whether or not to help us. However, She was grudgingly *a little bit* pleased that, even without Her, we had managed to overcome the Magoghe sisters.

'You were the right young people for the task, after all,' She purred.

'So *why* can't we get those women put away in a dark place?' I grumbled. 'After a thorough naming and shaming so?'

The Madonna sighed. 'A grand vengeful trial of these sisters would only prolong Venice's misery. Human justice all too often has a savage flavour. It merely embitters. No one is healed by it. There is already too much for Venetians to be ashamed of in these last desperate days. Every innocent Siracusan refugee in the city would become a scapegoat, accused of being their accomplices. No. Your task is to have the women swiftly removed from the city. With the utmost secrecy.'

Mr Bungus coughed and wriggled.

'You have a question, Englishman?' the Madonna asked.

'Please, My Lady, these admirable young people inform us that whether You are a marble statue in Santa Croce or a painting in Cannaregio, You are always the same person, and, well, personality?'

'Of course.'

'That's Venetian . . . magic?' asked Mr Bungus.

'No,' said the Madonna, 'that is *faith*.'

And She became as still and silent as a painting once more.

'So,' said Miss Mullvein, '*how* do we get these four blights of women out of Venice?'

Lily said, 'To get the Magoghe sisters officially exiled, we'd need to tell the Doge, the Three Inquisitors and the Council of Ten. That would not be very secret.'

'And the Doge is no use to us,' said Ivo. 'He's a Pisani, one of the Golden Book families. He won't want anything to change. He wouldn't want tales of false relics to stop tourists flocking here to see our churches. Anyway, he gambles with the Resident at the Ridotto.'

Then Ivo smiled. 'But Pisani's wife, the Dogaressa Elena Badoero, is a decent woman. She hated the way the Resident treated Eliah.'

It was then that Giacomo remembered something useful. 'My grandfather,' he told us, blushing, 'was a shoemaker. And the shoemakers of Venice have the honour to deliver a special pair of high-heeled slippers to the Dogaressa each year. My second cousin's making the slippers this time,' he said. 'They are to be presented to her tomorrow! It will be the simplest thing in the world to slip a note for her inside one shoe. It's customary for the Dogaressa to thank the shoemaker with a personal letter – so she can send back a signal that she understands and will help.'

Ivo nodded. 'She's known as a lady who gets things done.'

Back at the hotel, we composed the note, outlining the situation as economically as possible and without mentioning its magical aspects.

We asked the Dogaressa to have a red ribbon tied on the San Marco portal of the Doge's Palace when the tenth hour of night struck, if she would like us to deliver the Magoghes to the prison watergate at midnight.

Miss Mullvein said, 'I doubt the Venetians will want to be hosting the would-be stealers of Saint Lucy for long. The sisters will be on a galleon and pointed south to Sicily as quick as can be. And young Ivo must be exonerated of all false accusations of jewel theft.'

Within a day, the Dogaressa Elena Badoer had made Miss Mullvein's words come true, including a proclamation that Ivo Peruch was a boy of unstained character. Meanwhile, a secret Decree of Exile had been passed overnight upon the Sicilian women by the Council of Ten. The Magoghe sisters were never again to show their beautiful veinless faces in any Venetian territory. There was a price of ten thousand ducats on their heads if they dared to do so.

We convened in the mermaids' cavern to read a letter from the Dogaressa explaining all these matters. She also told us that the Council of Ten had decided *not* to unmask false relics the *badessa* had sold to so many Venetian churches. *The city is too fragile after recent painful events*, she explained. *Venice can take no more. She needs to heal*.

I turned to Lily, expecting fury. But her face was mild, her voice thoughtful. 'The *badessa* was selling lies, but those lies made people feel better. I've seen many stricken faces soothed after someone prayed in front a bone they thought to be the finger of Saint Agnes or the knee of Saint Joseph. That's how badly Venetians *need* to believe those wishing bones.' Then she looked straight at me. 'They were still real bones. They belonged to good people who deserved love and instead were cruelly and wrongly put to death. Why should they *not* be honoured?'

It was strange to imagine Uncle Red as a kind of saint. But then again, he had given his life in order to seek what was right and good. But it was still too painful to think what might have happened to his bones so I did not let my thoughts go in that direction.

Meanwhile, there was more unfinished business. I could see it in Ivo's face. I said, 'There's one villain still free and unpunished so. The English Resident is due a revenge or seven. That's Irish for—'

'Revenge be a tricksome business,' said the mermaid. 'One's best not hurting one's soul with it.'

'A few well-chosen words shall not hurt our souls though the air may turn a little blue,' I said. 'Ivo and I shall go to the Resident's palace. He shall hear that the Dogaressa knows exactly what he's been about. He'll realise that's the end of his place at noble tables in this city – dinner tables and gambling tables alike. He's a great one for his own grandeur, is he not? He shall see it as dust now. And that shall hurt him like vinegar in a cut finger. I'm not asking you if that is a good idea,' I told the mermaid. 'I am telling you that it is what we shall do.'

For a moment, the mermaid was as silent as an old shipwreck in deep water. Then she said, 'Do what ye must. I fear not for your souls. But don't dirty your hands by laying them on that man.'

As it happened, none of us needed to dirty our hands with the business of the Resident's just deserts.

CHAPTER FORTY-THREE

A white-haired maid greeted us at the door. 'Ivo! I never thought to see you again! Three years it's been, and not a word from you! What of our darling Eliah? Did he—?'

I interrupted, 'Eliah survives. And may one day do well—'

Ivo asked grimly, 'Where is *he*?'

'The Resident? Oh, himself's up chasing that bird of Eliah's, I expect. That's all he does these days. It still haunts the windows of this *palazzo*, like Eliah's own soul, faithful creature that it is.'

She turned to me. 'Miss, you never saw such a bird. Its breast is bright green, like emeralds, Miss—?'

'Dearworthy.' I smiled.

'Fancy, a *foreign* girlie, Ivo! Who'd have thought—'

'The bird?' Ivo asked tersely.

'Well, the remarkable thing was, after Saint Lucy was taken, even when everything else in Venice went grey, that bird stayed green as a field in springtime. It's still doing its uttermost to drive Milord the Resident mad. Yesterday he himself actually climbed on to the sill of his study window to try to grasp the creature. He's promised the bird, you see, stuffed as a hat ornament for that book-writing Scottish lady who's always making eyes at him, the trollop.'

'She!' I said, envenoming the word as I were a scorpion striking. 'The one who loved to see Eliah's crystal tears.'

'You know about that too? *Well.* You're obviously thick as thieves with young Ivo—'

Ivo interrupted, 'The *Resident*?'

'Oh, he's out on that window sill again now, on his knees, grabbing at the bird, as if he himself were not a grand gentleman. I told him only just now, "Sir, be careful!"'

'Let us go and urge him to be even more careful, shall we?' Ivo said.

He led the way up a grandiose staircase and through tapestried corridors to a room beset with glowering statues and vastly ugly portraits and smelling of tea, wine and sweat. At first, I thought the room was empty. Then in the window I made out the silhouette of the tall man and the tiny bird, dancing in the air around his head while he grabbed at it, ineffectually.

That bird is purely enjoying itself, I thought. The man, panting and swearing, was not.

Ivo called out, 'Sir?'

Perhaps the liquid music of the Grand Canal drowned out Ivo's voice. Or perhaps the Resident was dazzled by the bird's green breast. He did not even glance back. The bird fluttered temptingly close – so close – and then darted away. The Resident's hand closed on emptiness. He howled with frustration.

'Sir,' said Ivo. 'I don't think you should—'

'*You!*' shouted the Resident, looking back at last.

The hummingbird returned, circling the Resident's head in a blurred wreath of green. Then it hovered an elbow's length away. The Resident used both hands now to rake the air. But he overreached himself. One moment the window frame was full of his form; the next moment the sun glared in uninterrupted and a man's high-pitched scream echoed in my ears.

Ivo shouted at me, 'Stay where you are, Darling.'

He ran to the window. I heard a wet thump and another short scream.

'Ivo – no splash?' I asked.

Ivo leaned out. He looked down very briefly, and then away.

What has he seen? I wondered in a red flare of anger. *Just another of those Venetian things from Venice is it, from which I'm Irishly excluded, I suppose? After all we've been through together, I'm still on the outside, alone entirely.*

Ivo glanced back at me with sudden comprehension of my troubles.

'You know what's in the water below the palaces in Venice?' he asked gently.

'Surely. Boats, jetties, those pointy poles for moorings—'

'Those pointy *paline*,' said Ivo, meaningfully.

Back in the cavern, we told our story.

'Why that,' Giacomo said, 'is so wrong, and so right.'

'You know it is so,' said a rich voice softly.

Eliah sat up on his pallet and smiled at us all. And the tiny green bird soared through the gilded cavern to perch on his finger.

CHAPTER FORTY-FOUR

The four Magoghe sisters were already many leagues away on a southbound galleon. Elena Badoero had been to visit them in the Pozzi prisons before they embarked, making certain observations that had caused even those women to look at their toes, unable to meet her eyes. So the Dogaressa had told Miss Mullvein and Miss Birthwort, with whom she'd become very friendly. Watermelon and sweet Malvasia wine had been served to them at the Doge's Palace, and they'd returned to the hotel giggling like schoolgirls.

'There'll be many a dry eye now that they're gone,' I said bitterly. The Dogaressa had done everything right except that she'd failed to extract from the sisters the whereabouts of Uncle Red's body.

Aldo Momesso had also disappeared, pure unregretted. He had escaped from his cell by bribing a guard. A Decree of Exile was passed upon him too. At least Venice had seen the last of him.

The two corrupt jewellers were no longer profiting from their bloody side-trade. The *Signori di Notte* had raided their shops. When recently boiled human bones were discovered, both jewellers were dragged off to prison. In a bid for mercy, the jewellers implicated the Signorina's butcher. But he was long gone by then, his shop boarded up. His family told how he had screamed of a headless Flayed Man swooping down and trying to wrench his head off his body.

The Flayed Man himself was no more. The new *Incogniti* had received a report of a mysterious multicoloured heap of melted wax found at the city's largest bakery. 'We found teeth in there,' Sebastian Sourcollar told us. 'The creature must have tried to get warm, and it proved fatal.'

Also gone was the name of Lily's family. The *badessa* had taken that secret with her. Lily pretended she did not care. 'I've done without a birth family since forever,' she said.

'Not exactly flourished, though,' I said carefully.

'I intend to flourish mightily from now on,' she said.

Ivo said, 'And you shall, and you deserve to.'

And sure didn't Lily look pure startled to hear Ivo so kind? But I myself had lately seen a new Ivo emerging like a chick from an egg. Or perhaps it was the old Ivo – the person he was before the Resident distorted his soul with cruelty.

The Dogaressa herself had invited Ivo to return to the English Resident's palace. Ivo, with his perfect English, was to be the Consulente, an advisor to a new English Secretary yet to be appointed. Ivo was of course fierce young for such a task, but he seemed to have grown a whole hand taller in the last week.

And sure, I thought, *the seriousness on Ivo's face has always aged him. I wouldn't be sorry to see what a smile looks like on it.*

Ivo had also been appointed executor of the Resident's estate. He busied himself with the documentation of freeing the slaves on the sugar plantation in Jamaica. The Scottish lady disappeared hastily from Venice. Ironically, the Resident, like the guests at the Hotel of What You Want, had no one to attend his funeral, which was but a poor one, with no magnificence at all. Eliah was living with Ivo at the palace, receiving wages, not blows, for assisting in the office. Short shrift was given to any English visitor who expressed a desire for the services of 'the boy who weeps goodbye'.

I myself felt such a tenderness whenever I saw Eliah. He always clung to my hand trustingly and blessed me a dozen times at each visit. He taught his hummingbird to love me too. It consented to sit on my wrist, its little eyes glittering like dark sapphires. When, at considerable sacrifice to my own happiness, I offered to pay Eliah's passage back to Jamaica as a free boy, he declared, 'Thank you kindly but I shall never go ever again into the bowels of a ship, Miss Dearworthy. It would be like a tomb for me.'

I smiled, but the word 'tomb' made me swallow hard. The newborn *Incogniti* were still busy searching for Uncle Red's body.

CHAPTER FORTY-FIVE

Lily was as busy as Ivo. She was managing the Hotel of What You Want. She did not know it yet, but I had purchased the hotel for her, making a very tiny dent in Uncle Red's fortune. The deeds were in her name. I didn't want Lily to feel beholden to me, so I planned not to tell her until she'd made the hotel hers by making it a success.

Did I think I was buying her forever friendship that way? A little, yes. But I would do anything to keep Lily safe and close to me, to persuade her that my love for her had survived her part in Uncle Red's death. On bad days, I thought, *Darling Dearworthy, you have nothing but money and a great mouth on you.* But on good days, I was full sure I'd found the friend I'd craved, and that I would keep her.

Lily had emptied every last drop of the Signorina's Night Mixture into the canal. The black lionesses had been sent to a museum on the mainland where no one believed they were anything but marble. The witch's cats, now employed as ratters, were transforming into lap-sitting hotel pets. (Though they were not entirely reformed, being not without a bit of tongue about them.) Instead of sad English guests, the hotel now hosted orphans, many rescued from the convent of Saint Teresa on Murano. That was Lily's idea. A sign outside the hotel read: *Under New Management. Reasonable Rates for those of Moderate Means. Orphans Particularly Welcome and Petted Finely. Excellent dioramas to play with.*

'Where did you learn to be so soft-hearted?' I asked her. 'Did Giacomo have something to do with it?'

'Am I spoken of?' Giacomo strode into the room and took Lily's hand to his lips. 'Did you miss me?' he asked.

'What are you blethering on about?' asked one of the cats. 'You've been gone just half an hour, jackanapes.'

Lily laughed. She tousled Giacomo's hair and touched the tip of his nose with a gentle finger. 'You can practise your charms on me, but don't expect me to take you seriously.'

'I am *heartfully* serious about you, my loveliest girl of the infinite eyes.'

The cat muttered, 'Why does he always make such a truffled *omelette* out of it?'

Lily was wearing crimson, the first time I'd seen her in that colour. It fired up her green eyes, turning them into opals filled with that dancing light you see under Venetian bridges. *Sbarlusso*, it's called. Lovely word so. Lovely thing so. The dress followed the line of her body, which these days, though still slender, took up some space in the room, because of Lily's new belief that she was entitled to it. And not just on land. Lily had learned to love the water again. Incubina had even taught her to swim.

Lily never talked of herself as a rat now. She'd become a girl just a bit more alive than other people, a girl who'd fold me in a hug, and dance me round the room as often as she saw me.

She was so strong now, and I felt a little less in comparison. It was not Lily's fault. Mostly, it was because of Ivo, who these days treated me with exquisite and distant and very hurting politeness.

I wanted Ivo to be with me as he was with Eliah – as comfortable as a mother, as companionable as a brother. But I wanted something more too. I was desperate to bury the dark and destroyed things that had happened between us. For ever, and in a deep and quiet place so.

It was in fact Ivo, acting on a sudden hunch, who discovered the body of the Signorina's last victim – my Uncle Red. It turned out that Uncle Red had lain all this time in a cold sarcophagus at Saint Teresa's Convent of the Barefoot Carmelites on Murano. I'd been mere feet from him when the *badessa* tried to murder me there too.

I dared not ask, but Ivo told me: 'He is still whole, Darling.'

And now – reunited with his hair – Uncle Red lay in the *campo dei morti* by the Maddalena church, after a proper Irish wake at the hotel. The full Cohort of the *Incogniti*, Lily, Ivo, Giacomo and I ranged around his coffin, all exchanging memories of his kindness and intelligence, diluting our hot chocolate with tears. On his tombstone, above his too-short dates, I had the words carved: *Gregory Dearworthy, Truth-Seeker.*

After the wake, Ivo, Lily, Giacomo and I rushed off in different directions. There was so little time now to spend together. We were all eaten up by our various projects. Terrible as they had been, the Magoghe sisters had thrown us together for days and nights. Now there was no excuse to hide out with Ivo in the mermaid cavern. I had my old room at the hotel and was woken early each morning by the laughter of children.

Ivo did not exactly avoid me, but his eyes showed a preference for the floor if I was around. And I was running out of excuses to visit him at the palace of the former English Resident. Every time I was ushered into his office, I waited for him to say, 'Darling, we must talk, *really* talk.'

Yet every time Ivo asked with preposterous, exquisite formality, 'What may I do for you, Miss Dearworthy?'

I grew hot and stammery every time he pretended not to know. For it could hardly escape him. We needed to speak about Uncle Red and how he died.

It was Lily who suggested, 'Take him to the cave.'

The cat on her lap purred smugly as Lily explained, 'Here is for why: it's the site of painful memories and guilt, is what it is. At the cave, all things will crowd in on him until he bursts. It will be a relief. Not just for you. '

The cat said, 'A word of advice, miss. Stop imagining what you want him to say and then getting cross because he does not say it.'

Ivo must have guessed what I intended by taking him there. Yet he agreed. We sat by the shore late in the day, as the colours faded from the sky. The trees twitched their branches in the breeze. Leaves danced around us, wild and wanton. It was just what I craved: less tensely polite behaviour, more letting out of feelings.

'Ivo,' I began, 'how many drops of the Signorina's Night Mixture would kill a man dead so?'

'Twenty would do it,' he mumbled, his eyes on the horizon.

'How many drops did she give my Uncle Red on his last night?'

'Thirty.'

'So he had not one single chance of surviving?'

'But I—'

'You merely speeded him on his way to already certain death, Ivo. The Signorina murdered him. And now we also know that Uncle Red had *volunteered* to put his own life at risk investigating the hotel.'

'I did the final deed, the final disrespect,' Ivo said. 'I took the last person on earth who belonged to you. And I made Lily part of it. She was innocent before that.'

The dead weight of those words fell heavily on me. I could not contradict them. My task was to make them less potent. 'Look at me, Ivo. You won't? Well then, look at the sea and listen to me. Can you imagine how it feels to sit watching this war of Ivo against Ivo? It's maddening! It's . . . lonely, so it is! This war of Ivo against Ivo is pure selfish. It shuts out everyone else, completely. What if someone wanted in?'

'Who would want in here?' He jabbed at his chest with disgust.

'I understand it's *your* truth, and your truth's a knot surely tied and double tied. But it's not *my* truth about you.'

Ivo said, 'Perhaps the knot is tied too hard. It is too complicated to undo. Perhaps no one cares enough to undo it.'

'That sounds ridiculous, simply because it is so,' I said. He had turned away from me again. Wind shoved into the space between us, making me shiver. But I shoved it back and edged closer to Ivo.

I said, 'Every time I get a moment's clarity off you, Ivo, you slam the window down on my fingers. It is pure cruel. It hurts.'

He glanced at my hands. 'I see no wound,' he said.

If I'd had the *moretta* mask in my mouth then, I'd have bitten the button off in frustration so.

'Soon you'll be off back across the ocean to Ireland and your grand Young Ladies' Academy?' Ivo's voice was heavy as a gold ingot but without the shine. 'With all your money, back to your rich friends.'

Is that it? He thinks me someone who'd flit away, without a thought for him or Lily or Giacomo or Eliah?

'Rich *enemies* I left in Ireland, too many of them so. There's one called Esmeralda Sweeney who has a touch of the Magoghe about her any day of the week.'

'Of course, you don't *need* to be a Young Lady at an academy you hate when money's not a problem for you,' he stated flatly.

'Yes, as Uncle Red's heiress, I am free. I am no great shakes but I am not no one. I *could* travel in luxury and style to every far-flung city in the dioramas. I *could* hire a private tutor, rent a palace and live where I like, among . . . people that I . . . like.'

'That was never me, was it?' Ivo's voice was raw as radishes. 'You despised me from the moment you set eyes on me. You saw through me as if my eyes were windows. You always said to me, "Would it *kill* you to do this, or that?" Each time, I knew I was a killer. "Master Evil", you called me. You *named* me . . . for what I was, Darling.'

'Darling is not my name, actually. That's how little you know about me purely from the lack of wanting to know. I was christened Deirdre as in "dreary". Darling is the name I pulled out of my misery, out of cruel teasing and torture by Esmeralda Sweeney at that academy.'

'No,' said Ivo quietly. 'Darling is your true name. It suits you.'

On this soft turn in his tone, I spoke quickly. 'Here's my plan and there's no leaving Venice about it so. I want to open a school for languages! A happy school with more chatter than grammar. And more Venice than mathematics. My first pupils shall be Lily's orphans, none other. Then I shall set them up as guides to help lost and bewildered people of every nation. Young Venetians will learn to speak beautiful French, stylish German and sing-song Swedish so that they can describe Venice as she deserves to all those who wish to know her. No pretty lies, but the truth at every corner. Maybe I can even teach Mermaidtongue to new *Incogniti*. My own is starting to be more than functional, Incubina says.'

'May I offer my services for your school's paperwork, Darling? I can be . . . useful, in the Resident's office.'

'Sure that'll be grand.'

But that's not what I'm wishing, in my bones, for you to say.

'So you really mean to stay here?' Finally, Ivo turned his face to mine.

Again, as on the day that we thought Lily drowned, a flock of birds wheeled in the dim sky, a speckling of blackness. Once more, those birds were lifting their wings like heroes. With Ivo's eyes on mine, trusting and open, my heart was brave enough to watch those birds at last.

'You know it is so,' I said.

Sorrowful Lily's Farewell Letter to the Reader

Memories of my part in Mr Dearworthy's death still visit my dreams.

But in the daytime, I don't give them a place by the fire.

Now that you know what happened, Reader, can you forgive me my part in what befell that kind man?

But, Reader, before you answer that, think on this: have you yourself done something that needs forgiving? And I speak not merely of the chickens you've eaten and the wishing bones you've torn apart with no thought of the life that was given for your belly's pleasure.

For example, if mischancy people, cast out of their homes by war or disaster, ever came to your city – did you treat them as if they were rats?

Did you think of them as rats? Or, worse, did you not think of them at all?

I'll leave that with you, Reader.

I am less jealous of you than I once was.

After all, I am a girl with secret sacred ties to the incomparable city of Venice – and you, Reader, most likely are not. Where else in this world can you swim with mermaids and talk with cats? Nor am I alone here. I have at least one friend of my heart, whom I love enough to share, sometimes, with others.

When I think of those things, it is impossible not to feel rare smug.

Not to mention a great deal less sorrowful.

Lily

Historical Notes

WHAT IS TRUE AND WHAT IS MADE UP
VENICE IN 1739

At the time when this book is set, there were around 200,000 people living in the city – nearly four times as many Venetians as there are today. But there were far fewer tourists, who now number over 25 million annually. Venice was a city full of pleasures: gambling, balls and *Carnevale* six months a year. But there were also 30,000 nuns, monks and priests in Venice's many convents and monasteries. The Anatomy School, built in 1671, was drawing doctors from all over the world to observe the dissections of corpses.

In 1739, the Doge was Alvise Pisani. Elena Badoero was his wife. It was indeed the tradition for the *Calegheri*, or guild of shoemakers, to present a pair of slippers to the Dogaressa every year. The cruel English Resident in this book has nothing to do with any of the real men who occupied this post.

BAREFOOT CARMELITES

Carmelite friars and nuns practised the virtues of solitude, manual labour, prayer, contemplation, charity, fasting and abstaining from flesh of all kinds – unlike the badessa! The term 'Barefoot' ('*Scalzi*') usually meant that they went barefoot except for sandals. Without stockings or socks, Venice's freezing winters must have been a true penance.

Cruel nuns were made famous by Diderot's novel *The Nun*, published in 1796. I adapted some of Diderot's anecdotes for the trials Lily undergoes at the hands of the *badessa*.

THE WINDOW DIORAMAS AND CARNIVOROUS HOTELS

I am not the first person to imagine miniature tableaux inside an eyelid-shaped awning. The Spanish artist Mariano Fortuny y Madrazo (1871–1949), who moved to Venice in 1899, designed lighting and scenery for the theatre, including a structure like an eyelid that could open and close. Fortuny also made 'cloud machinery' of painted glass on tilting frames.

Nor am I the first person to think of a hotel as a useful place to kill guests and harvest their bodies for money. One of the first known serial killers in America, Herman Mudgett – who went by the name of Dr Henry Howard Holmes – was also a hotelier.

Mudgett opened a three-storey maze of a hotel in Chicago in 1893. He changed builders several times during its construction so that no one but himself knew all its secrets. These included airtight rooms set up as gas chambers, a soundproof vault and a greased chute for discreetly dropping the bodies of his victims down to the basement.

In the basement was a dissecting table and a kiln for incinerating bodies. He sold some remains to an 'articulator' who prepared the skeletons for sale to medical schools.

Suspicion was aroused by the large quantities of chloroform he bought and the number of missing girls who had at one time or another stayed at the hotel. Mudgett eventually confessed to 27 murders but he may have killed ten times that number.

The Chicago Times-Herald wrote: 'He is a prodigy of wickedness, a human demon, a being so unthinkable that no novelist would dare to invent such a character.'

I beg to differ! I had already conceived my Signorina before I learned about Mudgett.

He was hanged in Philadelphia on May 7th, 1896.

THE HOTEL OF WHAT YOU WANT AND THE CARRINGTON HOTEL, KATOOMBA, AUSTRALIA

When I was very little, my maternal grandparents ran a grand hotel in the delightfully named town of Katoomba in the Blue Mountains. The hotel was called the Carrington.

I adored the suit of armour in the hall, the grandfather clock, the stained-glass windows and the minstrels' gallery above the ballroom, which became the den for myself, my sister and my cousin.

Upstairs, the bedrooms were reached via endless corridors lined with sculptures of black lionesses. I was absolutely terrified of them. So my stays in the Carrington were a mixture of joy and fear – and were therefore the making of me as a writer. I suppose that for me the Carrington was the Hotel of What I Wanted, or at least it was until I was able to come to Venice.

NAMES

Amedeo Peruch and Violante Momesso are among the thirteen martyrs commemorated on a plaque near San Marco. They were partisans executed on July 28th, 1944, after causing an explosion at the nearby Fascist headquarters.

Barbarina Campani (1721–1799) was a famous dancer and a favourite of Emperor Frederick the Great. A beautiful portrait was made of her by the Venetian pastel artist Rosalba Carriera. Bastian Olivo and Isepo Luzzo were real jewellers in eighteenth-century Venice, but there is no record of their working in the false relic trade or indeed any kind of unpleasant business.

MERMAIDS AND MER-CREATURES IN VENICE

There are many strange watery creatures in Venice, some in unexpected places.

The most beautiful, in my opinion, are to be found at the church of Santa Maria dei Miracoli. The mermaids and tritons there were sculpted by the architect Pietro Lombardo, with his sons Tullio and Antonio.

Near the Ponte delle Guglie, there is the chemist still called 'Le Due Sirene' – the two mermaids. Originally, as in this book, it was called '*Le Due Sirene Scarpigliate*' – '*The Two Tousled Mermaids*'.

TETCHY MADONNAS

There are more than 500 *capitelli* in Venice, most of them devoted to the Madonna. At the time of *The Wishing Bones*, someone would have been in charge of lighting a lantern in each of these miniature chapels every night.

VENETIAN SUPERSTITIONS

I made up the superstition about colour vanishing in the absence of Saint Lucy. However, this book does reflect some other traditional Venetian beliefs, as explained by Horatio Brown, an Englishman who lived many years in the city. In his *Life on the*

Lagoons (1904), I discovered that anyone with an 'M' on the lines of their palm was considered fortunate because they bore the signature of the Madonna. Brown also recorded the Venetian ideas that everyone has a personal evil hour and that combing of hair plays an important role in various kinds of witchcraft.

SAINT LUCY AND SAINT EULALIA

Saint Lucy, whose name means 'light', lived in Siracusa in Sicily from approximately 280 to 303/304 AD. Many artists have shown Saint Lucy holding a dish or tray with a pair of eyes upon it. This refers to a legend that her pagan suitor was obsessed with her beautiful eyes so Lucy plucked them out and handed them to the man in order to make him leave her alone.

After many travels, most of Lucy's body ended up in Venice in 1204. Even within Venice, her body moved several times. Today she occupies a splendid glass tomb in the church of San Geremia in Cannaregio.

Saint Eulalia, born in the Spanish city of Merida, was only twelve when she was martyred for stoutly defending her faith. Her punishment brutal but she simply chanted blessings as she was burnt to death

GIACOMO GIROLAMO CASANOVA

Casanova is the only real historical character in this novel, apart from the Doge and Dogaressa. He was born in Venice in 1725. His mother, Zanetta, was an actress. His father, Gaetano, a dancer, died when Casanova was eight. With his mother was frequently away, performing at foreign courts, the boy was left in the care of his loving grandmother, Marzia. The story of his muteness and nosebleeds – and his visit to the witch on Murano – is recounted in the first part of his 3000-page memoir, *The Story of My Life*. I added a few extra details, such as the beating hearts in buckets.

In November 1737, aged twelve, Casanova entered the University of Padua to study law and graduated five years later. During the time this story is set, he was just fourteen, and had returned to Venice, where he was working for a lawyer.

SAINTS' RELICS

Relics began to feature in Christian worship sometime in the second century AD. There are two kinds. First-class relics consist of the bones or bodily parts of saints. Second-class relics are objects that once touched the body of the living or dead saint, and so include fragments of the cross on which Jesus was crucified and the nails that were used to fasten him to it.

Precious bones were housed in 'reliquaries' – silver or gold cases of great value. Relics became objects of huge value, of rivalry, of theft. The relics' great value meant that counterfeiting occurred. All the practices of the badessa have been recorded, and more. These days historical authentications are carried out by the Relic Office at the Vatican.

Michelle Lovric, Venice, July 2019

ACKNOWLEDGEMENTS

Many thanks to my agent Victoria Hobbs at A.M. Heath and to my editor Lena McCauley at Hachette Children's Publishing for steering this book through its long passage to publication.

I am grateful to Padre Ermanno Barucco for his help on the Carmelite nuns of Venice and to the artists Christine Morley and Deirdre Kelly for sharing with me their enthusiasm for and knowledge of the tetchy Madonnas in the *capitelli* of Venice. I am grateful to Tony Bird and Eugenio Rossaro for making everything possible for me in Venice, including the whole notion of peaceful, happy time to write.

Thanks to Kristina Blagojevitch, to Belinda Jones, the proofreader, and to Becca Allen, the copy-editor, for tidying up the manuscript. Any mistakes that remain are my responsibility alone.

For invaluable advice and support, *grazie infinite* to Lucy Coats, Mary Hoffman and the brilliant hive mind of the Scattered Authors' Society. This novel was immeasurably improved by the Sorrowful Lily Literary Agency and its eponymous heroine Lily L. And, at a particularly sorrowful moment, it was comforted with great kindness by Sarah Molloy.